THE MANY FUTURES OF MADDY HART

LAURA PEARSON

Boldwood

First published in Great Britain in 2025 by Boldwood Books Ltd.

Copyright © Laura Pearson, 2025

Cover Design by Lizzie Gardiner

Cover Images: Adobe Stock and Shutterstock

The moral right of Laura Pearson to be identified as the author of this work has been asserted in accordance with the Copyright, Designs and Patents Act 1988.

Every effort has been made to obtain the necessary permissions with reference to copyright material, both illustrative and quoted. We apologise for any omissions in this respect and will be pleased to make the appropriate acknowledgements in any future edition.

A CIP catalogue record for this book is available from the British Library.

Paperback ISBN 978-1-83603-455-1

Large Print ISBN 978-1-83603-456-8

Hardback ISBN 978-1-83603-454-4

Ebook ISBN 978-1-83603-457-5

Kindle ISBN 978-1-83603-458-2

Audio CD ISBN 978-1-83603-449-0

MP3 CD ISBN 978-1-83603-450-6

Digital audio download ISBN 978-1-83603-451-3

This book is printed on certified sustainable paper. Boldwood Books is dedicated to putting sustainability at the heart of our business. For more information please visit https://www.boldwoodbooks.com/about-us/sustainability/

Boldwood Books Ltd, 23 Bowerdean Street, London, SW6 3TN

www.boldwoodbooks.com

For Abi Rowson, Jodie Matthews and Lydia Howland.
And in memory of Deb Chambers.

PROLOGUE

MAY 2002

At the door, Mark pulls my hoody onto my shoulders, leans in and does up the zip. Half an hour ago we were naked, but strangely, this feels too intimate.

'You're quiet,' he says. 'Are you, I mean, are we, okay?'

I nod, but I don't speak. I can't meet his eyes. Those eyes that I used to feel on my skin like a burn, when he sat behind me in History and we weren't yet together.

He is standing inside his hallway and I'm just outside. The late spring air is warm and still.

'Okay,' he says. 'Well, I'll see you. Tomorrow?'

'Yeah,' I say. 'Tomorrow.'

It's true. Tomorrow is a Wednesday and we have Art together first thing. We've been working on this project, imitating artists from the 1960s. He's doing a Warhol and I'm doing a Lichtenstein. We sit together, often sharing brushes and other equipment. What will I say to him? How will I let him know it's over? I turn to go.

'Hey, Maddy,' he says. 'Don't I get a goodbye kiss?'

I let him tangle his hands in my hair and kiss me, knowing it is the last time. And then I walk away without looking back.

I don't go home, though. I go past my house and around the corner to Priya's. Her mum opens the door.

'Hi, Maddy. Priya's upstairs. Come on in.'

I take off my hoody and shoes and leave them in a messy pile in the hallway. Priya is lying on her bed with headphones on, and when she sees me, she pulls them down around her neck and smiles.

'I didn't know you were coming over. I thought tonight was the big night, with Mark?' She winks at me, and despite it all, I laugh.

'It was. I mean, that's where I was, until now. And now I'm here.'

'So how did it go? Did you do it?'

'Yeah, we... yeah. We did.'

Priya sits up, crosses her legs. 'You're being weird. Was it not okay? Tell me.'

I am still standing in the doorway, but before I speak again I move across the room and join her on her double bed. We lie on our backs, side by side, the way we have at countless sleepovers over the years. She turns her face to look at me. I know she will know there's something wrong. I tell her everything, always have.

'Priya,' I say. I don't know how to start. But then I do. 'Is there something about sex that you didn't tell me? Something that nobody talks about?'

Her eyes widen and she looks over to check the door is closed. Then she screws up her face. 'What, that it hurts? It will get better, I promise.'

'Not that. There's really nothing else? Because when it happened, something else happened, too.'

'What was it?'

'I don't know, exactly. It's like I travelled, somehow. I was with Mark. He was older. We were sitting on this ratty blue sofa watching TV. Not speaking. It was really unsettling.'

Priya sits up again, looks at me until I meet her gaze. 'You saw all that, while you were actually having sex with him?'

'Not so much saw it as lived it. I was there, in the scene. That's weird, right? That's not something that happens?'

'I mean, it certainly hasn't happened to me.'

This is what I was expecting her to say, but it still feels like a blow. 'So maybe some kind of vision of the future or something?'

'I guess...'

'How old were you?'

'I don't know. I wasn't watching myself. I was there.'

'And Mark?'

I close my eyes and picture the scene again. Look at Mark. He's heavier, and he's holding a pint of lager on the slight dome of his belly. Are we... married? Is that what this is?

'Mid-twenties, maybe.'

'So.' Priya thinks for a moment. 'Maybe ten years from now?'

'Yes, about that.'

We are quiet. I can hear the tinny sound of music coming through the headphones Priya pulled off when I came in the room.

'Do you think there's something wrong with me?' I ask.

It is our greatest fear, that something is wrong with us. With our bodies, our brains. We are obsessed with it.

'No,' my friend says. 'No. I'm sure you're fine. I'm sure it won't happen again.'

But it does. It happens again and again and again.

1

NOW (NOVEMBER 2011)

'What the hell is this?' I ask the man who's standing in front of me dressed as an elf. He's holding out a bag and we're both looking down at it. There's a pair of pointy elf ears sticking out of the top.

'It's your outfit,' he says, and as soon as I take it from him, he holds both hands up. 'Don't blame me.'

'This is supposed to be an acting job!' I know I'm directing my fury at the wrong person, but he's the only one here right now.

'Well, it turns out it's more of a dress-like-an-elf-and-hand-presents-to-kids-whose-parents-have-paid-for-them-to-see-Father-Christmas job, and I'm as happy about that as you are.'

I check my phone for the email asking me to come here. 'Where's Mac?'

The elf man shrugs. 'He went to get coffee or something. He told me to tell you – assuming you're Maddy – to put this on and meet him and SC by the big tree on the first floor.'

'SC?'

'Santa Claus.'

We're in a shopping centre, round the back, in a room that's clearly used for storage. There are piles of boxes and huge signs propped against walls, but there is no privacy. 'I'm not getting changed here, in front of you,' I say. And then it comes to me. 'Are you Mac? Is this all some kind of trick? Are you just some pervert who has a thing for elves?'

He goes pale. 'No. NO! I'm Oliver. I'm an actor too. I've told you everything I know. Seriously. And there are toilets over there.' He points. 'For getting changed.'

'Oh. Well, then.' I go in the direction he indicated. When I emerge, I'm wearing a short green dress, red and white striped tights, the aforementioned ears and a green hat with a white pompom at its point, my own clothes shoved unceremoniously into my thankfully large handbag. Oliver's still where I left him, shuffling about a bit uncomfortably. 'Shall we go?'

We don't talk on our way to the escalators. Oliver points out the big tree, which is so big you can surely see it from anywhere in the building, and we head in that direction. I keep my eyes low, hoping to avoid seeing or being seen by anyone I've ever met.

'Ah, there you both are,' a big, beefy man says, rubbing his hands together. 'A bit late but I'll overlook it.'

'Are you Mac?' I ask, my anger returning.

'The very same. And you must be Mindy.'

'Maddy.'

'Of course, Maddy.'

'You advertised this as an acting job. You said you were looking for extras.'

'Ah!' He holds up a finger as thick as a sausage and I look over at Santa for the first time. He's pulled his beard and moustache down under his chin and looks about as happy as I feel. 'That I did. And that's what you are. This gentleman here is Father Christmas, as I'm sure you can see, and you and Oscar—'

'Oliver,' Oliver says.

'That's right, Oliver. You and Oliver are the extras.'

I open my mouth to argue that if he was looking to people a grotto he should just have said so, but there are children starting to form a queue and I can tell this Mac guy is the type who'll wriggle out of anything I throw at him. Suddenly, I've lost all my fight.

'I'll be back in a couple of hours to see how you're getting on,' Mac says, already walking away. 'The presents are in those sacks. Don't forget to smile!'

I turn to Oliver and roll my eyes, and he crosses his and sticks out his tongue, and it makes me laugh despite the shitty situation.

'Let's get this show on the road,' he says, and Father Christmas reluctantly tugs his beard into place and takes a seat on the rocking chair provided.

Two hours later, I never want to see a child or a Christmas present again. I've been told the presents are crap, which is absolutely true. This Mac guy is a total scam artist, charging parents ten pounds for a meet and greet with the big guy and then fobbing them off with us lot and a present from the pound shop.

I've been sneezed on. I've very nearly been vomited over, the oddly purple spray reaching to just a few centimetres shy of my left foot. And I've had enough. Oliver's been trying to keep my spirits up with friendly chat, but there's only so much he can do. There's a lull in the queue and I tell the others I'm leaving.

'What about your money?' Oliver asks.

He has a good point. I'm not really in a position to throw away the money I'll have made for this morning, but my feet are aching and I feel like a prize idiot and I don't think I can keep this up for another four hours. 'Forget it,' I say.

'Give me your number,' Oliver says. 'I'll get it to you. I'll tell Mac you were taken ill.'

I'm stunned. 'Why would you do that, when I'm leaving you in the lurch?'

Oliver shrugs. 'I just... I don't know, it seems like the right thing to do.'

I'm taken aback, and for a few seconds I just stand there, unsure what to do. It's then that I notice how blue his eyes are, how tall he is, and I start to think about what he might look like if he wasn't an elf. He hands me his phone and I save my number in it under 'Maddy (Elf)' and it seems like it's all settled, so I walk away.

I don't walk far. Just outside the shopping centre is the café where Priya works, and it isn't until I see her through the window and she makes a 'what the hell?' kind of face at me that I realise I'm still dressed up. Luckily, I'd remembered my handbag, containing my real clothes. I push open the door and go inside.

'What can I get you?' Priya asks. 'Our soup today is carrot and coriander. And our toastie of the day is cheddar and mushroom.' She does not comment on the costume I'm wearing or the hat and ears I've hastily pulled off and am holding in my hands, and I love her for it.

Priya's boss, Ellen, looks over. 'Priya, how many times do I have to tell you, you don't have to pretend not to know your friends. Although...' She shoots a look at me. 'I can kind of see why you might want to pretend that, in this instance.'

I look hopefully into the coin compartment of my purse, as if the coins might have helpfully multiplied since I counted them this morning. 'Just a tea,' I say.

'I'll bring it over. One pound fifty please.'

I hand her two fifty pence pieces, two twenties and a ten, and find a table for two. Sit down, exhale. It's not a hip café, this one where Priya works. It's called Time for Tea and the majority of customers are retired or in the building trade. Right now, it's almost empty. In one corner, there are two women in their sixties chatting quietly. Behind me, there's a middle-aged guy in a high-vis jacket eating a baked potato. There are a lot of signs that say things like 'Live Laugh Love' and 'Home is Where the Heart is'. Priya's tried making suggestions over the two years she's worked here, but this is Ellen's place and Ellen's vision is the only one that matters. I've grown to like it. They play Radio 2 and will always plug your phone in for you if you're low on charge. Plus Ellen makes the world's best flapjacks.

When Priya brings my tea over, she pulls out the chair opposite mine and sits down. 'Ellen told me to take ten minutes. Apparently she can handle all this.' She throws her arm wide to indicate the sparsely populated café. 'So, tell me what the hell happened to you this morning.'

'It wasn't an acting job,' I say.

'No, I got that.'

'I was an elf.'

'Of course. And you liked the costume so much you asked to bring it home with you?'

I can't help but smile. 'I walked out. Forgot I was wearing it.'

'How will you get it back to them?'

'Don't know, don't care.'

Priya shrugs. 'Want to change in our tiny toilet?'

'I really do, but I'm going to have this tea first.'

'Do you know what sucks?' Priya asks.

'Everything?'

'Well yes, that. But I was thinking about the fact that this bit only lasts such a short time in all the films.'

'What bit?'

'This bit where the protagonists are paying their dues by doing crap jobs to cover the rent, before becoming incredibly successful in their chosen career. It's usually covered in one montage-type scene, with a peppy crowd-pleaser of a song and our gutsy lead making the best of a bad situation by falling in love with someone unsuitable and having lots of great sex. My adolescence led me to believe that working in a café would just be a fun, blink-and-you-miss-it stop on the way to my eventual career as a doctor.'

'I mean, it is just a stop, but it's a bloody long one.'

'I thought you'd be in a soap opera by now.'

'Did you? Which one?'

'*Hollyoaks*.'

I reach across the table and tap her hand playfully. 'If you'd said that when I was at drama school, I would have been devastated. But now I'd kind of welcome something steady like that. Regular money. Colleagues.'

'I have regular money and colleagues and it's still pretty rubbish,' Priya says quietly.

'But not as rubbish as turning up expecting to be some kind of extra and being handed an elf suit and made to hand out crap presents to small children.'

'No. You win, today. Although it ain't over just yet.'

As she says that, the door opens, the bell jangles, and Oliver – also still dressed as an elf – comes inside and heads straight for my table. He hands me three ten-pound notes. 'Here.'

'How did you find me?' I ask.

Priya looks back and forth from him to me as if she's watching tennis.

'I mean, you haven't exactly come far. Also, do you remember telling me your best friend works at this place?'

Now he says it, I do remember. We were talking about our favourite places to go out to eat, and I mentioned the flapjacks. 'Have you walked out too?'

'I'm on a break.'

'Who are you?' Priya asks.

'I'm Oliver,' he says. 'Do you work here? Could I get a cup of tea?'

'Of course,' she says, giving me a look that I can't quite interpret. She goes back over to the counter and Oliver sits on the chair she's just vacated.

'Why?' I ask.

'Why what?'

'Why did you find me?'

'Because Mac gave me your pay and I thought it would be easier to give it to you in person than call you and arrange to meet somewhere between our two flats, so I thought I'd come in and check, on the off chance. Also, he said you have to return the costume, when you're feeling better.'

'What did you tell him I had?'

'Sickness bug. There was still a faint aroma of vomit, so it seemed like the obvious choice. Also, you know, it's the kind of thing that comes on quickly.'

'Was he pissed off with me?'

'Not really. He's only paid you for the time you did.'

'I owe you one,' I say, and he nods, and there's something like shyness in his expression.

There's a strange shift in the air between us, because it's the first hint that our acquaintance will extend beyond this day.

Priya comes over with Oliver's tea then, and a second one for me. 'On the house,' she says when I give her a panicked look.

'So tell me,' Oliver says, once Priya's gone again. 'What do you get up to when you're not being an elf?'

I lean forward, prop my right arm up on my elbow and rest my chin in my hand. 'To be honest,' I say, 'I'm always being an elf.'

He looks confused.

'I mean, not literally. But I'm always chasing jobs that turn out to be shit and doing humiliating things to pay the rent.'

'Join the club.'

'You said you're an actor too?'

He nods.

I hate myself for asking the next question, but what the hell. I get asked the same at least once a day. 'Anything I'd have seen you in?'

'Maybe *Hollyoaks*,' he says.

'No way.'

'Yeah, I was this cool young lecturer who started getting a bit too close to the students, if you know what I mean.'

'A wrong 'un.'

'Exactly.'

'How many episodes?'

'Oh, a few months.'

I'm impressed, but I try not to show it.

'So this is a bit of a comedown for you?' I gesture at his green felt waistcoat and elf ears.

'Wouldn't this be a comedown for anyone? But no, it's how it is, isn't it? Ups and downs. Dreams don't just come true like that.' He drains his cup and takes it over to the counter, puts his hand up in a wave and walks out of the door. 'See you, Maddy.'

I count the seconds until Priya is back with me. Four. 'So, he seemed nice.'

I look at her with disdain. 'You only like him because he brought his cup over.'

She raises one eyebrow at the two empty cups now sitting in front of me.

'I will too,' I say, but she shakes her head and picks them up, leaving me alone at the table with nothing to drink and no one to talk to. I take my bag through to the tiny toilet and wrestle myself out of the costume, banging against the walls as I do. When I've finished, I am sweating and my hair is in complete disarray. I pull it into a ponytail and secure it with the band I always have around my wrist. And then I shove the elf costume back in the bag.

Priya's serving someone when I emerge, so I give her a quick wave and head out of the door. But just as I'm shutting it behind me, she appears.

'Pub?' she asks. 'Later? Seven or so?'

I think about the money I just earned, how I need it for rent and food and bills and probably other important things I haven't thought of yet. 'Sure,' I say. 'Will I see you at home first?'

'Not sure. I might go straight there.'

'Okay, see you at seven.'

On the bus home, I try to think about the audition I have in three days' time. It's for a daytime medical drama. Patient two. I'll go over my lines again before I meet Priya. When Oliver pops into my head, I'm sort of surprised. I picture the way his hair was flattened against his head when he appeared at the cafe because of the stupid hat. The way we connected, how easy it was to chat. But what are the chances that I'll ever see him again? And besides, I'm not looking for that. Whatever *that* might be. Friendship. Companionship. An acting buddy. A boyfriend. A lover. I am not looking for any of those things. Because all of them hold the possibility of sex, and the bad thing that happens when I have sex.

2

NOW (NOVEMBER 2011)

It started with Mark, of course, the night I lost my virginity at the age of sixteen. That weird vision I had, of me and him, older and in some kind of depressing relationship. It freaked me out so much that I ended things with him the next day and didn't allow myself to so much as kiss a boy for the next two years.

Then, when I was in my first year at drama school, I became friends with a course-mate called Drew. I knew from the start that he was interested in a romantic relationship, and I tried to tell him that I wasn't, but perhaps inevitably, one night we drank a lot of wine and ended up in bed together. It had been so long that it felt like losing my virginity again. I was nervous, despite the inebriation. But Drew was sweet and courteous, asking whether I was alright, whether this was what I wanted. And it was, because by then I had to know whether the vision was a weird one-off. It wasn't.

This time, though, it was different. I was in a theatre, on the front row. I looked up, and there was Drew, on the stage. Older, with a full beard. He was pleading with a red-haired woman to keep his baby. I felt uncomfortably hot, and I needed to clear my throat. I picked up the programme in my lap and fanned my face with it a bit. And then I saw Drew noticing the movement, saw his concentration break. After that, his lines didn't ring true. And a feeling of fear ran through me, though I didn't know why. I was jolted back to the present. When it was over, Drew kissed my cheek in a strangely chaste way and said he really liked me, that he'd wanted this to happen for a long time. I couldn't look at him without feeling the echo of that fear. What did it mean? Was there a meanness in Drew that I hadn't seen yet? If we got together properly, would I be scared of him, of his reaction to things?

I lay awake next to him while he slept, and as soon as he left the next morning, I called Priya, told her it had happened again. I didn't need to say what I meant. But she did want the details, and I gave them to her, and she went quiet for a bit.

'It's like you see a possible future with this guy,' she said.

'Do you think it's the truth? It feels like the truth.'

'God, how would I know? It's the strangest thing I've ever heard of. You promise you're not just making it up to test how gullible I am?'

She was joking. She knew how long it had taken me to do this again, after what had happened with Mark.

'I keep thinking about the Facebook thing,' I said. 'I feel like that proves it's real.'

It had taken me a while to remember it, but during that first vision, with Mark, he'd said something about someone being a 'Facebook friend'. I'd debated endlessly with Priya about what it could mean. And then a few years later, I heard that word again when a drama school friend asked if I was on Facebook.

'I don't know about proof. Why don't you find out the national lottery numbers and we'll see. But seriously, I feel like we'll know more each time it happens,' Priya said. 'Like, we'll be able to build up a picture.'

'I'm not just going to sleep around to get case studies,' I said.

'I mean, you could. Uni seems like the perfect time and place to do that.'

'Do you think it would happen if I was sleeping with women?'

Priya was silent, but only for a moment. 'I don't know. It doesn't happen when you're, you know, alone, does it? I think it's something to do with the penis. It's a very heteronormative sort of condition you have, for better or worse.'

I was in London; Priya was in Birmingham. We saw each other every couple of months – it was an easy train journey. But it wasn't the same as having her down the road, as seeing her every day. I'd made new friends, but I didn't love any of them the way I loved her.

Does it go without saying that I didn't sleep with Drew again? The next time it happened was about six months later. His name was Anton. I met him in a student bar – he was in his final year, studying Economics. We went on a few dates and then, after one of them, in the middle of the afternoon, I went back to the flat he shared with three friends. Into his bedroom. For a moment, I thought about telling him. *There's this thing that happens to me when I have sex...* But it was impossible. Who would believe me? Priya did. But I'd known her forever and that counted for a lot. And even she had doubts. Anton leaned in and kissed me, put his hands on my waist, and I tried to relax into the moment, tried to clear my mind.

It didn't do any good. As soon as it started, I found myself in a tiny flat, holding a screaming baby. That was a shock. I held the little creature out in front of me, terrified I would drop it. I could see that its eyes were the same shade of blue as mine. I could see my grandmother in the curve of its cheek. Could I see Anton? It was hard to say. I spotted something out of the corner of my eye; a mobile phone. It looked like some space age piece of kit from the future, which it was, of course. When I picked it up, the date and time flashed up on the screen. 3.06 p.m., 23 March 2017. It was ten years to the day – to the minute? Quite possibly – into the future. The phone in my hand rang as I was trying to adjust to this and I looked for a button to press to answer it. I worked out that it required a swipe just in time.

'Hello?'

'Hi, babe.' Anton. 'How's Ella doing today?'

I looked down at the baby in my arms. At Ella. She'd stopped screaming, but only because she was sucking furiously on one of her fingers. 'Hungry,' I said.

'I won't keep you, then. I just wanted to say I'm going to be home late. I've got this dinner thing that I can't really get out of.'

I wanted to say that he could. That he could use me – us – as an excuse. But I didn't know whether this was a one-off or a regular occurrence.

'What time will you get here?' I asked.

'It won't be late. Maybe ten or so?'

I thought about the hours that stretched ahead. All that time taking care of this baby – my daughter – on my own. But I wouldn't be here for all that time, would I? I wouldn't have to face those long hours for years. Or possibly ever.

'See you then,' I said, ending the call without saying goodbye.

Ella had lost her fingers and was screaming again. I pulled my top up and my bra down and tried to position her mouth by my nipple. It was the strangest feeling, but luckily she knew what she was doing even though I didn't. I studied her, the top of her head and her small fingers, which were splayed across my chest. She looked about six months old. I felt terribly, horribly lonely, and I didn't really know why. But while I sat with that thought, I was whipped back to the present, to Anton, lying on top of me. I wanted to push him off.

'Babe,' he said afterwards. 'That was magic. You're really something, you know?'

I felt trapped, and I wriggled a bit until he rolled off me.

'Cup of tea?' he asked.

I nodded gratefully, because I wanted him out of the room so I could get dressed. Ten minutes later, after burning my mouth on a too-hot mug of tea, I made an excuse and left. The next time he called, I said I didn't think it was working out, and I never saw him again.

'Here's a question,' Priya said, after I told her about that one. 'Are you effectively gone for the whole time it's happening? Like, you're in the future with the baby for ten or twenty minutes, and when you come back to the present, the same amount of time has passed?'

I didn't know the answer. But I wanted to. The next time was a quiet man called Jonathan who I met at a bar job. He was a stand-up comedian, drily funny and fiercely intelligent. When we went to bed together, I made sure to look at the alarm clock on his bedside table before I 'disappeared': 1.22 p.m. In the vision, I was having lunch with my mum. Unexpected. We were having paella and wine and she was saying that she worried about me, that she wished I was more financially stable. I didn't know what to say, because I didn't know how financially unstable we were talking. And then she said it.

'I don't know that I think Jonathan's the right man for you, sweetie. It's been years now, and no proposal, no talk of babies. I feel like you're waiting around for something that might never happen.'

I was back in the present before I had to answer, and it was still 1.22 p.m. Jonathan was behind me, his arm hooked around my waist, and I was glad I couldn't see his face.

'So time doesn't pass while you're away,' Priya said. 'Interesting.'

'Is it? I mean, I guess it's good, otherwise I'd be sort of absent for the whole act, which feels a bit creepy. But why do you think the guy I was sleeping with wasn't in the vision this time?'

'Because you weren't with him exactly ten years on from that moment,' she said.

'Huh.' I was relieved, then, that I didn't have to work this stuff out on my own.

'Are you going to see him again?' she asked.

'Maybe.'

I didn't, though. I saw him, at work, but when he asked me to go for a drink with him I told him I didn't see it working out, and soon enough we just passed each other glasses and divided up the bar queue like any other colleagues.

I am twenty-five now. There have been other men. But only two. Danny was a DJ with a pretty serious coke habit and that vision was the most terrifying of all. We were on the streets, sitting in a shop doorway, and he was holding my hand but there was no comfort in it. We had a sign made from an old cardboard box, a hat with a scattering of coins in it.

When I told Priya about that one, she took my hand. 'That's really scary,' she said.

'I wish I could know for certain,' I said, 'what these visions actually are. Whether they're what will happen or what could happen, or what I imagine might happen.'

Priya didn't say anything, but she didn't need to, because I knew what she thought. We'd talked about it endlessly. I was convinced that these visions were a true reflection of my future, if I stayed with this particular man. But Priya wasn't so sure.

Perhaps because she's never experienced it, the solidity of it, the depth and the realness.

And then there was Aidan. We'd been at school with him and when I met him, by chance, in a bar, he told me that he'd always had a thing for me. He was sweet but uninspiring. Had a boring-sounding job in IT. With him, for the first time ever, there was no vision at all. And even though that was what I'd always wanted, it was unsettling. Priya and I talked about it often.

'What if there can't be a vision, because he isn't going to be around in ten years' time?' Priya suggested.

I knew we'd both thought about it, but saying it felt dangerous, somehow.

'Or maybe there's just no chance of us having a future together that spans that length of time,' I said. But my heart wasn't in it. I thought she was probably right.

And we only had to wait a few months. Priya came to me, ashen, and took my hands in hers.

'It's Aidan,' she said.

And I didn't need her to say anything else. He'd taken his own life, and once I knew that, it felt like I'd always known he would, in a way.

So, I've never slept with anyone more than once. And in recent years, I've tried to avoid the whole dating scene entirely, with a pretty high success rate.

My thoughts are interrupted by the buzz of my phone. Mum.

'Hey,' I say.

'Maddy, how are you? How was the job?'

I wish I hadn't told her about it, but she was talking about how unreliable the whole acting business was and I thought telling her I had a job as an extra coming up would placate her. I briefly consider lying to her, but there's really no point. She has this sense when it comes to me, always has. Must be a mother thing. She knew when I was out drinking vodka in the park with Priya when I was supposed to be doing my GCSE Science revision, just like now she'll know I haven't spent my day in the background of some scenes in a big-budget British film.

'It was kind of a trick,' I say. 'It was stupid. A Christmas grotto thing.'

She laughs, but it's not unkind. If anyone else reacted to my misfortune that way, I'd be furious. But with Mum, it's just so nice to hear her laughing, after everything that's happened, that I find myself smiling too.

'I was a bloody elf,' I say, wanting to hear it again.

'Oh, Maddy.' And now the disappointment.

'But I have a real audition on Thursday,' I find myself saying. 'I'm just looking over the lines now.'

'Oh, well I'll be sure to call you on Thursday, then, see how it's gone.'

Damnit. If I didn't feel the need to feed her scraps of hope in the form of upcoming auditions, I wouldn't then have to tell her when I didn't get any of them. Why can't I just tell her nothing, and then hopefully surprise her with a secured part at some point? If I ever get one.

I change the subject, ask her how she is, and she launches into a story about my stepdad's sandwiches and how someone else at work has been taking them from the fridge. How she's adding more and more mustard to the ham in an attempt to catch them out. She doesn't mention Henry, and I don't bring him up. When there's an opportunity, I tell her I need to go. I only have an hour before I've agreed to meet Priya, and I need to shower and eat something.

'Good luck for Thursday,' she says, and I wish she didn't have the memory of an elephant.

3

NOW (NOVEMBER 2011)

When I get to the Rose, the pub Priya and I always mean when we say 'pub?' to one another, she's already there, sitting on a bar stool, waving her hands around. Behind the bar, her boyfriend Nic is leaning back with his arms folded across his chest, a huge smile on his face. I wonder what she's telling him as I approach. And then I'm within earshot and I hear her say 'that bloke from Asda' and 'nineteen cups of tea' and 'big inflatable alligator' while showing just how big she's talking with her arms. There's a temptation, with someone like Priya, to ask her to back up, to tell the story again. But she has a seemingly endless supply of them, so there's no need.

'Hey,' Nic says, noticing me. It seems like he has to physically tear his eyes away from his girlfriend. So it's one of their good days.

'Hey, Nic. A glass of your cheapest, driest white wine, please.'

'Come on, Maddy. You know that the cheapest is the Chardonnay but the driest is the Sauvignon Blanc.'

I make a face. 'Remind me how much cheaper the Chardonnay is?'

'Fifty pence a glass.'

'Cheapest wins.'

Priya stands up then, and pulls me in for a hug.

'Priya told me, about the whole grotto thing.' Nic slides my wine across the bar.

I sit down on the stool next to her and drink half the glass in one go. 'You win some, you lose some. Or, no, actually. I can't remember the last time I won one.'

'What about when you got to play the big sister in that advert for washing powder?' Priya asks.

She mimes holding a towel up to her face and I say the line along with her. 'Mmmm, smells like summer.'

'How was your day?' I ask Nic.

By day, Nic is doing a training contract to qualify as a solicitor. Priya is training to be a doctor, after doing a degree in Biology and then deciding medicine was the route for her after all. We're all of us waiting to be the thing we want to be.

'Same old.'

'Listen,' Priya says, signalling to Nic to get us both another glass of wine. 'We've got something we wanted to talk to you about.'

Three things flash through my mind. They are getting married. They are having a baby. They are moving in together. The first two seem highly unlikely. They've always said they'd wait until they'd both finished studying and they were a bit more settled, financially. And Priya's told me countless times that her parents would actually disown her if she had a baby before getting married. Plus, there's the fact that I can't bring myself to believe Nic is the one for Priya. She doesn't know that, because I know just how she'd look at me if I told her. I can't help it, though. He's handsome and charming and funny, but he isn't always that nice to her, and for me, that's the dealbreaker. I try to arrange my features in a neutral curious expression, but Priya's reaction suggests I haven't managed it. She tilts her head to one side.

'You look weird. Can you go back to normal?'

'Are you moving in together?' I ask.

Priya looks a bit pained.

'Yes,' Nic says, sliding my second wine across the bar to soften the blow. 'That's the plan. I hope you're okay with it.'

I know that Priya loves Nic, and he's the best of the boyfriends she's had. And yet... Priya and I have shared a series of flats since we graduated four years ago and she moved down to London, and I'd be lying if I said I wasn't sad about that coming to an end.

'Wow,' I say. 'Wow, that's huge.' I picture myself sitting alone in our current flat, try to imagine who I might possibly bring in as a Priya replacement.

But then Priya reaches a hand out to cover mine. 'We'll help you find a place, if you want us to.'

Oh. So we're all moving out? 'Won't you be busy finding your own place?'

They exchange a look, and it's Nic who says it. 'We thought we'd stay where you guys are at the moment. It's the right sort of size for us, and it's familiar.'

Nic practically lives at our flat as it is, so it strikes me that this isn't so much about him moving in as it is about me moving out. Everyone knows that finding a place in a flat share with strangers is horrendous. I feel daunted at the prospect of it. But they seem happy, and I don't want to piss all over it.

'Sure,' I say. 'I'll find somewhere else. How long were you thinking?'

'There's no rush,' Priya says. 'Nic's about to give notice on his place, but he can move in before you move out, if necessary. It's not like anyone will be sleeping in the other room regularly.'

A small part of me wants to point out that if no one is going to be sleeping in the other room regularly, perhaps I might just stay there. But they've made it clear that they want to live together, alone, and I have enough dignity not to plead with them to include me. I drain my glass, suddenly feeling a bit cold, a bit lost. 'I think I'll go home,' I say.

'Maddy,' Priya says, and her voice sounds like a plea. She's asking me to be okay with this, to not blame her. To let her know that it won't change things. But I'm not sure I can.

'You stay,' I tell her. 'I'm fine. I just need a clear head for that audition tomorrow.'

'Thursday,' Priya says.

'What?'

'Your audition. It's on Thursday.'

Damn her for knowing everything about me, including how I hide myself away when I'm sad and need to process something.

'I just... I have to go, okay? But it's fine, honestly. I'll start looking for a place. I'll keep you posted. I'm happy for you guys.'

I give Priya a hug, and it's a comfort.

Nic leans across the bar and kisses my cheek. 'Try to be happy for us,' he whispers in my ear, and it pisses me off, but what can I say?

I'm pulling my coat on when Priya asks if I'll be alright walking home on my own, and I tell her I will, that she should stay. It's clear that she wants to stay, and besides, I want to be alone.

It's a ten-minute walk back to the flat, and I stomp through the soggy leaves on the pavement, my mood low. It's not Priya's fault that I can't have a boyfriend. But when we were younger, it didn't really matter because none of her relationships were serious and I knew she'd always come back to me and our friendship in the end. And then Nic came along, and it was clear quite early on that things had shifted, that this wasn't a fling or a short-lived affair. It was all leading here. So why didn't I see this coming?

I round the corner onto our street and up my pace until I get to our front door. Mrs Aziz, who lives upstairs, is rooting through her bag for her keys. I call out to her to avoid alarming her, and she turns with an armful of flowers and asks me if I could possibly come up to water her spider plants. She keeps them on a shelf that's too high for her to reach, for some reason, and every week or so I call round and give them a drink.

While I'm filling the watering can she keeps on the kitchen worktop, she puts the kettle on and offers me tea. And I'm about to politely turn her down when I realise I'd enjoy half an hour in her company. She's wise, Mrs Aziz. And she gives it to you straight. I fill her in on what's happening.

'So that tall boy is moving in?' she asks.

We're sitting on her sofa, which has seen better days, and I feel like I'm gradually sinking in closer to her. I hold on to the armrest in a bid to keep myself in one place.

'Yes.'

'And you're moving out?'

'Right.'

'Oh, my dear. But who will look after my spider plants?'

I laugh. 'I'll come back from wherever I'm living. Or I could help you move them to somewhere more accessible. I'm easy.'

She sips her tea. 'You are sad about this.'

'I am. It's just, Priya and I have lived together for a long time. And there are so many awful flats out there, and so many terrible housemates. It's just so easy, with Priya. And it's a great street...'

'Great neighbours,' she says.

Mrs Aziz is a great neighbour. Our flats were once a Victorian house. We have the downstairs; she has the upstairs. Everyone who's lived in a flat conversion like that knows that the downstairs neighbours can hear every move the upstairs neighbours make, but Mrs Aziz goes to bed at about nine o'clock in the evening and sleeps in until nine o'clock in the morning, so she's never once kept us up. She doesn't play loud music, she doesn't have a car to park inconsiderately. She's neat and clean and she's kind. Every year, for Eid, she brings us food she's made.

'Great neighbours,' I say.

'Still, you'll find something, and it could lead to a great adventure.'

'What do you mean?'

'Well, you might meet someone you fall in love with, or a fabulous new friend. You might have a new neighbour who also pretends to need help with watering her plants, because she likes your company.'

I'm touched by her sweetness. I want to tell her that if she wanted to spend a bit of time with me, she could just have said that. But I recognise that that's not quite true. I am always busy, always bustling around from one thing to the next. Auditions and jobs and hobbies and even, very occasionally, dates.

'Well,' I say, taking deep breaths to keep my voice steady. 'I'm not going anywhere just yet. And I'll tell you more when I know it.'

'Okay, dear,' she says. 'Now, do you and that flatmate of yours need cookies? I made cookies earlier, and I can't eat them all myself.'

I let myself into our flat with a plastic tub of cinnamon and raisin cookies in one hand, and when I go into my room and see the elf costume from earlier, I'm reminded of what a shitty day it's been all round. I sit on my bed, open the cookies, and eat one and then another, and then a third. When I'm reaching for the fourth and final cookie, I tell myself that Priya doesn't have to know they ever existed. After all, my need is greater right now.

4

NOW (JANUARY 2012)

I lean against the wall, slightly out of breath from walking up three flights of stairs. Should have taken the lift. The guy I'm meeting here buzzed me into the building, so he knows I'm on my way up. I knock on the door. This is the sixth property of the day, and the other five have left a lot to be desired. The first was a house share with four girls, who all looked like they didn't eat often enough. They told me they were dancers. The house was clean and tidy but I could just tell they hated me, and as I was leaving one of them let slip that the room had become available because their friend had died. I marked it on the list on my phone as a no, but later changed it to a maybe after seeing the flat full of pet snakes and the flat that looked like it was last cleaned in the 1980s. In every instance, either the place or the people have put me off.

And this is the last one. The last one of the six I emailed hopefully, after reading their ads with Priya online. Now that Christmas has been and gone, it's time to get serious. I know that Priya and Nic said they didn't mind how long it took me, but I also know they were just being polite. They want me out, so they can start their cohabiting life together properly. I'm getting in the way of them having sex in the kitchen and watching TV naked.

This place is on the top floor of a small, purpose-built block, and the stairwell didn't smell so I'm expecting terrible things from the flatmates. I wasn't sure how I felt about moving in with a couple, but Priya persuaded me it was worth a look. The name of the guy I'm meeting has escaped me, so I root around in my bag for my notebook, where I wrote down all the names and phone numbers and addresses. And then the door swings open.

'Hi,' a man says.

He's young and handsome and he looks familiar, but I can't immediately place him. I look down at my notebook, try to decipher the name I've scrawled. Oliver.

'It's you!' he says. 'Maddy, right?'

Well, this is embarrassing. Where do I know him from? A cold wave of dread crashes over me as I contemplate the possibility that we've been on a date, but I know almost immediately that it's impossible. I barely date. Work, then?

'What, you don't recognise me without the elf costume?'

Oliver! From the grotty grotto job. 'Hi!' I try to use enthusiasm to detract from how long it took me to answer him. 'I'm just shocked, that's all. What are the chances?'

'Come in,' he says. 'Shall I put the kettle on?'

I wonder whether his partner is here too, but I decide it's unlikely that they'd both be available on a Tuesday afternoon. He's an actor; it makes sense that he's the one showing people around. Inside, the flat's bright and airy, and there are plants and pictures on the walls so that it looks like someone's actual home rather than a crack den. 'This is... nice.'

'You sound surprised.'

'Believe me, if you'd seen some of the places I've seen today, you'd be surprised, too. So why is the room free, if you don't mind me asking? I've been in one dead girl's room today and don't much fancy seeing another.'

Oliver widens his eyes. 'Well, we just decided it was time to let it out. We could do with the money.' He's led me into the kitchen, which is small but clean, with cookbooks lining one wall. 'So, tea? Tell me how you take it and I'll make it while you look around. I don't know about you, but I hate having to follow someone around making small talk.'

I'm so relieved. I'm nosy and love poking around other people's homes, but being shown around is its own kind of hell. I tell him milk and no sugar, and I head into the living room. There are three doors – all slightly ajar – in a row at one end of the room. Two bedrooms and a bathroom, I'm guessing.

I open the first door and put my head inside, realise it's his room – their room – and don't back out immediately. It's tidy, for the most part. Bed made, curtains drawn. There's something I can't put my finger on at first, and then I realise what it is. The clothes on the chair in the corner all look like men's things. There's no makeup or jewellery or women's clothes in evidence. Maybe she's just very tidy.

The bathroom, in between the two bedrooms, is the best one I've seen today, and actually about on a par with the one at home. Which just leaves the room that would be my bedroom. I open the door and step inside. There's light flooding in, and on the double bed, there's a black cat lying fast asleep. I go over to the bed, and the cat jerks awake, stares at me with yellow eyes. I put a hand out tentatively, and it gives me a sniff before curling up again in the sunshine. The room's a little smaller than Oliver and his girlfriend's room, but it's big enough. I picture my furniture in it – wardrobe against that wall, chest of drawers here. I might just fit in the armchair that I like to sit and read in, too.

'Ah, I see you've met Marjorie,' Oliver says. 'I hope you're not allergic.'

I hadn't realised he was behind me and I jump.

'Shit, sorry. I didn't mean to sneak up.'

'Not allergic. She's beautiful. How long have you had her?'

He frowns and I can't decide whether he's trying to work it out or whether there's a painful memory attached. 'Just over a year. She was from a rescue, so we don't know how old she is, but they thought she was about two at the time. Tea's ready.'

We go back into the living room and I sink into one of the sofas while he takes the other one.

'This is a really nice place,' I say. 'Have you had lots of people coming to look round?'

'Not yet, but there are lots booked in.' He seems a bit uncomfortable, like there's something he needs to get off his chest.

Of all the places I've seen today, which appeared to be the best of what the internet had to offer in this part of London, this is the only place that I can see myself living in. I tell him that, and he smiles a bit thinly.

'Full disclosure,' he says. 'The ad said that you'd be sharing with a couple, but actually it's just me.'

I stand up immediately. 'So you lied about who lived here to entice people in?'

'No, no, it's not like that. I promise. My girlfriend just left me.' He breaks off, and for the first time I see the sadness in his eyes, and I worry that he's going to cry, but he holds it together. 'It'd been her idea to let the room, but I didn't know it was because she was planning to leave. She literally just told me – and went – yesterday.'

I am still standing, and I'm studying him. Do I believe him? If he lied about having a girlfriend, if he's lying now, that's really creepy. But if he's telling the truth? Well, this place is a hundred times better than anything else I've seen. And I know Oliver a bit. He's not a complete stranger.

'I know how women might feel about sharing with a guy they don't know. And I'd rather live with a woman, to be honest. Most men are animals. I like to keep the place nice. I've emailed the people who were booked in for tomorrow, and more than half of the women have cancelled. So I thought I'd just test the water, with you. And then I was blindsided because we'd met before. I mean, what are the chances?'

Without really making a decision one way or the other, I find myself sitting down again. Oliver smiles. And then I'm thinking about how it must feel to share a flat with a partner – to get a cat together – and then to have to find someone else to move in. We're both a bit bruised in our own different ways, and perhaps we can help one another. Plus, I know he's an actor. We could run lines for auditions.

'I'll take it,' I say.

He splutters, spills a bit of his tea, goes to fetch a cloth. 'Wow, you don't need to think about it?'

'Trust me, this is the best place I'm going to see. And if I wait, and let other people see it, you might find someone you like better. What do you think? I'm pretty easy to live with. I keep myself to myself, I'm usually in bed before midnight and I do my fair share of cleaning. Oh, and I can cook.'

'Do you have a car? There's one parking space with the flat and I have one, so...'

'No car.'

'You're okay with Marjorie?' he asks.

Marjorie appears at that moment, slinking over to where we're sitting, tail high. She comes straight to me and jumps up onto my lap. I laugh. 'Fine with Marjorie.'

'And it looks like she's fine with you. Let's do this, Maddy.'

If it wasn't for Marjorie, I would stand up. I might hug him. But instead, we hold our mugs of tea up and towards each other, as if in a toast.

Soon after that, I leave. I walk home to see how long it takes, and it's just over ten minutes.

Priya and Nic are in the kitchen. He's cooking and she's opening bottles of beer.

'I found a place!'

'Already?' Nic turns away from the hob.

'Already.' I turn to Priya. 'Remember that elf guy who came into the café after I did that awful grotto job? I'm going to be living with him.'

'Wow, that's funny, that he was looking for someone just as you needed a place.'

There's something underneath what she's saying. It's like she's somehow unhappy with how things have worked out, which doesn't make sense because she was the one who wanted me to go.

'I know, I couldn't believe it. But he lives in this really nice, homely flat and he has a cat called Marjorie. He's just split up with his girlfriend.'

'Will it be just the two of you?'

'Yep. But I really think it will be fine. I have a good feeling about it.'

Priya goes to the fridge and gets another bottle of beer for me. 'Great. When do you move in?'

'He said as soon as I want to, basically. So I wondered what you guys thought. Fancy helping me move?'

'We've hired a van next weekend to move me,' Nic says. 'We can just move both of us!'

'That feels really fast,' Priya says.

Nic frowns. 'But if it's the right place, and she's happy, isn't that the main thing?'

'Yeah, of course, it's just...'

She doesn't finish the sentence and I think I know what's bothering her. Priya likes to adjust to things slowly. She's never liked surprises, or being spontaneous. She wants to move in with Nic, I know that, and she wants me to go, but she just wants it all to happen at a glacial pace, so she can get used to it. In the past, I would have pandered to her, but not this time. I don't want to let this flat go.

'It's fine,' I say, crossing the room and putting a hand on her back. 'It'll all be fine, okay?'

She doesn't answer, but she gives me a small smile. I go to my room, let them have dinner in peace, and I only go out to make myself something when I hear they've moved into the living room to watch TV. I feel exhausted from the day, and I'm tempted to have a bowl of cereal, but I know I'll feel better if I eat something proper, so I root around in the fridge and make a quick mushroom stir-fry, then I take it back to my room and eat it on my bed listening to a radio play.

Much later, when I'm ready for bed, I take my bowl out to the kitchen and find Priya in there in a pair of Nic's boxers and a vest top, the light off.

'What are you doing in the dark?' I ask.

'I don't know,' she says, going to the fridge and opening it. 'I was hungry, and I just feel weird about everything changing.' She takes out a big bar of Milka and holds it up.

'Sure,' I say, pulling a chair out and sitting down at the kitchen table. I'm not sure how to ask what I want to, so I just blurt it out. 'The whole moving in thing, was it Nic's idea?'

She shakes her head vigorously, as if trying to dislodge the very suggestion. 'No, I mean, not only his. I love him, Maddy, and it just seems like the obvious next step, but I don't know, it's been a long time that I've lived with you and you know I hate it when things change.'

'Do your parents know?' I ask.

She looks at me. Priya's parents have let go of thinking she'll marry a nice Hindu boy. They've known about Nic for a long time. But this – moving in together – is big. 'They know.'

'And they're okay with it?'

'I mean, they'd much rather I had a ring on my finger, but they haven't forbidden it or anything.'

I take a big chunk of the chocolate she's broken up. 'My new place is less than fifteen minutes away,' I say.

She brightens a bit at that. 'Walking, or on the Tube?'

'Walking. I'll be here all the time, and you can come there. It's a new era, but it doesn't have to be the end of anything.' But it's not quite true, and we both know it.

When I go back to my room, I lie awake for a long time, hoping that we're all doing the right thing.

5

NOW (JANUARY 2012)

'Whatever you do,' Priya says, 'don't sleep with him.'

'Why would she sleep with him?' Nic asks.

We're sitting in a row in the front seat of a hired van, Nic at the wheel, my worldly possessions in the back.

'I don't know, sometimes people sleep together. Especially when they're young and attractive.'

Last night, Priya found a photo of Oliver on his agent's website, because she said she didn't remember what he looked like properly. We sat side by side, studying him.

'Was he in *Hollyoaks*?'

'Yes!'

'I thought so. Hot but inappropriate lecturer.'

'I'm not going to sleep with him,' I say now.

Nic doesn't know about the whole ten-year vision thing, of course. He often asks why I never go on dates, never show much interest in anyone. There's only so many times you can say you're trying to focus on your career, especially when your career is as much of a shambles as mine is right now.

'Left here,' I say, pointing. 'And then you can pull in behind that Toyota.'

The Toyota pulls out without indicating just as Nic's starting to park and he leans on the horn and makes gestures through the window. I'm glad to get out.

We stretch our legs and I notice that it's cold enough to see your breath. We've only been in the van for a few minutes, but our limbs are tired and aching from lifting and moving all of Nic's possessions and then mine. I don't have a key yet, so we go up in the lift empty-handed and I press the buzzer, and when Oliver opens the door, he's all smiles.

'These are my friends,' I tell him. 'Priya and Nic.'

Oliver shakes their hands, and it feels a bit formal. A bit awkward. But then he's asking who wants a drink and we're heading down to bring up some boxes, and I relax. He has a way, I think, of putting me at ease, and that's a great trait for a flatmate to have.

By the time we're done, I'm absolutely shattered. Oliver made us all tea and then pitched in, and after we've made the last trip, all four of us collapse onto the sofas in the living room.

'That's it,' Nic says. 'Everyone stays where they are now, forever.'

When I glance over at Oliver, I catch him looking at me, and I can't quite interpret the expression on his face. Just then, Marjorie comes into the room and Priya makes that kissing sort of noise while holding out her hand, and Marjorie goes to her and she squeals.

'What a beautiful cat! Can I move in?' Priya asks.

'What about everyone staying where they are forever?' I ask.

'Oh yes. Well, I'll have to visit a lot to see this beautiful kitty.'

'Right,' Nic says, standing up and brushing off his jeans. 'Let's go, Priya.'

I feel suddenly as though I might cry. It feels a bit like the day Priya and I went off to separate universities. But no, I'm being stupid. She's going to be a short walk away, not a train journey. And it's nice here. I've really landed on my feet. We hug for a long time and I notice Nic rolling his eyes at Oliver over our heads. When they leave, I stand by the door for a moment, gathering myself.

Oliver comes out into the hallway and clears his throat. 'I thought maybe we could have some wine?'

I know it's not a good idea, that I'll drink too much, too fast, and get all sad and open up slightly more than is comfortable. 'We should definitely have some wine,' I say.

'And did you have any plans for dinner? Because it's been quite a day and I thought maybe I'd order a pizza.'

Pizza and wine. It sounds heavenly. 'I like anything other than pineapple,' I say. 'Okay if I have a shower? I feel disgusting.'

Oliver laughs. 'Maddy, you live here. You don't have to ask for permission to have a shower.'

The shower is hot and has great pressure and I realise, afterwards, when I'm putting my pyjamas on, that I'm sort of tensed, waiting to find out what's wrong with this setup. Because it feels a bit too good to be true. The clean flat, the nice flatmate, the cat. But then I remember that I had to move out of the place I loved. So maybe that was my bad luck, and this is my good. I tell myself not to be so cynical, to just be happy that it's all worked out well. And then I run a brush through my wet hair and go into the living room, where Oliver's sitting on one sofa with his legs crossed, two glasses of white wine on the coffee table.

Four glasses of wine later, I'm officially drunk. 'So you see, that's what really cemented our friendship, I think.' I stumble a bit over the word 'cemented'. I've only eaten a couple of slices of the pizza, because we've been chatting, and it's easier to drink than eat when you're in the middle of a conversation.

Oliver has told me about his acting successes and failures, and I've shared mine. He's told me why he got into acting in the first place – he joined a drama club to spend time with a girl he liked, but then he completely fell in love with it and can't imagine doing anything else. I've said that it was similar for me, GCSE Drama chosen on a whim and then getting up on stage and being totally surprised by the feeling of being at home. In the right place. I've told him a bit about my non-existent love life, too (but I haven't told him why that's the case), and my friendship with Priya. He's easy to talk to. He pays attention, sometimes looping back to something I said a while ago, always letting me go first if we start to speak at the same time.

'She seems nice,' Oliver says. 'And him.'

'Between you and me... I'm not really his biggest fan.'

'Because he took your flat, or because he's not right for your friend?'

I think. 'Mostly the latter.' I stand up to top us both up, but he covers his glass.

'I've had enough.'

He's right. We've both had enough. But there's only a dribble left, so I pour it into my glass and take the empty bottle through to the kitchen. When I get back, Oliver is staring into space.

'Tell me about your girlfriend,' I say, suddenly wanting to know the full story. 'I mean, ex-girlfriend. If you want to, of course.'

'There isn't much to tell, I don't think. We met about eighteen months ago and got very serious very quickly. We were both living in these really awful house shares, so it just made sense for us to get a place together, even though it was a big step, looking back. We were twenty-five. And gradually, we just grew to be more like friends than lovers. You don't always notice it happening, until it's pointed out to you. When she came to me and said she was moving out, I was crushed but I think I knew straight away that it was the right thing, too. We weren't doing each other any favours, letting things stagnate like that. We both deserved better. So yeah, she's gone and there are no hard feelings.'

It seems like a very grown-up outlook. I watch him as he speaks, and it's clear that he's telling the truth. He loved this girl, and they grew apart. No one's fault. And for some reason, it's like that's the moment I see him clearly for the first time. Not when he introduced himself, dressed as an elf. Not when I came to look at the flat. But now, sitting across from him, having drunk a bit too much wine. He is so handsome, with his thick, slightly messy hair and a jawline to die for, and it doesn't hurt that Marjorie is curled up in his lap and he's stroking the top of her head.

For the most part, it's been pretty easy to stay away from men, because most of the men I've met haven't been attractive to me for one reason or another. Too much ego, or unkind, or boring. And here, for the first time in a long time, I'm sitting with a man who seems to strike just the right balance. Very little ego (despite being an actor), kind, interesting. We lock eyes and he moves across the room, gently placing Marjorie on the floor, and sits beside me, and I can feel the heat of his leg against mine and I'm suddenly aware that I haven't so much as kissed a man for months.

It's slow, deliberate. We're both careful to give the other person adequate chance to back out. But neither of us does, and eventually we are kissing, and it doesn't feel like kissing sometimes does, where you're worried about the position of your head or whether your eyes are closed. It feels like the magical kind, where you forget about everything and just give in to the feeling of it, and you're unaware of your entire body because all you know is that your mouth and this other person's mouth belong together, and must ideally never be apart again. But then he pulls away, and I dip my head, ready for him to say it was a mistake.

'That was a mistake.'

I'm gutted, but I nod. I won't let him see. I hear Priya saying, *Whatever you do, don't sleep with him.*

He clears his throat, and it brings me back to the room, and I'm so embarrassed I could cry. Am I going to have to move out now?

'I shouldn't have done that, Maddy. Not because I didn't want to – I think it was quite clear that I wanted to – but it puts us in such a strange position. We've literally just moved in together, and I've only just come out of another relationship, and I don't want us to sleep together and then not be able to look at each other in the kitchen the next day. It's my fault. I shouldn't have let it happen.'

It's quite the speech. I open my mouth to say that I wouldn't have let it go as far as us sleeping together, but I'm not entirely convinced that's true. There was something about that kiss. I'm not sure I would have wanted to stop it at all. But he's right, of course.

'I'm sorry,' I say. 'Can we just pretend it didn't happen?'

'Yes, I think we should. I'm so glad we're on the same page about it, because I really want you to feel at home here, Maddy. I really want this to work out.'

I stand up, feel a bit wobbly. My face is flushed and I can't look at him. 'I'm going to go to bed, and maybe tomorrow we could just start again?'

'Absolutely.'

I turn and walk to my room, hear Marjorie pattering after me on the wood floor. And when I throw myself onto the bed, she comes up alongside me, as if in solidarity. I stroke her silky-smooth ears. 'Bollocks,' I say, but only quietly because I'm not yet sure how sound travels in this place. 'That wasn't great, was it?'

6

NOW (JANUARY 2012)

When I wake the next morning, I can't put my finger on the sense of unease in my gut for about thirty seconds. Then I remember. Oliver, the kiss, the agreement to chalk it up to insanity. Shit. I want to go into the kitchen for water but I also don't really want to run into him. How have I turned this nice flat share into an awkward situation in less than twenty-four hours? But then, I hear the front door click shut. Was that him coming in or going out? Surely going out. It's – I check my phone – just after seven thirty. No one has already been out at that time on a Sunday in January, have they?

I open the door slowly. The main living space is empty. I scuttle out, feeling like an idiot, and then I see a movement out of the corner of my eye and let out an involuntary yelp. But it's just Marjorie. I go over and give her a bit of a fuss, and then I seek out some bread and put a couple of slices in the toaster. Food shopping. Must do some food shopping. While I'm at the kitchen table eating the toast with a scraping of Oliver's jam, which I vow inwardly to replace, I call Priya.

'If I hang up without warning, don't worry,' I tell her.

'Why? What's going on? Tell me you didn't sleep with him.'

'No!'

'So what then?'

'We kissed. But I swear it wasn't my doing. Or not only mine. And then we agreed to act like it hadn't happened, and now I'm eating toast in my pyjamas and talking to you and he's out, but if he comes back I need to either end the call immediately or change the subject.'

'Let's talk about CANDLE syndrome.'

'What?'

'If we have to change the subject. It's a rare disease I learned about last week.'

I have no idea what to say.

'Anyway,' she goes on, 'I'm sort of torn between being cross with you for putting yourself in this position and excited, because Oliver seems really nice and you haven't kissed anyone for ages, so I know it must have meant something, even if you're now going to pretend it didn't.'

In the background, I hear Nic's voice. 'Wait? She kissed him?'

And then I hear something else. The rustle of a key. 'So what's CANDLE syndrome all about, then?'

She doesn't miss a beat. 'It's this thing that usually occurs in the first year of life. Autoinflammatory. Nasty.'

'Right, so...'

Oliver appears in the room, all smiles. He has a paper bag that he puts down on the kitchen worktop.

'Is he right there?' Priya asks.

'Yep.'

'And do you fancy him? Would you, if none of this whole awkward flatmates situation was in the equation, kiss him again?'

I think back to the kiss. The rightness of it. It's never felt like that for me before. And it makes me wonder whether I've just kissed the wrong people. And if he's somehow right for me. But how can I possibly find out without letting it happen again? And he was very clear about not wanting that. I mean, I was, too. But he's the one who's just come out of a serious relationship, and all of this is before I've even started to think about the future vision thing. 'Yes.'

Priya squeals, and I have to hold the phone a bit away from my ear. Oliver smiles and motions to the kettle, and I nod.

'I should go,' I tell her.

'Okay, but message me later and tell me everything. Promise?'

'I mean, there's nothing else to tell, but sure.'

'Not now, but there might be later. Okay, I'm going. Have a great day.'

I end the call and get up but I'm not sure where I'm planning to go.

'Morning,' Oliver says. He doesn't seem awkward at all. He's wearing running clothes and he's sweaty. 'I brought pastries.' He gestures to the paper bag. 'Force of habit. Every Sunday I would go for a run and pick up pastries on the way home. Anyway, there are too many for just me. Help yourself. I'm going for a shower. I'll do the tea when I come out.'

I don't say a word. I just stay where I am, wondering whether we can really sit here drinking tea and eating pastries and pretending that we didn't kiss last night. But that's just what we do. He reappears ten minutes later with wet hair, and I ask him about his run while he makes the tea, and I get a plate out for the pastries, and we sit down opposite one another and I think that we're behaving like a couple, and I don't know what to do about it.

'Any work on?' I ask. We didn't get into the specifics of our current situations last night.

He pulls a face. 'I've got auditions for a couple of adverts, and there's this play I've been asked to do, but there's pretty much zero budget. You?'

'Similar. I'm down to the last two for an advert and my agent's heard about a bit part in a sitcom so she's going to put me forward for that. Plus the side hustle, of course.'

Most actors have a side hustle. Bar or restaurant work, on the whole. I find it exhausting to deal with people for hours on end, so I've tended towards online work. Things I can do from home, in my pyjamas. Copywriting. I write descriptions of hotels I've never visited, lists of top ten attractions for cities I have to google to spell correctly. I write website copy for garden centres and, sometimes, the government.

'And is that the only kind of writing you do?' Oliver asks when I've explained.

'What do you mean?'

'I mean, do you write scripts or anything like that?'

I feel my skin redden as I remember telling people as a teenager that I was going to write scripts for film and TV. Before I knew how hard it was to break in. And before I knew how it felt to be in front of the camera or on the stage.

'No, just the copywriting. These pastries are amazing. Where did you get them?'

'Deli across the road. They do great coffee too.'

I pick up the flaky pieces of pastry with my fingertip, making sure to savour every last bit. Oliver notices this and immediately reaches into the bag and puts another pain au chocolat on my plate. I laugh, not intending to eat it, but then I realise that I want it, this delicious thing he's offering, so I do.

'What's your side hustle?' I ask. 'Assuming *Hollyoaks* actors still have one.'

'Well, I'm not sure about that guy who's played Tony for

about thirty years, but us bit-parters definitely do. I teach people to swim. Mostly kids.'

I wasn't expecting that. 'Wow, that sounds—'

'Noisy? Frustrating? Hard work? It's all those things, but it's pretty great, too. That moment when you see a child go from not being able to do something to being able to do it, and it's down to you. That's really something.'

'I was going to say brilliant,' I say, though I'm not sure it's true.

Back in my room, lying on my bed with a novel, I struggle to concentrate. Who is this man who likes cats and cleans and brings pastries and teaches children to swim, for Christ's sake? And why couldn't I have met him in a bar or something?

In the late morning, he knocks on my door, and I get up and open it, putting a hand to my hair to try to smooth it down.

'I'm just going out for a bit,' he says.

We don't know what kind of flatmates we are to each other yet. The kind who live independently and move around each other largely in silence, or the kind who are good friends, who tell each other where they're going and what they're doing, or somewhere in between. So it's nice of him to tell me he's going out. I didn't expect it.

'Have a good time,' I say.

He smiles at me, meets my eye and catches the side of his bottom lip in his teeth, and the effect it has on me is powerful. I really like this guy. There's no point pretending I don't. To myself, at least.

'Well,' he says, 'see you later.'

And then he's gone, leaving me to wonder whether he's going on a date or to serve soup to homeless people or something else equally charming and wholesome. I try to get back into the book, but it's not happening, so after ten minutes I give up and head over to my old flat. I need a coffee and I need Priya's wisdom.

She's in the kitchen, making soup. Nic's playing on his Xbox, and Priya whispers that he's in a mood. I make hot drinks for us and don't offer him one.

'How's it going?' Priya asks. 'With the dreamboat?' She has her hands on her hips and an apron on, her hair tied up on top of her head.

I can't help but laugh. 'Who says "dreamboat"?'

'Don't try to change the subject.' She turns back to the hob, puts the lid on the pan and comes to sit down with me at the table.

'It's like someone made him for me,' I say. 'It's like someone crept into my brain and accessed all my hidden thoughts about what I want in a man and made him.'

Priya claps her hands excitedly.

'No,' I tell her, 'it's not good. I have literally just moved in with him, and also, you know I don't do this.'

'Don't do what? Falling in love?'

It sounds ludicrous, when she says that. Firstly because that's not what this is, is it? It's just lust. Just attraction. And also because who doesn't 'do' falling in love? 'I can't let it happen, for so many reasons. He's just come out of a relationship, he's my flatmate and if we have sex, I will see a miserable future with him and it will be so depressing.'

'What if you don't?'

'What if I don't what?'

'What if what you see isn't miserable? Come on, Maddy. The fact that it's always been miserable before doesn't mean it always will be. He could be the one. You could see everything you've ever wanted. And even if you don't, who's to say that what you see is what's going to happen?'

I focus on the part about seeing everything I've ever wanted. What would that look like? I don't know, at first, because I've pushed the idea of romantic love so far to the back of my mind. I've locked it away. But when I was younger, before I'd ever found out about this stupid ability I have, there were things I wanted. A loving relationship, a nice home. A child?

'I can't,' I say. Because I'm scared of how much I'm starting to like him, and I'm scared that we'll sleep together and it will be a disaster, and I won't even be able to tell him what the problem is. And then I'll have to find somewhere else to live and it will be awful and I'll probably get murdered in my sleep.

Priya shrugs. 'Sometimes you have to take a chance. You know, you can't always control everything.'

'I don't try to control everything.'

She snorts a laugh, and I hit her on the arm, but not hard.

On the walk back to Oliver's place – because that's how I think of it, even though I'm trying to think of it as home – I go back through my catalogue of awful sexual encounters, start to finish. I won't add Oliver to that catalogue. I can't. I like him too much. Damn it.

7

NOW (APRIL 2012)

For the first few months of living together, Oliver and I are polite and courteous and we keep each other informed about where we're going and when we'll be home. Neither of us keeps regular hours, because of auditions and side hustles, but we leave each other notes on the whiteboard on the kitchen wall if we don't see each other to say goodbye. When we're both around for dinner, we take it in turns to cook. I make him my Thai green curry; he makes me something with prawns and noodles. We talk about things that are safe. Work, friendships, ambitions. In the evenings, we sometimes watch TV together (mostly crime dramas and films of all kinds that we pull to pieces, either guessing the ending or suggesting how they could have been better) and sometimes we read. When I tell Priya about all this, she says it sounds very much like we're a couple, and when I point out that we don't have sex, she says that lots of couples don't have sex, and there's nothing I can really say to that.

I've been there three months and it's turned from winter to spring when he knocks on my door one Sunday afternoon and asks if I have time to run some lines with him for an audition he has the next day. It's an advert for a new chocolate bar called Zoom, and the money's better than average, so he really wants it. I take the crumpled page he hands me and go out into the living room. We stand opposite each other and he says his first line.

'I know it hasn't been that long but there's something I've been wanting to say to you.'

I clear my throat. 'I think I know what you're going to say.'

'I love you.'

Even though I can see it there on the page, and I know it's not real, it brings me up short. His eyes are fixed on mine and he looks serious.

'And I love a Zoom.'

We're silent, and I fold the page into a small square for something to do.

'Is it the worst script you've ever read?' he asks.

'I mean, it's pretty bad, but I've seen worse.'

'How do you think I should play it? The "I love you" part? Straight and sincere, or jokey?'

I think for a moment. 'I think the way you did it was fine.'

'Okay, can we do it again? I'll try a few different ways and you can see which you think is best.'

I agree, of course, because all he's asking me for is ten minutes or so of my time, but it's quite awkward to stand there and have him tell me he loves me over and over, with different intonations. To have to rate them for him. When he's happy, he takes the piece of paper from me and says thank you. I'm about to go back to my room but he asks if I want a cup of tea, and I do, so we go into the kitchen, and he flicks the kettle on while I get the mugs out and root around in my cupboard for chocolate digestives.

'When will you know, about the ad?' I ask.

'Not sure. Pretty soon, I think. And then I'll know whether I can afford to go on holiday this year.'

His voice is light, but he knows I understand this way of living. Being broke and worried about rent one day and having enough to pay for a holiday the next. There's so much heartbreak in it, so many near misses, and you have to keep bouncing back, keep going for things even when you think there's no chance you'll get them, because you just never know.

'Do you have anything coming up?' he asks.

'I got that sitcom part. Did I say? It's only two episodes.' I know I didn't say, because the day it happened he was turned down for a play he'd been counting on.

'No! That's great news.' He comes over and puts his arms around me and he smells incredible, like wood and coffee and mint. 'Well done, Maddy.'

When he releases me, I feel stunned, like I might trip and fall. So I'm not expecting what he says next.

'I think you should try writing something.'

'What, other than the website stuff I do?'

'Yeah, I mean, like a script. I think you'd be really good at it. When we watch films, you always have such good ideas.'

Sometimes, in the evenings, I go to my room and get in bed with my laptop and work on something I've been toying with for a few years. But nobody knows about that. 'Thank you. Do you have writing ambitions?'

He gives a quick shake of his head, and then he goes to get the milk out of the fridge, and I wonder whether it's something I could be open with him about, in time. He might even be good for some input. By the time he speaks again, in my head we're a successful screenwriting duo, so I'm caught off guard.

'I'm seeing Gemma later.'

'Gemma?' I don't actually need him to clarify; I'm stalling for time. Because Gemma is the ex, the one who lived here until a few months ago.

'My ex.'

'How did that come about?'

He hands me a steaming mug and sits down opposite me. Then he puts a hand to the back of his hair and looks down at the table. 'She called me. She wants to talk.'

I feel a cold clutch of dread. What if she wants him back? And then I interrogate myself – what if she does? Am I worried about losing the flat, or losing him?

'How do you feel about it all?' It's such a vague question, and there are so many ways he could choose to answer it.

'I want to hear what she's got to say. I want to know if she left me for someone else, or if it was just the fact that we'd drifted.'

'Do you think there was someone else?'

He looks past me, to the wall, and I wish I could move over to him and put my arms around him. But it would be the worst possible time to do something like that.

'Maybe,' he says. 'There was this guy she worked with, who I sometimes wondered about.'

'Will it make you feel any better, to know?'

He snaps his eyes back to meet mine. 'That's a really good question. And honestly, I don't know. I just don't know.'

Soon after that, he gets ready and goes. I want to tell him that he looks nice, but the words catch in my throat. And as soon as he's left, I feel inexplicably lonely. I curl up on the sofa with Marjorie and turn on the TV. There's a new BBC drama I'm dying to watch but I know Oliver will like it, so I decide to wait for him. Instead, I watch three back-to-back episodes of a reality show about a semi-famous family, stopping every now and again to make tea.

Priya and I message back and forth about some of the

patients she's been looking after, and it snaps me out of feeling sorry for myself. I'll make dinner, I think. It's coming up for seven, and he's bound to be back soon. I root through the fridge and the cupboards, find a pack of sausages and some potatoes and a butternut squash, and I start preparing a sort of traybake. But even though the veg take an eternity to roast, he's still not here when it's ready. I take a portion for myself and leave the rest in the cooling oven, and I eat it sitting in front of the TV.

I'm in bed with a book when I hear the door open and crashing noises in the hallway.

'Sorry!' he calls. 'Sorry, Maddy.'

I get up, intending to go out there and see him, because he sounds strange, possibly drunk, and he's been gone for about eight hours. But then I second-guess it. Will that look strange, me going out to meet him in my pyjamas, desperate to hear about his afternoon and evening? I'm standing near my bedroom door, unsure, when there's a light knocking. If I'd been asleep, I would have missed it.

'Come in,' I say, and my voice is a bit croaky from not having spoken to anyone for hours.

The door opens and he almost falls into the room. 'Maddy!' he says, as if we are old friends and it's been years since we saw each other. He pulls me into an enormous hug and the tightness of it is comforting. He reeks of alcohol.

'How did it go?' I ask. 'With Gemma?'

He screws up his face. I'm guessing not well. I want to ask if he's been with her all this time, but it isn't my place.

'She wanted to tell me all the things she didn't like about me,' he says, finally letting go of me. 'It was a long list.'

I feel simultaneously devastated for him and pleased that she wasn't asking him to give things another go, and I don't really know what to do with either feeling.

'Must have been,' I say. 'You were a long time.'

'Oh, that only took an hour, but then I felt like drowning my sorrows, so I called my friend Matt and I've been with him since.'

I don't examine the relief I feel. 'Do you need anything?'

He furrows his brow. His facial expressions are exaggerated and slow to form, like he's a cartoon of himself. And in a way, I like the fact that I've seen drunk Oliver now. I like adding things to the knowledge I have of him.

'What would I need?'

'It's just, you knocked, on my door?' I say it like it's a question.

'I just wanted to say hello. Lovely Maddy.' He lunges forward then and puts his arms around me at the waist. I'm so surprised I don't move and the next thing I know, his face is looming and I know he's going to kiss me and I want so much for him to kiss me, but not here. Not like this.

'No, Oliver,' I say, and he steps back immediately.

'Shit, I'm sorry,' he says, turning and leaving the room.

I stay frozen to the spot, unsure whether to follow him. He needs to drink some water and take some painkillers, but it's surely not down to me to remind him of these things. He has that audition tomorrow. Maybe he's one of those people who don't really get hangovers. Because if he's not, he's screwed. I go out, find him standing at the kitchen sink, looking out of the window into blackness.

'Oliver,' I say.

He spins around. 'I'm really sorry. I shouldn't have done that. It's just... I like you so much, Maddy. I thought it would be fine, living together, but the more I get to know you, the more I like you. And it's hard, seeing you every day and wishing we could be together.'

I'm blindsided by this. And at the same time, I know he

wouldn't have said it if he wasn't wasted. 'I think you should go to bed,' I say. 'You have your audition at ten. Drink some water.'

I don't wait for him to answer, just turn and go back to my room. But once I'm there, the light switched off and the covers pulled up, there's nothing but my thoughts. I repeat what he said, over and over. He likes me. And he's unsure about our living situation. But he likes me. I find that I'm grinning, there in the dark. What if I'd let him kiss me, if I'd let him into my bed and just given it a chance? It doesn't have to always be a disaster, like Priya always says. One day, I could see a future that I like the look of. My mind snags on the idea of a future with Oliver. In this flat, or elsewhere. With Marjorie. Supporting each other's creative work and making each other laugh. I think back to the kiss we shared on the sofa. And I go to sleep like that, thinking about possibilities I've never allowed myself to consider before.

8

NOW (APRIL 2012)

The next morning, Oliver hasn't surfaced by nine and I know I'm going to have to wake him. I knock on his bedroom door, softly at first, the way he knocked on mine last night. But there's no response, so I knock again, harder. I hear a sound that's somewhere between a groan and a wail.

'It's nine o'clock,' I say. 'I just thought – I didn't want you to miss your audition.'

I wait there for a minute or so and then I go to the kitchen and put bread in the toaster. I've done as much as I can. Five minutes later, he emerges, his eyes red and his skin puffy. He goes into the bathroom and I hear the shower come on. It isn't until he's dressed and ready to leave that he speaks to me.

'I messed up,' he says. 'Last night. I'm so sorry, Maddy.'

He still smells like old booze. I go to my handbag and root around until I find a packet of Polos. 'Have one of these. We can talk about it later. Good luck.'

He nods, accepts the mint and goes to the door with his head low. I want to call out to him, to prompt him to say his lines one final time, to be sure he remembers, but I can't. I can't effectively ask him to say he loves me after what happened the previous night. I go into my room, turn on my laptop and bury myself in property descriptions. But a couple of hours later, when I'm thinking about breaking for a snack, my phone rings. Priya. And when I answer, I can hear that she's crying.

'What's happened?'

'It's Nic. I think it might be over. Can I come round?'

She's at the door in less than fifteen minutes and I usher her in, trying not to fire questions at her. But I don't need to, anyway, because the words are pouring out of her like she's a leaking tap. I find the bag of Haribo that I always keep in for emergencies and tear it open, and gummy bears and fried eggs spill out on the table. Priya picks at them half-heartedly.

'Maybe we weren't ready to live together,' she says. 'It's like every little thing that either of us does annoys the other one.'

'But you were practically living together anyway.'

'But we had you, didn't we? Maybe you acted as a sort of buffer.'

She gives me a half smile and then her face collapses again. 'What am I going to do, Maddy? He walked out last night, said he needed some time to think. Probably slept on someone's sofa. Will you come back, if he's gone for good? I don't want to be on my own.'

I hold my hands up. 'That's a lot, Priya. I feel like maybe you need to talk to him and work out what's going on. What happened before he left? Walk me through it.'

'We were having dinner, and I just realised that he makes so much noise when he's eating. How have I never noticed that before? Have you noticed that?'

I haven't. 'No. So, did you say something about it?'

'Yes, I told him to eat more quietly. And he put his fork down and said if we were going to start bringing up annoying habits, perhaps I could stop putting the toilet roll on the wrong way round.'

'You don't put it on the wrong way round,' I say.

'I know I don't! He does! Everyone knows it should be over, not under. So I said I hated the fact that he calls his mum every two minutes, to get her opinion on whether he needs a coat or what he should eat for breakfast, and then he said that at least he made time for his family, because there was this one time that my mum called me and I forgot to call her back for a couple of days. And then he said he was going.'

It sounds ridiculous. It's not unusual for the two of them to argue like this. They're both short-tempered, both stubborn. Their relationship swings from safety to danger constantly. But they love each other, too.

'Sounds like teething problems. I bet he'll be back when you get home.'

Priya tries to smile but it doesn't quite come off. 'But if he's not, if he never comes back, will you move back in?'

It strikes me that I could get offended at this. She asked me to move out so that she could live with her boyfriend and now, at the first sign of trouble, she's trying to make sure she has her bases covered on the flatmate front.

Just then, Oliver arrives home. He looks a bit more human, but dejected.

'How did it go?' I ask him, swivelling round in my chair to face him.

'Hi, Priya,' he says, and then he shakes his head at me and I feel so sad for him that I want to gather him up in a hug. But I don't know where we stand.

'I'm just asking Maddy to move back in with me,' Priya says.

I glare at her.

'What?' Oliver's eyes are a bit wild, a bit panicky.

'She's had an argument with Nic,' I say, trying to reassure him. 'It's not a big deal. They're going to kiss and make up.'

It's Priya's turn to glare at me.

'Why don't I walk you back?' I say. 'We'll see if he's there, and what sort of mood he's in.'

Oliver's standing in the kitchen doorway. 'What sort of mood he's in? Is this Nic guy a potential threat?'

Priya and I try to assure him that Nic's not dangerous, but he still insists on walking us both there and coming into the flat. Nic's in the kitchen, whistling. When he hears the footsteps and bustle of us all arriving, he steps out into the narrow hallway.

'Hey, Maddy, hey, Oliver.' He turns from us to Priya and I see her fury melt in front of my eyes. 'I was an idiot, Priya, I'm so sorry.'

She walks over to him and they kiss, Oliver and I trapped in the hallway with nothing to do but watch them. He gives me an 'Are they always like this?' look and I return it with an 'Afraid so' one. When they break apart, I clear my throat, and they both jump slightly as if they've completely forgotten that we're here.

'We should get back,' I say.

Priya walks back to me and takes hold of both my hands. 'Thank you,' she says.

'Do you think you might have overreacted slightly?' I ask. It's a question I've been asking her whenever she behaves dramatically since we were teenagers. She's never once admitted to it.

'Me, overreact? I don't know what you're talking about.'

Oliver and I say goodbye and step outside. It's warm but there's a bit of a breeze, and I see Oliver notice me rubbing at my bare arms to warm them.

'About last night,' he says, and I turn to see he's looking at me intently.

'Yes?'

'I meant what I said.'

I wasn't expecting this. I thought he'd apologise again, and I would accept his apology, and we would add it to our list of things that are never to be mentioned again. But that's not what's happening.

'You were really drunk,' I say.

'I was, but I did mean it. I know it's difficult, because we're flatmates, and I know it's not that long since I came out of a relationship, but this energy between us, it feels different to me. And I think we should take a chance on it, because I think you feel the same way. But if you don't, I'll be absolutely mortified and Marjorie and I will help you find somewhere else to live.'

I laugh. Without agreeing to do so, we both stop walking and turn to face each other. We're on a residential street and I can hear the clipping of high heels in the distance, but it's otherwise quiet. The air smells like spring. Daffodils and cut grass. Somewhere nearby, there's a barbecue going on. Oliver reaches for my hand and I let him hold it.

'What do you say?'

And I don't know I'm going to say it until the very moment that I do. 'Let's give it a shot.'

He breaks into a huge grin and leans down to kiss me and I'm back in that moment, our first kiss on the sofa, and this time feels just as magical, just as rare and special. I feel like my legs are going to cave, and I hold on to his arms for support. And suddenly, I can't wait to get back to the flat, where I know we'll take this forward, where we'll fall onto the sofa or one of our beds and undress. And I want it to happen so badly, in a way I never have before, and it's all I can do to push the invasive thoughts about what I'll see out of my mind.

'Let's go home,' I say, and we start walking a little faster, holding hands this time.

When we get to the front door of the flat, Oliver takes his keys from his pocket and fumbles with them, and I see that his hands are shaking slightly. It's a welcome reminder that I'm not the only one who's nervous. Although he, presumably, doesn't have the same reason as me for his apprehension. Inside, we take our shoes off.

'Are you sure about this?' I ask.

He looks dejected. 'Are you not sure?'

'I'm sure,' I say.

'Me too.'

And then we're kissing again, me pressed up against the hallway wall, and he's running his hands down the sides of my body and over my hips, and I never want it to stop. But it does stop, and he pulls away and looks at me, his eyes full of want, and I feel like my lips are stinging from the kissing. Or perhaps from the absence of it. I reach for his hand and pull him into my room.

9

TEN YEARS FROM NOW (APRIL 2022)

For a few seconds, I think it's not going to happen. That I'm just going to be able to live in the moment like everyone else. But that's not how it is. That's never how it is.

Oliver and I are in a flat, but it's not this one. He's aged a bit, and it suits him. Lines around his eyes, flecks of grey in his hair. There's an open bottle of red wine on the coffee table and we each have a glass in our hands. And – oh! – there's Marjorie, snuggled up by Oliver's feet.

'What have you got on tomorrow?' he asks.

I freeze for a moment. How can I answer this? I have no idea what my tomorrow looks like.

'Mads? Are you writing?'

'Yes, sorry, I was miles away. Writing, yes.' Something inside me sinks. Still copywriting. Still trying to sell things and make things clear and explain things. I change the subject. 'What about you?'

'We're filming that restaurant scene. Want to run my lines with me?'

I take a minute to reply, because I'm absorbing the information that Oliver is still an actor, and I'm not. Or if I am, it's still not my main or only gig. It's like a blow to the gut. 'Sure.'

Oliver goes off to retrieve them from somewhere, and I reach my hand down to Marjorie and she comes over and rubs her beautiful face against me. She's a bit thinner, and there's a patch of fur missing from one of her back legs. But she's here, and there is such comfort in that. I take the opportunity to look around the room. It's spacious and homely, with big windows and a high ceiling and a beautiful, tiled fireplace. Victorian. That's all I manage to glean before Oliver returns and hands me his script.

'Do you even need this?' He laughs.

I guess we've been doing this a lot. He plays his part and I play everyone else and I'm oddly surprised by how good he is. It's not just that he knows his lines or that he expresses them with real emotion. He seems to embody the part, somehow.

'Think I'm ready?' he asks.

'Definitely.'

'I'm kind of nervous. It's the first time I've worked with such big stars.'

Wow, so Oliver's not only hung in there with this acting thing, but he's become successful at it. While I've... what? Stepped back? Stepped away? Given up?

'You'll do great,' I say, and I mean it.

'I think I'm going to get an early night.'

'Me too.' For a moment, I wonder what would happen if we went to bed and had sex – would I be transported *twenty* years into the future? The thought makes me laugh and Oliver gives me a curious look. 'I was just thinking about something I heard today. Doesn't matter.'

He shrugs, and we go through to the bedroom together. He starts to take his clothes off, and I go into the bathroom to brush my teeth.

10

NOW (APRIL 2012)

And then I'm back, in 2012, in my bed, in Oliver's arms. He kisses me, runs his fingers through my hair.

'Well,' he says, 'we've really done it now, Maddy.'

And I laugh, because he's right, we have. And it isn't until he's fallen asleep and I'm lying on my back, staring at the ceiling, that I put my finger on why I feel so light and carefree. It was so happy, that future. It was so comfortable. I've never had anything like that before. So maybe this is it. Maybe I can let myself get into this thing, for real, because if I'm heading towards a future like that with Oliver, that's definitely something I can live with. The only part that snags is the career stuff. It hurts to know that I haven't managed to keep going, that I haven't broken through. Especially when Oliver so clearly has. I lie there, wired, wishing it wasn't too late to call Priya to talk it all through. Just before I go to sleep, I resolve to catch her at the café in the morning.

Priya claps a hand to her mouth. 'You did not!'

I feel my cheeks flushing, look around. There are a handful of customers but none of them are looking at us. Still, I put a finger to my lips to indicate that she should keep it down.

'Tell me everything!' she says, in a slightly quieter voice.

'Well, we were walking home from your place and...'

'Not that! I mean, I do want to hear all that but first I want to hear what you saw. You know, in the future. Did you get me those lottery numbers I've been waiting for?'

It strikes me how bizarre this conversation would sound to an onlooker. This is the kind of thing I would never believe in if it didn't happen to me.

'We lived in this Victorian flat, and it was lovely. And we still had the cat!'

Priya widens her eyes. 'So it was good? You finally saw a future that was good?'

I mull this over for a moment. 'Yes, it was good. I felt really content. Just, at ease and comfortable. But there was one thing.'

'What?'

'I was still copywriting. I'm not sure whether I was acting at all.'

'Oh.' I can tell she wasn't expecting that.

'I don't know what to do,' I say. 'I really, really like him.'

Ellen calls Priya's name and she holds up a finger to say she'll be there in a second. 'This might sound a bit wild, but have you thought about telling him?'

The truth is I've never thought about telling anyone other than Priya. Telling her wasn't something I'd had to consider, because when it happened that first time I was so freaked out and I needed to find out whether it was just me. And once it was clear it was, I've always had her to discuss it with and I've never been tempted to talk to anyone else about it. Who would I tell? My parents? Who wants to talk to their parents about sex? The men I sleep with? I know how it would sound. They probably wouldn't believe me and, on top of that, I'd seem a bit like I was obsessed with them. *Ten years, babe? I'm not really looking for anything that serious.* But now, while Priya goes over to see what Ellen wants – presumably for her to do some work – I think about the possibility of telling Oliver. I know he'd listen and take me seriously, but I know, too, that he'd think it was a load of nonsense.

I drain my cup of tea and go over to the counter. 'I can't tell him.'

Priya shrugs. 'Your call, of course. I just…'

She breaks off and then reaches across the counter to clutch my arm, opens her eyes really wide.

'What?' I ask.

'I've just realised, you've never slept with someone more than once because all the ten-year futures were so shitty. This is your chance to find out what happens next.'

She's right. I guess I've always thought this is a one-off thing, that after it's happened once with a person, I get to be normal. But what if it's not? What if I see ten years into the future every single time Oliver and I sleep together? It's daunting, thinking of it, but it's sort of exciting too. It feels like looking ahead in a book to check all the characters you like are doing okay a hundred pages down the line. It's like getting a preview.

'Well, you'll be the first to know,' I say, keeping my tone light. I pass her my mug and she turns and drops it into a bowl of soapy water behind her.

'Have you talked to Kelly recently?' she asks.

Kelly's a girl we went to school with, and for a while the three of us were close. She was always more Priya's friend than mine, though. 'No, why? Is she okay?'

'She's pregnant.'

'Like, on purpose?'

'Not planned, exactly. But she's keeping it.'

Wow. I'm not ready for the idea that people our age are doing this yet. But before I can say anything else, Priya gives me a cheery wave and turns to her washing up.

When I get home, Oliver's there. He's been at the pool doing swimming lessons and his hair is wet. He greets me the way he always does, but I don't know how to act around him, because we haven't had a chance to talk about what all this is. This morning, he went for a run before I woke up, and then I left to see Priya before he came back. But now we're both in the small kitchen, and everything feels charged. The way he reaches across me to open a drawer. The way I wait behind him to put something in the bin.

'I guess we should talk,' he says.

I feel a lurch in my stomach because this is what people say when they want to backtrack or get out of something, isn't it? And it's that lurch that makes me realise how much I want this. How much I want him.

'We should,' I say, trying not to let any emotion into my voice.

He's made a sandwich, but he doesn't go to eat it. Instead, he stands with his back to the counter, both hands resting on it, his legs crossed. Marjorie comes into the room, looks at him and then me and walks out again, as if she can sense something in the air between us and she doesn't want any part of it.

'I don't know how we navigate this,' he says, 'but I really like you. I don't want things to be awkward or tense. I just want to give this thing a go.'

I exhale. There's a tiny blob of what I think is conditioner on his left earlobe, and I reach up to wipe it away, and when I touch him, it feels electric. He looks at me, puzzled.

'You had this,' I say, showing him my finger before going to the sink to wash my hands. When I return to where I was standing, opposite him, he hasn't moved.

'I feel the same,' I say. 'But I'm nervous.'

'Why?'

I can't tell him about the visions, but I want to tell him something that's true. 'Because I've never been in a relationship.'

'Never?'

I shake my head. 'Nope. I've just... never liked anyone enough. Do you think that's weird?'

He considers this. 'Not weird. Unusual, maybe. Does it bother you that I was in a serious relationship quite recently?'

'I don't think so. From what you've said, it sounds like that was on its way out for a while. So I don't feel quite like you've jumped straight from one thing to another.'

He kisses me lightly. 'Want to hang out and watch bad horror films all weekend?'

I do want this. 'I'm sorry, I can't. I'm going home.'

'Home, as in, to your parents?' he asks, and it's a reminder that we really don't know each other that well.

'Yes. Except that it's my mum and stepdad, and my brother. They're near St Albans. I need to go and pack a bag, but I'll be back tomorrow afternoon.'

He watches me leave the room and I feel as if he knows I'm holding something back. I haven't told him about Henry, his accident. Because while he doesn't know, I can pretend it didn't happen. But I'm starting to wonder how long I can keep these two huge parts of my life separate.

When I'm ready to leave, Oliver asks what time my train is, and when I say I have an open ticket he takes the handle of my suitcase out of my hand and kisses me very firmly, his hands either side of my face. And I know we're going back to my bedroom, or his, and I won't be leaving any time soon.

11

TEN YEARS FROM NOW (APRIL 2022)

I'm alone, reading in the late afternoon sun, Marjorie curled on my lap. I close the book, using my finger to keep my place, but I don't recognise the author's name. It's been nominated for a big award, and I read a couple of sentences and they are truly beautiful, but I'm halfway through so I have no idea what's happening. I lay the book down on the sofa and stroke Marjorie between her ears until she purrs with gratitude.

I wonder where Oliver is. But of course, we have our separate lives as well as our joined one, and he could be anywhere. There's an iPhone on the coffee table and it doesn't look wildly different from the one I'm used to. I guess the password easily. But the functionality is alien to me so it takes me a minute or so to find what I'm looking for. Photos. I scroll through. Oliver and me at the theatre, smiles wide. Me standing next to a sign that says 'Don't Forget to Vote', my thumb raised. Restaurants and beaches and the inside of this flat and Priya and a lipstick named Coral Blush. But more than anyone else, far more than me, a little girl. A girl I've never seen before, with shiny brown hair and no front teeth. I have photographed her all over London. But who is she? Could she possibly be mine?

12

NOW (APRIL 2012)

'Is that you, love?' Mum calls, as if anyone else would be letting themselves in to her house on a Friday evening.

'It's me.'

She's in the kitchen, wiping the tops down. The whole room smells like her chilli, and pure comfort, and there are daffodils on the kitchen windowsill. I'm ashamed that I haven't been back here since Christmas. When she turns to look at me, she takes me in, head to toe, the way she always does. I tell her on the phone that I'm fine, but she needs to see it for herself. She looks so tired. Older than her fifty-two years. I go to her and we hug, and she feels a bit fragile, a bit light. And it's strange, because she's the strongest person I know.

'How are things?' she asks.

We sit down at the kitchen table and I tell her an edited version of how things are going in the new flat. She was worried about me moving in with a man I didn't know, but she sounds pleased when I tell her that we've been sharing the cooking and watching films together in the evenings. She doesn't ask why it's taken me so long to come home.

'You must miss Priya,' she says.

It isn't a question. It's a fact.

'When you two first became friends, I didn't think it would last. Just shows what I know.'

The house feels quiet. The washing machine is running and the radio's on low, but there are no creaks or footsteps.

'Where are Alan and Henry?' I ask.

'They've gone to McDonalds for a milkshake. Henry had a tough physio session this afternoon. Alan promised him a treat after it. But they'll be back soon. Are you hungry? I've made chilli.'

I smile at the familiarity. She makes chilli every time I come home. I sometimes think she's getting the kidney beans and the spices out of the cupboard before we've even finished talking about a visit on the phone. I'm pretty confident there'll be a lemon cheesecake in the fridge, too.

'Always hungry for your chilli.'

I hear the door go then, and I get up and go into the hall to greet my stepdad and my brother. Alan's pushing Henry's wheelchair, and he seems a bit out of breath.

'Hello, love,' he says, breaking into a smile.

It is the nicest thing, to have a place to come back to where you're always welcome, where people are always pleased to see you. I have to remind myself, sometimes, that not everyone has that. When Mum met Alan, less than a year after she split from my dad, I wasn't sure how it would be with this stranger in my home. But he made such an effort with me. Friends had stepdads who bought them stuff, but Alan took the time to learn about the music I liked, the plays I read. He even took me shopping, traipsing from one clothes shop to another in the drizzling rain, holding the bags and offering opinions on different combinations when they were sought, keeping quiet when they weren't.

And then, when I was sixteen and they were both in their early forties, they had Henry. The surprise and joy of all our lives.

'Hi, Alan. Henry.' I give Alan a hug and then lean down to hug Henry, but his body language makes it clear he doesn't want to be touched. I stand up again, trying to catch his eye, but he's sullen.

'Right,' Alan says, glossing over the awkwardness. 'Where am I taking you? Living room?'

'I can do it,' Henry says, and then he's propelling himself towards the back of the house, to the room that used to be the dining room and is now a makeshift bedroom for him while we wait for the house to be properly adapted.

Alan and I exchange a look, and he shrugs and smiles. 'Your mother in the kitchen, is she?'

We go through, and I watch as Alan kisses Mum's cheek and they exchange pieces of information about the time they've been apart. They're a team. A really good one. While Mum weighs out rice and finds a pan to boil it in, Alan cuts a loaf of fresh bread into chunky slices. They move around each other as required, sometimes touching each other's arm or waist lightly to indicate that a small movement is required. I try to remember Mum and Dad being in this kitchen together, and can't. I was devastated when they told me they were splitting up, but it only took a few years before I could see what a marriage should look like. And by then Dad had moved to Spain and I'd realised that Alan was more of a dad to me than my actual father was.

'How is he?' I ask. 'Henry?'

They know I mean Henry. My sweet and happy little brother, who was doted on as a baby by me and Priya and all of our friends. I remember feeling unsure when Mum was pregnant with him. This was going to make them a family, the three of them. And where did that leave me? But Mum and Alan must have anticipated this and they made it clear that it was the four of us, that I was an important cog in that machine. I was in the hospital when he was born. I was the first to change his nappy.

'He has good and bad days,' Mum says. She's stirring the rice and her back is to me, and I'm pleased that I can't see how much all of this is taking out of her.

'And today's a bad one, I'm guessing?'

Alan takes knives and forks out of the drawer, reaching around Mum to get the salt and pepper shakers. 'We don't know how many more sessions of physio we can have. The funding we applied for runs out soon, and we'll apply for more, but it's not guaranteed.'

For the thousandth time, I ask why this had to happen to Henry. My brother, who I watched countless times on the football pitch, running so fast he was little more than a streak of colour. But then, almost a year ago, he was knocked off his bike by a car and it damaged his spinal cord. He was in hospital for six months. His life has changed completely, and Mum's and Alan's lives have, too. The toll it's taken is etched on their faces.

'Have they talked about him walking?' I ask.

Mum looks at me and there's pain in her eyes. 'Walking's a long way away, if it ever happens at all. For now we're focusing on the everyday challenges, like bowel and bladder routines.'

I don't know the ins and outs of all of this, but I can imagine how hard it must be for Henry, how demoralising to need their help with something he's been able to manage himself for years.

I know, suddenly, that I'm going to cry, so I excuse myself and go to the downstairs toilet, where I stand with my hands on the sides of the sink, staring at myself in the little mirror. Telling myself I don't have a right to feel sorry for myself, when I'm the one least affected by all of this. When I feel a bit steadier, I go to find Henry. He's playing FIFA, his shoulders hunched.

'Can I play?' I ask.

He shrugs. So I take the other controller from the shelf and wait for him to finish his game and start up a two-player one. He's Chelsea. He's always Chelsea. I let him choose my team, and he goes for Liverpool.

'How's school?'

He turns to look at me for the first time since he got home. 'School's school.'

'What did Mrs Bellamy think of your *Sunflowers* cake?'

He'd had this homework the week before, to make a famous work of art out of anything he wanted. Mum had thrown her hands up, said what did she know about art and why did they have to make life so difficult for everyone? Baking was my idea. They'd found most of the things they needed in the kitchen cupboards and Alan had gone to the Tesco down the road for the other bits. When they showed me, on a Skype call, I could see how proud Henry was of it.

'Nobody could eat it, because we hadn't listed the ingredients.'

'What? No way. It didn't get thrown away, did it?'

'No. I brought it home. Dad ate most of it.'

He's winning, three nil, but then I manage to get control of the ball and my player runs with it, takes a shot at goal. Misses.

'Good try,' Henry says.

'You know I'm letting you win, right?'

And when I look over at him, he's smiling, because he knows, as well as I do, that he's been able to walk all over me in video games since he was about six. Mum calls us in for dinner and we shout back that we're just finishing the game, and it looks for a minute like I might make a comeback but the game finishes five nil.

'What's your news?' Alan asks, passing me the basket of

bread. 'I feel like we don't know much about this new flatmate of yours.'

I realise I haven't thought about Oliver since I got here, haven't checked my phone. And the thought that there might be messages from him, waiting, makes me feel a bit light-headed. I try not to think about the recent developments in our relationship, worried it will show on my face. 'He's nice. Another actor.'

'Christ, how will you pay the rent?' He smiles, winks at me across the table.

The truth is, both Mum and Alan were worried when I said I wanted to go to drama school and become an actor, but I told them I would do whatever it took alongside the auditions to keep myself afloat, and I have.

I tell them a bit about Oliver, and I wonder whether they'll guess how I feel about him. Mum's astute. Later, she might pull me into the kitchen while she's making coffee and demand all the details. And if we'd met in any other circumstances, I'd be happy to share them. But I feel a bit protective over this fledgling relationship, given our living situation.

'And on the work front,' Mum says. 'How are things there?'

'I had an audition for a small part in a new play last week.'

'And when will you hear?'

'Oh, I already know I didn't get it. But what I mean is that I am getting auditions.'

Mum flashes Alan a look and I know, instantly, that this is something they've discussed, that they've decided to talk about it while I'm home. They want me to give it all up and do something less competitive. They always have.

'I'm not giving up acting,' I say, cutting to the chase.

'No one's saying you should give it up,' Alan says, scratching the corner of his nose with one finger. 'Your mum and me, we just wonder sometimes whether it should be more of a hobby. Whether you should start looking at different career options.'

'I'm getting on okay, aren't I? I never have to ask you to bail me out, with money.'

'It's not about that,' he says. And then he turns to Mum, silently asking her to take over.

'Love,' she says, 'we just don't want you to get to thirty, or forty, and realise it's too late to start a career you can really get passionate about, rather than something you do to pay the bills while you're looking for acting work.'

They'd be so happy if I told them I was going to train to be a teacher, or a journalist, or an editor of some kind. They would worry so much less about me. And don't they deserve to not have to worry about one of us? But dreams are dreams, and they're not easy to let go of. When you've found the thing that feels like coming home, you cling to it.

'It would be nice,' I say, 'if you even thought there was a tiny chance that I'd make it. If you didn't see it as a foregone conclusion that, at some point, I'll fail at this.'

Mum looks as if I've reached across the table and slapped her. Alan looks worried. And Henry. Henry looks really sad.

'It isn't like that,' Mum says, but she doesn't carry on, because we all know that it is.

Perhaps it's impossible to have blind faith in your children and their ambitions, because you're so caught up in wanting them to be okay, so fearful of them taking the wrong path.

'I'll work it all out,' I say. 'I'm still only twenty-six. I don't want to turn my back on this. I still believe I can maybe make a life out of it. And if I can't, I'll handle that. And I'll find something else that works. Please just trust me.'

'She's right,' Henry says, and we all turn to look at him. He has to sit at the end of the table because it's the only place his wheelchair will fit. He used to sit next to me, but there's an empty space there now.

'What do you mean?' Alan asks him.

'It's just all so stupid, you thinking she should do something else when acting is what she loves, just because she might never be able to make a living from it. None of us know what's going to happen, or what we're going to be able to do or not do in the future, so she should just do the thing she loves while she can.'

None of us can look directly at him, because it's so clear he's talking about his accident and the football he misses desperately.

'We just worry,' Mum says.

And I nod and tell her I understand, because I do, to an extent. I know that she wants me to be happy and safe and free from anxiety, and that all her advice and interference stems from that. Stems from her wanting the best for me, and wanting to help me in any way she can. That's all part of being a mother, isn't it?

'You don't have to,' I say. 'And if you ever do, I'll tell you. Okay?'

'Shall we have that lemon cheesecake?' Alan asks, and I know that we'll change the subject, move on to lighter things.

13

NOW (APRIL 2012)

I go to bed early, saying that I want to read my book, but really I want to scroll on my phone and read the messages from Oliver that I can see stacked up, waiting.

OLIVER

Let me know you got there okay.

I guess you haven't looked at your phone. Will assume you're still alive.

God, I sort of miss you. Is that weird?

I know I'm talking to myself. I guess at some point you'll look at these and when you do, know that I would love to hear your voice, no matter what time of the day or night it is.

I hit call, and when he answers I keep my voice low. 'Hey. Sorry about the messages. I just got caught up with all the catching up.'

'No problem. So how's everyone there?'

'They're okay. Kind of... tired.' I'm opening the door a crack, letting him in.

'Tired, right. I guess your mum did the whole kid thing with you, and then started again with your brother.'

This is true. But it's not why she's tired.

'Still,' he says, 'it must be fun having a nine-year-old around?'

I think about Henry, about how it used to be. Chasing him in the garden, curling up next to him on the sofa to watch Christmas films. I used to feel like I was getting a second childhood, in a way. But now, it's like a light's gone out in him and it's so hard to see that. I should tell Oliver, and I want to, but at the moment he never asks how Henry is with that worried look everyone has since the accident, and I don't want to lose that.

'I have to go,' I say, and then I can't think of an excuse. It's ten at night, so I can't really say there's a meal ready or someone's calling me. 'I need to go to sleep.'

'Okay, Maddy. But listen, are you alright? You sound a bit distant.'

'I'm okay. I'll see you tomorrow.'

After we end the call, I feel sort of hollowed out. I want to share things with Oliver, to offer him things. I want to have a real relationship, to be a partner, but it's scary, because I haven't done any of those things before. I message Priya, tell her I'm at home. Straight away, she replies and asks how Henry is. I tell her he's just the same. And then I must fall asleep, because the next thing I know, it's gone midnight and I haven't got in my pyjamas or brushed my teeth. There's a reply from Priya.

PRIYA

I love you, Maddy.

Priya knows that there's really nothing to say about a nine-year-old boy who can no longer walk. She knows how sad it makes me, how it's changed the dynamics of my little family. She's just there, for the good and the bad of it, and I feel so lucky to have her. But letting someone else in to all of it, letting Oliver see all the messy and devastated parts of me – what would that be like?

* * *

When I go down for breakfast, Henry asks if I want to come to football training, and I don't know what to say.

'Didn't I tell you?' Mum asks, holding up a loaf of bread.

I nod and she puts two slices in the toaster for me. She knows I like it barely browned, with a thick layer of butter. 'What?'

'Henry's helping the coach. Remember Pete?'

I do remember Pete. He's coached Henry since he was five, since that first time he went along on a Saturday morning and was too scared to join in for a good half an hour. That day, Alan and I stood with him on the sidelines, asking now and then if he was ready to play. He was holding a ball, and his hands still had some of that baby chubbiness to them. Pete set up a drill and then came over, asked if he could have a look at Henry's ball. Henry handed it to him, and pretty soon they were passing it back and forth, Henry's shots wildly inaccurate but Pete managing to return most of them. After the accident, Pete visited Henry in the hospital weekly, bringing him football cards and magazines.

'That's great,' I say. I look at Henry's face but he's not giving anything away. I wonder how hard it is for him to go to training and not be able to play. I can see why they've done this, given him this coaching position, but I wonder whether it's harder for him than staying away altogether.

When Henry's finished his breakfast and gone off to brush his teeth, I make tea for me and Mum. 'I can take him to football. Why don't you and Alan have a break?'

She looks at me, gratitude in her eyes. 'Are you sure?'

I stand up and put my hands on her shoulders, try to rub away some of the tension there. 'Of course.'

On the way to training, I ask Henry how Mum and Alan seem to him. He's propelling himself, his arms strong and steady. Sometimes, if there's a hill, he needs a hand, but he's mostly got this. The way he's adapted is incredible.

'They're okay,' he says. 'I mean, mostly. Sometimes they argue.'

I think about the arguments my parents used to have before my dad left. I've always thought things were straightforward between Mum and Alan. But then, I don't live there. Everyone argues sometimes, don't they?

'What do they argue about?'

'Money.'

Mum went part-time at work after Henry's accident because of all the support he needs. I think again about them worrying over me, about my acting. It's bigger now, that worry, because money's tighter, so they're not in a position to help me out if I need it. The fact of it sits in my stomach like a rock.

'Over there,' Henry says, pointing. 'Can you push me once we're on the grass?' I see Pete and some of Henry's teammates. He calls out to them as we approach and they come over, give him high fives and call his name.

'Haven't seen you here in a while.'

I look up and Pete is beside me. 'Home for the weekend. Thanks for what you're doing, with Henry.'

'He's a good coach,' he says. 'Wouldn't want to be without him.'

I stand on the sidelines as Pete blows his whistle and the boys run over to him. He tells them to run around the edge of the pitch three times to warm up, and then he stands with Henry and they chat about the plan for the session. There's nothing patronising about it, the way Pete consults him, asks for his opinion. And Henry is engaged, focused. Both of them have found a way for him to be part of the team, and I could cry with gratitude.

Henry's quiet on the way home. We're almost back when he speaks. 'I wish you lived here.'

It's like a knife to the gut. I left home to go to university when Henry was two years old, and I've never gone back there to live. I've always gone home often, not least because I wanted to see him change and grow. And he's never asked anything of me, but this is something I can't give.

'I can't work as an actor here,' I say.

'Would you? If you could?'

I think about this. I don't want to lie. 'I'm not sure I would. But it's nothing to do with you, or Mum and Alan. I think I just need to explore right now, and it's easier to do that in a big city.'

'What are you exploring?'

It's a good question. We're back home, and I slip my key into the lock as I try to formulate a worthy response. 'I'm trying to find out who I am, I suppose. And where I want to be, and what my place is in the world. What I can do, how I can be helpful. Who I want to spend time with, and why. All of that. You'll want to find out all those things too, when you're older.'

'I might be stuck here,' he says.

I snap my head around to look at him, but he doesn't say anything else because Mum appears in the hallway, oven gloves on her hands. 'Good session? Lunch is almost ready.'

I think about what Henry said all the way back to London on the train. He might be stuck there. Will he? If he's always in a wheelchair, then maybe. But not necessarily. Still, it's a reminder not to take what I have for granted. My freedom, my endless choices.

When I'm on the train back to London, Oliver and I message back and forth, and when I get off the train at St Pancras, he's there waiting for me. It's such a surprise, and I throw my arms around him, before he takes my bag from my shoulder.

'Fancy a drink?' he asks.

We go to the champagne bar in the station, sit on high stools and drink from long-stemmed glasses, and I keep knocking my knee against his because I find it hard to be close to him without us touching. He hasn't kissed me, and he doesn't. Not while we walk to the Tube or when we're on it, not while we walk up the three flights of stairs to get to our flat. I wonder whether he's doing it on purpose, to build the anticipation, or whether he's had a change of heart. But no, surely he wouldn't have surprised me at the station and taken me for champagne if he was about to end things. My question is answered as soon as we've let ourselves in and he's dropped my bag in the hall.

'Maddy Hart,' he says, smoothing my hair with his fingers. 'I'm so glad you're home.'

I think about that word, home, about what it means. When I go to Mum's, I talk about going home, and when I'm there, I talk about going back to London. But this flat has become home, in all the really significant ways, in a few short months. I feel comfortable here. And I feel missed, when I go.

'Me too,' I say. I can feel the champagne fizzing inside me, or maybe it's nerves. Is it always this hard, when you haven't been seeing someone very long and you've been apart for a time, to kiss them? He's looking at my lips and I lean towards him, taking matters into my own hands. We start off slow but speed up quickly – mouths open, hands sliding, clothes pushed off shoulders or over heads. He pushes me gently back against the hallway wall, his fingers interlaced with mine, pressed up against the wall either side of my head. And I forget everything that's been worrying me, about Mum, about Henry. Everything but how it feels to be kissed like this.

14

TEN YEARS FROM NOW (APRIL 2022)

I'm walking hand in hand with a little girl. And it's *the* little girl, the one from the photos. I sneak quick looks at her and determine that she's about six or seven.

She stops walking and I realise I must have missed a question she asked.

'Sorry?' I say.

'Do you think it was my fault or George's?'

I shake my head slightly, as if willing an answer to appear from somewhere in the dark reaches of my brain. I don't know this girl's name, let alone who George is or what either of them have done.

'I'm not sure,' I say. 'I wasn't there. Let's just forget about it now.' I hope it's the right thing, and she seems to accept it.

'What's for tea?'

I panic, before realising that no matter what I say, this almost certainly won't be my problem to deal with. I mean, it will in ten years' time, but not today. 'Sausages,' I say, and she gives a little cheer. Her hand is warm in mine and her long brown hair is in two braids that look like they're about to fall out. I wonder how neat they were this morning, whether I was the one who sat her down and brushed it for her. There's a squeezing sort of feeling in the general area of my heart.

'Mum, you're going past our flat!'

And there it is. *Mum.* I stop walking, make a 'silly me' sort of face, and walk down the path I just almost missed. It's a mansion block with trees at either side of the front door. I reach into the pocket of my jeans and find a key. I'm a bit relieved, when we get inside, to see that it's the same flat I've been to in previous visions. But of course it is. It's just that there's so much to take in that any scrap of familiarity feels good. Marjorie comes into the hallway to greet us and the little girl drops to her knees and coos over her. While she's not looking, I search her bag until I find a book with her name on the front. Isla Swanson. Swanson is Oliver's last name. But Isla? That can't be right, can it? Isla has been Priya's baby name for years and years. How could I have just taken it from her? A feeling of dread washes over me. It feels like I've swallowed a rock, and it's lodged in my throat. Could I have chosen this name because Priya couldn't? Wasn't around to? I don't dwell on it. Can't.

'Isla,' I say, testing it out in my mouth.

She looks up, and I try to compare her features to mine, but mostly I'm overcome by how beautiful she is. Her front teeth are coming through, and they look too big for her, and she has freckles and wide, blue eyes. Are they like mine, her eyes? Mine are blue, but hers are a shade lighter. More like Oliver's.

'What, Mum?' she asks.

'I just wondered whether you'd like a drink,' I say, and it's only when I speak that I feel how close I am to crying.

15

NOW (APRIL 2012)

Back in the present, when it's over, I disentangle myself from Oliver but stay close. I don't want him to think there's something wrong.

'Okay?' he asks.

What can I say? 'Okay.'

He kisses my forehead and we are quiet for a few minutes, and all the time my mind is racing. A little girl. A daughter. And if she is six or seven, that means she'll be born in two or three years. Before I'm thirty. It doesn't feel quite true, but then, of course it doesn't. It's a huge change to my life. But people make huge changes like having children, don't they? People do it every day.

When Oliver goes to have a shower, I send Priya a message. I need to check she's still here. It's stupid, but I can't help it.

MADDY

In the latest vision, there was a little girl.

She replies immediately:

PRIYA
Yours?

MADDY
Yes.

PRIYA
Wow.

MADDY
I know.

PRIYA
Please remember that you don't know whether it's all real, Maddy.

She wouldn't say that if she'd been there, if she'd seen Isla. I can't have just made her up. I find I don't want to tell Priya about Isla's name just yet. I know it will hurt her. And besides, I need to understand why I did it. I think of the times I've heard her say that word. Isla. How she relishes it. But then she sends another message and it's not what I expected.

PRIYA
What do you think happens to the you in the future when the you from the present is there?

I don't know what she means at first. But then I read it again and I do. When I'm having the vision, when I'm moving around and speaking and being myself in ten years from now, does that future version of myself know? Does she zone out? Are both of us inside her, battling for space?

MADDY
I guess I'll tell you in ten years' time.

And then I hear Oliver coming back so I push my phone under the pillow and turn to look at him, smiling.

'Do you know what I think we should do?' he asks.

'What?'

'I think we should get dressed and go out for dinner. Somewhere nice, with napkins and stuff. Drink some wine, let people cook for us. What do you say?'

It strikes me, as he says it, that we haven't been on a date. And yet we're all in, in some mystifying way. 'Give me twenty minutes,' I say, and he leans down and kisses my lips, droplets of water falling from his skin onto mine.

He takes me to a place he knows on one of the quieter commercial streets in Balham. It's small, intimate. When we step inside, the lighting is so low that it takes me a few seconds to adjust to it. There's an aroma of garlic and rosemary, and we are shown to a corner table by a serious-looking waitress who's around our age.

'Why have I never seen this place?' I ask.

'It's kind of tucked away. But it's great. They do this garlic bread that is to die for.'

I think about eating garlic, being embarrassed about my breath afterwards. And, as if he can read my mind, he says: 'If we both have it, neither of us will notice the smell.'

I look through the menu, and all the time, I can feel his eyes on me. 'You don't need to choose?'

'I know what I'm having already. Duck cassoulet, with garlic bread on the side.'

The words on the menu are swimming in and out of focus, so I say I'll have the same and close it. And then there's nowhere to look but straight at him, and we maintain eye contact, smiles twitching at the corners of our mouths, until the waitress who seated us returns to take our drinks order.

While we wait for our food, we drink red wine and ask each other questions. There is still so much we don't know. We take it in turns, and he promises he'll answer anything, which I'm not quite ready to agree to. He tilts his head when I say this, as if I've revealed that I'm the keeper of a sweet little secret and he's confident that he'll get to the bottom of it. If only he knew. Really, there's only one thing I want to ask him right now, because I can't get the encounter with our future child out of my mind. Does he want to have children? And when does he see himself taking that step? But it isn't the kind of question you can ask on a first date, even a first date that comes four months into living together, so I stick to learning about his taste in films, music, and food.

'What's the deal with you and Priya?' Oliver asks, just after our food has arrived.

'What do you mean?'

'Just that you seem really close. Have you always been? Where did you meet?'

This feels like safe and easy ground. 'We met at the start of secondary school. We were in the same tutor group and we'd both come from small schools and it seemed like everyone else had come from the same big school in the town. Our tutor teacher put us together when we had to do something in pairs, and we just got on.'

'Wow,' he says. 'So that's, what, about fifteen years?'

I do the maths in my head. 'Yep, fifteen.'

'Do you ever feel like you've had enough of each other?'

I think back over the arguments we've had. There have been plenty, but none of them have lasted more than a day or so. 'I think we balance each other. She's dramatic, as you've seen, and I'm quite grounded. She's insanely academic and I'm more creative.'

'That makes sense.'

'Who's *your* best friend?'

'Probably Matt, who I got drunk with the other day after

seeing Gemma. But he's a university friend who just happened to end up in this part of London, and I sometimes feel like it's about circumstances more than deep compatibility. And to be honest, when I was with Gemma, we became quite insular. It wasn't healthy, and it's struck me since it ended how many of my friends have sort of drifted away.'

All the time he's speaking, I'm watching him. The way he gesticulates with his hands when he's making a point, the way his face is animated, always changing. I am asking myself whether I could see myself with him, really see it. Because in the past, it's never been like this. It's not only the fact that the ten-year vision appeals, but it's also how I feel right now, sitting opposite him in this dimly lit French restaurant. Giddy, and a bit flushed. Like I'm right on the edge of having had too much to drink. I reach for my glass and drain it, but when Oliver moves to pour me another, I put my hand over it. I feel pleasantly fuzzy, and it's enough.

When our waitress asks if we want to see the dessert menu, Oliver says they do a crème brûlée that he would sell a kidney for, and I say we'll take two of those, and the waitress nods and disappears again. And he's right. It's like nothing I've ever tasted. Light as air but somehow creamy too, perfectly caramelised sugar on top.

'This has been so lovely,' I say.

He puts one elbow on the table and rests his chin in his cupped hand. 'There's something I should say.'

I flinch internally, wondering what it's going to be. That he's changed his mind, that this is some kind of farewell meal? But no, it's not possible. Not the way he's been looking at me, the way his foot has been sliding up and down my leg under the table. I brace myself, expecting something bad.

'I don't really do casual,' he says. 'I don't see the point. Sure, I had the odd one-night stand when I was at university, but now I don't want that. I know from your perspective I've jumped from a serious relationship into... this... But I swear it's not like me. I'm only interested in being with someone if I really like them. And I really like you.'

It's not what I expected, and I have to adjust my face and body language accordingly. I was on the verge of curling up, turning away. And it's all I can do not to grab hold of him right here in the restaurant, because he's all I can think about, and he's telling me he feels the same way. He's being open, and clear, and straightforward, and all those things I expect men not to be.

'Me too,' I say, and we grin at each other like little kids who've just heard their school is closed for snow.

'Shall we go home?' he asks.

It sounds nice, like something a real couple would do. Going back together to the home they share. But it's so fast, isn't it? Something at the back of my mind is warning me. It's no match, though, for the giddiness I'm awash with. And that's what wins out. We hold hands, stop every few minutes to kiss, and by the time we get back to the flat our hands are straying and I know we'll go to bed the second we get inside.

16

TEN YEARS FROM NOW (APRIL 2022)

'I don't know why you said it was sausages,' Isla says. She is in Spiderman pyjamas, delirious with tiredness. It is gone nine o'clock.

Oliver puts his head in his hands, then stands up. 'Baby, it doesn't matter. Mum got mixed up. It's not the end of the world. But you have to go to sleep now, or you'll be so tired in the morning you'll fall asleep on your desk and miss breaktime.'

'What if I fall asleep after breaktime?'

'Then you'll miss lunch.'

She stands on one leg, her pyjama trousers ruched up to the knees, and tips her head the opposite way as if to balance herself.

'Shall I tuck you in?' I ask.

'Yes please.'

I go to her, take her hand, and lead her back into her bedroom. Her bed is covered with soft toys, and there is a space just big enough for her to settle in amongst them. I pull back the cover and she gets in, wriggles around a bit until she's comfortable.

'Please try to sleep,' I say, kissing her on the forehead.

'I will. Will it be sausages tomorrow?'

I don't want to make the same mistake again, so I tell her the truth. 'I don't know, baby.'

She nods as if I've just said something profound and she's trying to take it in.

I stand in the doorway for a couple of minutes, watch her eyelids droop and fall. And I have this strange sense of having accomplished something, despite having done nothing but stand here. When I go back to the living room, Oliver raises his eyebrows to ask how I did.

'She's asleep,' I say.

'Thank Christ for that. That might be a new record. Please never tell her it's sausages for tea when it isn't again.'

'I don't know what I was thinking,' I say. 'It was stupid.'

He holds out his arms and I go to him. We lie together on the sofa, him behind and me in front, and he strokes my hair absent-mindedly.

'So how was your day?' he asks.

I feel a rising sense of panic, because I don't know. The only bits I know about are walking Isla home from school and this extended bedtime. Can I bluff it? 'You know, same as always.'

There's a stretch of silence and I expect him to challenge me in some way, but he doesn't. He shifts around a bit behind me, rests a hand on my hip. And I feel myself drifting off to sleep.

17

NOW (NOVEMBER 2012)

Spring turns to summer and summer to autumn, and things with Oliver are good. More than good; right. We fit together, whether we're brushing our teeth side by side at the small sink in our bathroom or cooking a meal together or lying on the sofa, my body tucked into his. There's a part of me that doesn't trust it, but I try to override it. Sometimes things just work, don't they? Sometimes things are just right. What if every small choice I've made across the years has been leading me here, to him? In the future I see, he is my family, my co-parent. And that's a powerful thing.

The only sticking point is Henry. I still haven't told Oliver about his accident, because I want to keep a corner of my life where there is no tragedy. Every time I go home, I sense that Oliver is willing me to ask him to join me, and I know I have to do it soon.

And the visions. The visions are exhausting. I learned pretty early on, when we were in that stage where we were always touching, that if I needed a break, it was best to make sure most of the sex happened late at night, when I would just find the two of us asleep. I am always putting Oliver off until later, and he never seems to question it.

Priya knows it all, every twist and turn. On a phone call in November, we discuss my future.

'I wonder why you only have one child,' she says.

'I don't know. I mean, at the moment I don't even know whether I want any, so one seems less daunting to me than two or three.'

Everyone talks about only children being lonely, always wishing for a brother or sister. Is that how Isla will feel? I hope not. I try to tell myself that it's not a foregone conclusion, that it's not the same for everyone.

'What's her name?' Priya asks.

I cannot believe I've managed to avoid this for all these months. I am silent, and she knows almost immediately that there is something behind it.

'Maddy, what's her name?'

'It's Isla,' I say, because I can't keep it from her forever.

It's her turn to go quiet.

'Priya, I don't know why I did that. I don't understand it.'

'No.'

It's so hard to know what to say. I'm sorry, of course I am, but it's for a decision I haven't made yet. 'Talk to me, Priya. How can I make this better?'

'You can't,' she says, her voice a little frosty. 'Unless...'

'What?'

'Could you somehow find out if I have children too?' she asks.

I'm relieved that she hasn't come to the same conclusion I did. That the naming of Isla might be some kind of tribute to her.

I consider it. 'When I'm there, I don't know the things I

should know. Like, I think I'd only know what was going on with you if I happened to be with you in one of the visions. I could ask Oliver, but how would I do it without him knowing something weird was going on?'

'I don't know.'

'Can we talk about something else?' I ask. 'I feel a bit worn out from it all.'

* * *

Later, I'm waiting to audition for a part I know I won't get, and I should be going over my lines, but there's only one and I'm pretty sure I've got it nailed, so I think, instead, about what Priya said. About finding out whether she has children in the future. Somehow, it's never occurred to me to use these visions to find out anything other than how my relationship is going, despite Priya's unrelenting teasing about lottery numbers. But, of course, I do find out other things. Like the fact that I have a daughter. And the fact that Marjorie is still alive. If I happened to time it so that I was with Priya, I guess I'd find out things about her too, wouldn't I? It could change everything. Because if I could find out what's going on in Priya's life, I could find out all sorts of things. That's what I tell myself. All sorts of things. But it isn't what I mean. There's only one thing, really. I could find out whether Henry is walking again.

It's intoxicating, the thought of it. Why hasn't it come up before? I think it's because I've never had a sense of having any control over the visions. But I do have control over when I have them, of course.

I'm called into the tiny audition room and I spend a few minutes saying the single line with varying emotions and emphases. The casting director doesn't look at me when he says he'll be in touch, and when I get off the Tube there's a voicemail from my agent to say that I didn't get it. When I get home, Oliver is stretched out on the sofa with a book. He looks up, questioningly. I shake my head, and he comes over and takes me in his arms, kisses me on the forehead.

'Do you ever think about giving up?' I ask him. Whenever I say those words, Mum's worried face flashes into my head.

'What, acting?'

I nod.

'No, not really. I mean, I would if I stopped being able to afford to live like this, but it's going okay for the time being. Do you?'

'Hardly ever. But sometimes.'

I think about having the kind of job where I'd know exactly what I was going to be paid each month. About knowing which hours I'd be working and which I'd be free, about being part of the daily rush hour commute. It's never appealed, it's something I've fought against my entire life, but wouldn't it be easier, in many ways? Wouldn't it feel safer, and more secure, and wouldn't my time off feel more like my own, if there weren't lines to learn and auditions to seek out and awkward conversations to be had with my agent? And how much of this questioning is about me having seen that I'm no longer doing this in ten years' time?

'You just have to trust that it's going to happen,' Oliver says into my hair. 'The big break. It might take a long time, but it will come, if you stick with it.'

I feel overwhelmingly tired suddenly. How does he know? How can he be so sure? But then, my visions back it up, for him. So maybe he's right. 'I'll be okay in the morning. It just feels a bit relentless sometimes.'

He nods, and I know he gets it. The last job he had was as part of a reenactment for Crimewatch. And this job I didn't get today, it was a throwaway bit-part in a sitcom. It's not what we dreamed of, when we battled for our places at drama school. It's not what we hoped for.

'Christmas is coming up,' he says. 'There might be further grotto opportunities.'

I laugh. 'Do you want a cup of tea?'

We sit in front of the TV for a bit. 'I went to drama school with her,' Oliver says.

The woman on the screen looks a little older than us, and a bit familiar. I've probably seen her in a handful of different things. This one is an old episode of a wartime drama. Why her, I want to say, and not us? But there's just no knowing.

That night, we go to bed and we don't have sex. He reaches across the space on the sheet between us and links his fingers through mine, and it's a comfort.

'Something will come up,' he says.

And I don't know whether it's true, but I love that he believes it. We fall asleep like that, hands held. But when we wake up, he's on his back and I'm on my side, turned away from him. I've had a dream about Henry, a dream in which he never had his accident. It happens fairly often, and it always takes me a bit of time to get over it. When it's my turn in the bathroom, I have a cry in the shower, and come out ready to face the day.

18

NOW (NOVEMBER 2012)

'I still feel like I don't really know him,' Oliver says. 'Nic.'

I know what he means, because I've known Nic for three years and occasionally he still feels like a near stranger.

'Trainee lawyer, right?'

'Yes.'

It's a reminder that the four of us haven't spent much time together in this first year of my relationship with Oliver. Priya and I go to the cinema every Tuesday, and we've met them in bars a couple of times, but this might just be the first dinner.

'So he's going to be a lawyer and she's going to be a doctor. In ten years from now, they'll be some big power couple. And we'll still be chasing after parts in adverts for toothpaste or soup.'

Ten years from now. It's a lot to take in, what he just said, because he's alluding to us being together in ten years' time. But also, I want to tell him that in ten years, I think he'll be starring in a major TV show. That I'll be out of the game altogether. That we'll have a child. But I can't.

'Something like that,' I say. 'But for now they're as broke as we are.'

'And you don't like him.'

It isn't a question. We're walking from our flat to theirs, and I stop when he says this. 'I don't not like him, as such…'

'You do this thing with your shoulders when you mention him. Sort of tensing up.'

'Huh. Well, I'm just not 100 per cent sure he's the one.'

'For Priya?'

'Yes, for Priya.'

We're going over for a takeaway curry. It's Friday night, late November, and Oliver's holding my hand loosely, a plastic bag full of glass bottles of beer hanging from his other hand, clinking as we walk. I feel more hopeful about things than I have lately. I spent all day writing house descriptions, but I have an audition lined up for next week for a returning character in a drama series. Oliver's promised to run lines with me all weekend.

As we approach the door, I see that Mrs Aziz is there, about to let herself in.

'Mrs Aziz,' I call, and she turns, breaks into a smile.

'Maddy! Are you here to check in on my spider plants?'

I laugh. 'Well, partly. Also thought I'd call in on Priya and Nic, you know how it is.'

'And who's this handsome chap?' She looks up at Oliver, who reaches out a hand.

'Oliver,' I say. 'This is Oliver. He's my flatmate. And my boyfriend. Oliver, this is Mrs Aziz, my former neighbour.'

We nip up to her flat first, and I water the plants while Oliver asks Mrs Aziz all about her family and her past, which she loves. She wants us to stay for tea but I tell her we're late, that Priya's expecting us, that she'll never forgive us if her jalfrezi goes cold.

'She's nice,' Oliver says as we go back down the stairs.

'The nicest.'

Priya and Nic are both in the kitchen surrounded by brown

paper bags full of food containers. I messaged our order over so they could have it ready for when we arrived.

'Damn,' Nic says. 'They're going to know we didn't cook it all from scratch.'

Priya, Nic and I have sat around this table countless times, so it feels familiar. But I expected the addition of Oliver to change the dynamic, to make things feel a little strange, and it doesn't. That's the thing about Oliver. He's easy-going. He fits in. He makes you feel like he's been around forever.

'So what's going on with you two, acting wise?' Priya asks.

'Maddy has this great audition next week,' Oliver says.

'Which is why,' I say, holding my hand over my wine glass, 'I'm taking it easy tonight. I need to spend all weekend preparing.'

'What's it for?' Nic asks.

And I tell them, how it's called *Summing Up* and is about a group of accountants and how it doesn't have great ratings yet, but there are a couple of people joining the cast who were previously in Eastenders, which should raise its profile. About the part, which is a scatty waitress with a heart of gold, who goes on a couple of dates with one of the main characters. My agent had said that they were leaving their options open, to see how the character went down. That there was potential for further work. I've been chasing this kind of thing for years, and I know that everyone sat at this table knows how much it means to me.

'Tell us the second you know,' Priya says. 'I mean, tell me. The second. Promise? I know *he* is your boyfriend, but I've been around longer and I need you to tell me first.' She gives Oliver a pointed look, and he laughs.

'What's the back-up plan, Maddy?' Nic asks, then.

'What do you mean?'

'I mean, it never really seems to come off, does it? What will you do for a career if it never does?'

I feel like he's slapped my cheek. I'm stunned. But both Oliver and Priya start talking animatedly at once, and I know without hearing exactly what they're saying that they're backing me up, telling him he's out of line. Nic holds his hands up as if to say he didn't mean anything by it, and we go back to our food, but there's an atmosphere.

When we've all finished eating, Priya grabs my hand and pulls me into the kitchen with her under the pretence of clearing the dishes away.

'Sorry about Nic,' she says once we're out of earshot. 'He's got a lot on, and he hasn't been himself.'

'It's okay,' I say. It's not, really, but it's also not her fault. I turn the tap on and hold the dishes under it to rinse them.

'Does it freak you out?' she asks. 'Knowing that the two of you are going to have a baby in the next few years?'

Priya rarely brings this up, since I told her about Isla's name. I suspect she's still bothered about it but she's pushing those feelings to one side, acknowledging that there are more serious matters at stake.

'Kind of. I mean, there's no way I'm ready for a baby. And yet, when I'm there, with her, it feels so normal. So right. So I guess I just have to wait and see how it all plays out. What else can I do?'

Priya takes another bottle of wine from the fridge, presses the cold glass against her arm. 'Is it hot in here, or is it the food? I'm boiling. Anyway, let's go back before they realise we're talking about them.'

We find Nic and Oliver discussing films. There's one about a Romantic poet and his lover on at the local arts cinema and Oliver and I have been talking about going. Nic says he's seen it, that he thinks it will win big prizes, but that his personal opinion is that it's shit. Oliver laughs at that.

'So,' Priya says, topping up everyone's glasses. I let her fill mine halfway – it's only my second of the evening. Everyone else has had a few. Their eyes are glazed, their movements loose. 'How's Henry doing?'

All three of them turn their gaze on me, and I can feel Oliver's eyes burning on my skin. I still haven't told him, about Henry's accident. I don't know why. Or maybe I do. It's because I want him to know the family I had before the accident, not this broken one I have now. What Priya's asked doesn't actually give anything away, but we've landed on the topic of Henry, and I know it's only a matter of time.

'No change,' I say.

'How is he in himself?' she asks.

'Just... you know. Hurt. Sad.' I turn to Oliver, and there's a puzzled expression on his face.

'Your brother Henry?' he asks, but he knows that's the Henry we're talking about, knows there's something I've kept from him.

I clear my throat. 'Henry had an accident.'

Priya claps a hand to her mouth. 'I'm sorry, guys, I just assumed you'd have talked about it.'

'We haven't,' Oliver says, his voice calm but with a warning in it, his expression wounded. 'Why haven't we, Maddy?'

'I... I don't know. I try not to dwell on it.'

He raises his eyebrows, and I know he thinks it's a lame excuse. 'So what happened?'

'Spinal cord injury. He was knocked off his bike by a car. Nobody's fault, just one of those things. He's paralysed from the waist down.'

How many times have I said this, since it happened? There are always people to tell, it seems. People to fill in. And then once they know, they ask after him endlessly. They're doing it to be kind, just like Priya is this evening, but it's hard to keep saying that there's no change, that he's still just the same, still waiting and hoping for an improvement.

'I'm sorry,' Oliver says. And I know he means it. Of course he's sorry, everyone's sorry. But he's hurt, too, that I didn't confide in him about this.

'Just awful,' Priya says, 'and he's such a nice kid, too. Not that it would be okay if he was a little shit, but he just isn't.' She's rambling. She looks at me, and her eyes apologise for making things awkward.

It's a conversation stopper, bringing up a paralysed child. I watch as everyone reaches for their glass at the same time.

When Oliver and I get up to go, a couple of hours later, I have a heavy feeling of dread sitting on my chest. I know he'll ask me why I didn't tell him. And sure enough, he does, almost as soon as we've turned off Priya and Nic's street.

'I guess I felt like if I didn't tell you, at least for a while, it would be like it hadn't happened, when I was with you.'

Oliver stops walking, looks at me with a slight squint. 'Really? That's why?'

'It's the worst thing that's ever happened in my life. And I can never get away from it, and sometimes that's all I want. To pretend it didn't happen, pretend that Henry's still playing football and moaning about having to tidy his room. That Mum and Alan aren't waiting to have their home converted so he can get upstairs. It's just a lot, you know? He's so little, and I remember holding him as a baby and not being able to believe how perfect he was. And sometimes, it feels like he's adjusted to it better than I have. Every time I go home it's like a kick in the teeth, the reality of it. So I didn't tell you, because I didn't know what to say.'

Oliver stares at me, says nothing.

'I would have told you, at some point,' I say. And I hear how weak it sounds.

'Good,' he says. 'Because I'm hoping I'll get to meet them, this family of yours.'

I don't know what to say to that.

'I don't get it,' he says. 'I haven't been through anything like it. But if you'll let me, I'll try to be there, to help you with it.'

I nod, and we start walking again. Not for the first time, I wonder how I got to be so lucky. With Oliver, but not just that. Why am I the one who still gets to walk along these London streets late at night after a good meal with good friends? Why am I the one who can run for a bus when I'm late for an audition? Why him, and not me? I feel tears prick at my eyes, and I blink them away.

'I'll take you to meet them. My family.'

Out of the corner of my eye, I see that he's smiling. 'Thank you.'

When we get back to our building, three flights of stairs seem like too much effort so we take the lift. We don't speak while we're in it. Inside the flat, Oliver puts the kettle on and we sit in the living room drinking peppermint tea.

'Listen, Maddy, about the whole Henry thing. It's okay, that you didn't feel like you could tell me. I'm sure there are other things too. But just know that I'm here, and I don't intend to go anywhere, and I'm ready to hear these things when you're ready to talk about them.'

'Do you have things?' I ask. 'Secrets, I mean.'

He doesn't look away from me. 'Everyone has secrets. But I'm a pretty open book. You can ask me anything and I'll be as honest as I can.'

'I'm ready for bed,' I say, swinging my legs off the sofa and onto the carpet. I pick up our mugs and take them through to the kitchen.

Oliver follows me into the bedroom, puts his arms around my body from behind, and kisses the back of my neck. And I thought I was too tired for this, but it rouses something in me, and I turn around and kiss him back, already reaching to peel off my clothes.

19

TEN YEARS FROM NOW (NOVEMBER 2022)

'We should definitely think about it,' Oliver is saying. 'I mean, just look at how great Isla is.'

We are in bed, facing each other, our noses inches apart. It's disconcerting, to rush from one bed to another like this. I turn my attention to what Oliver just said. What is it he's suggesting? I say nothing, stalling for time. Hoping he'll give it away the next time he speaks.

'I know you're scared, Maddy, and I know babies are hard work, but we're such a great team.'

A baby. A second child. I haven't given too much thought to why we only have one. The wonder of Isla existing at all has been enough for me. Do I want another one? It's so hard to know, because this thirty-six-year-old brain isn't the one I'm used to consulting.

'I'll think about it,' I say. It's not much, not a commitment, and Oliver's face tells me I've fobbed him off like this before.

'The longer we wait, the bigger the gap,' he says.

'I mean, obviously.'

'Think of Isla being a big sister. She would be so good at it.'

I'm sure he's right. But can I commit to having another baby for that reason alone? But no, I admonish myself, that wouldn't be the only reason, would it? I try to search through my brain like it's a filing cabinet, looking for Isla's early days. The sleep deprivation. The boredom. But I don't have access to any of it. I'm starting to learn that when I'm in the future, I still only have my current memories and experiences. It's not helpful.

'I have to go to sleep,' I say. 'Can we talk about it another time?'

Oliver nods, tries to smile, but there's a frustration in his eyes that is plain to see. I turn away from him, pull the cover up to my chin, and close my eyes.

20

NOW (DECEMBER 2012)

I open the door to Priya and she does a sort of 'ta da!' pose. God knows where she's got it from but she's wearing a skintight, shiny red jumpsuit. When she sees my blue air hostess outfit, she claps a hand to her mouth.

'Kelly is going to freak out,' she says.

'But do you think everyone will be doing this?' I ask, looking down at myself, unsure.

'No, most people will be doing the school uniform thing. Because it's easy.'

We're going to our friend's Britney-themed baby shower, and I'm not quite ready so I usher Priya into the kitchen. I'm grabbing my bag when Oliver comes out of his room and does a wolf whistle. Priya juts a hip and breaks into a dance routine, which I'm pretty sure is lost on Oliver.

'Is this... normal for a baby shower?' he asks.

'I'm not sure. It's the first one I've been to.' I was surprised when Priya first told me Kelly was having a baby. I wasn't sure we were 'there' yet. But I've had a few months to get used to it.

'I went to one for my cousin, but it was very boring,' Priya says.

'No Britney?'

'No Britney at all. In fact, just no fun whatsoever.'

'What would you do?' I ask. I'm not expecting her to have an answer ready.

'I don't think I'd have one. They just feel a bit cheap, somehow. Although I am not mad that Kelly's gone the whole hog. It's not often you get to wear something like this. You?'

I feel my cheeks reddening. I look from her to Oliver, back again. 'I have no idea.'

'Babies, hey? Where do you stand on babies, Oliver?'

It feels like time stands still. And it feels unfair, too, that Priya and I know that there is a baby in Oliver's near future, and he doesn't.

'I don't think it's for me,' he says.

It's so casual, like he's said he doesn't want a cup of tea. Could I have misheard him? But no, Priya is giving me a wide-eyed, panicked look.

'Ever?' I ask, because the silence in the room feels loaded. I can't look at him while I ask it.

'I don't think so, no.'

It would be one thing to find this out about your boyfriend, who you've fallen hard for, while you were lying on the sofa or in bed, limbs tangled, but it's quite another to find out in the kitchen, with your best friend present, while you're both dressed as different iterations of Britney Spears. I feel like someone's taken a sledgehammer to my heart, and it's ridiculous, because a year ago I would have said I wasn't sure either way about children. And yet now, there is Isla, the seemingly solid fact of her. And I know that she loves sausages and fights sleep and that her hair is always tangled and wild no matter what you do with it.

'We should go,' I say.

Priya walks out into the hall ahead of me, and Oliver pulls me back into the kitchen for a moment, his voice low.

'I guess that's something we should have talked about.'

'Maybe,' I say. But I understand why we haven't. We're both still in our twenties, having fun, and though the relationship feels serious and solid, we're not even a year in. It's just felt like longer because of us living together.

'Yeah, I just, I know it might be a bit of a shock.'

'We can talk about it later,' I say, and there's a slight shake to my voice and I know he's heard it.

He pulls me around to face him, kisses me on the lips in a way that is both gentle and hard, and I want to cry into his neck, but I pull away instead and follow Priya out of the door.

On the Tube, we scroll through Britney images, trying to match our friends to different looks. We're pretty sure Kelly will have that vest top with 'I have the Golden Ticket' on it and an arrow to her bump.

'Stay classy, Britney,' Priya says.

I know she wants to bring up the conversation with Oliver, but she's waiting for me to mention it first. It's a game we play, sometimes. And I don't crack for five stops. Almost six. When I do, there's no introduction, but she knows just what I mean.

'It's not even as if I know I want children myself,' I say.

Priya uncrosses her legs, recrosses them the other way. There are two boys in their late teens sitting opposite us who can't take their eyes off her. She looks about as good as you can possibly look in a shiny, red catsuit.

'I know, for me it would be a disaster. But you've never been sure.'

'And if it wasn't for—'

'Isla,' she cuts in, saying the name with such tenderness that I give it a bit of space before speaking again.

'Yes, Isla. If I didn't know about her, I would just let it slide.'

'But you can't.'

'And yet, what can I do, really? And please don't say I should tell him everything, because that's just not an option.'

'Sometimes I feel like these visions are ruling your life, and you don't—'

'I do know,' I interrupt. 'I do, Priya. I can't explain it, but there's no way all of this could be in my mind.'

Priya looks at me with wide eyes and I know she doesn't know what to say. We pull into our final stop and stand up to get off, and the conversation never gets restarted. Not while we're walking to the flat Kelly shares with her older boyfriend, not while we're playing games involving nappies smeared with different types of chocolate and drinking non-alcoholic cocktails.

The party's drawing to a close by the time Kelly comes to find the two of us. She's dressed as we predicted, her bump big and round and obvious, and she looks deliriously happy.

'You next?' she asks Priya, nudging her.

'Steady. I may be quite settled but having a baby before I've qualified is not in the plan.'

'But then once you qualify, you'll be on that whole doctor treadmill and there won't be an obvious time to do it,' Kelly says.

I know what she's doing. She's happy that she's taking this step, but she wishes someone else was taking it with her. Or at least looking likely to in the next couple of years.

'Oh, I'll make time,' Priya says.

Priya and Nic talk about their future children casually and often. They want three. They talk about being the kind of parents who have busy jobs but cram loads of love into the spaces. Camping trips and theme parks. Bike rides and swimming, that sort of thing.

'What about you?' Kelly asks.

She knows about Oliver but she hasn't met him. 'No babies on the cards,' I say. 'But I think I love him.'

Kelly makes a dramatic shocked face. 'Not Maddy Hart, in love?'

I feel a redness creeping up my neck. Priya gives me a look that is all sympathy, and I have to push past them and go to the toilet before the tears start spilling out. As I'm walking away, I hear Priya telling Kelly how nice Oliver is, how she thinks it might be serious with us.

For a minute or two, I stand in the bathroom giving myself stern looks in the mirror. How would I feel about this news that Oliver doesn't want children if I hadn't seen into our future? I think it would be fine, honestly. I try to tune into that, because I don't want to react in a hysterical way when Oliver and I talk about it again. I have to remember that what I know and what he knows are two totally different things.

* * *

Later, I'm on the sofa eating crisps and Oliver's getting us beers. The non-alcoholic cocktails were nice, but overly sweet, and I need something with a bit of a kick.

'So,' Oliver says, passing me a bottle of Corona that he's wedged a piece of lime into, 'about what I said earlier.'

I have to stop myself waving a hand and saying it's nothing. Because it isn't nothing. It's a conversation that needs to be had at some point, so why not now?

'My mum left, when I was about three,' he says.

I sort of knew this, but he's never said it outright. I look straight at him, encouraging him to keep talking. My feet are on the sofa and he reaches for them, moves them into his lap, holds on to my toes in a way that makes me feel secure, somehow.

'It was just me and my dad, and he wasn't the best when it came to anything emotional. So I just feel like I don't know how to be a part of a family, like I don't know how to be a parent. And because of that, I've always assumed I won't take that path.'

I take a moment to let this settle. 'I'm sorry, about your mum.'

'Yeah, well.'

He must have been telling this story his whole life. Must have had endless sympathy from teachers and parents of friends. He seems to find my apology uncomfortable, and I know that I would, too.

'Do you have any kind of relationship with her?'

'No, nothing. Dad doesn't talk about it much, but he tries to tell me it's not about me. That she just wasn't suited to being a mum, that she couldn't cope with it. But it's hard not to blame yourself, sometimes. I mean, it's pretty unusual, isn't it, for a mum to walk away like that, so completely? You have to wonder what you did.'

'It could have been more about her relationship with your dad,' I say.

He shakes his head, and it's clear he's been over and over this.

'But then she would have kept in touch. It was definitely motherhood she was walking away from. But it's okay, I've accepted it. I just don't know how I would turn that sort of past into a future with a happy family. But it doesn't change how I feel about you, you know? I like what we're building here. I really do. But I understand, too, if not wanting to have children is a dealbreaker.'

'It's not a dealbreaker,' I say, without realising I'm going to.

He does a slow nod, keeps his eyes fixed on mine while he takes a drink from his bottle. 'It's not?'

'No, it's not. I've always been unsure about it. Priya just knows, she's always known, and Nic seems to know too. And Kelly, who we were with today, she said the pregnancy wasn't planned but she knew the minute she found out that she wanted to go ahead with it. I've just never had that certainty. And you know, at the party today, there were these older women there who Kelly works with, and it was like they had nothing good to say about mothering. It was all no sleep and no peace and no time to yourself and yet they were all telling Kelly it would be the best thing she's ever done. I don't really get it.'

Oliver rubs the arches of my feet and it makes me shiver. 'You might change your mind,' he says.

I nod, conceding that this is a possibility. 'So might you.'

He doesn't say anything, but I know he's thinking that he won't.

21

NOW (DECEMBER 2012)

One Tuesday afternoon in December, while the wind blows a gale outside and I'm trying to think of a new and interesting way to describe a three-bedroom, 1950s semi-detached house, Oliver appears in the doorway to my room with a cupcake in his hand.

'For me?'

'For you.'

He comes in, stands by my bed. 'I was just thinking, about how it's been over a year since we met.'

I'm confused at first, because I count things from when I moved in, but of course we met before that. The grotto job. The elves.

I think of those early months of living together, after that initial kiss and before we gave in to how we feel. Now, we've settled into something comfortable and easy. We always sleep in Oliver's room, but I still work in this one. And I am living in two worlds. Mostly in this one, but also in the one where we have Isla. Where we're a family.

I stand and go to him, our bodies meeting at our toes and our hips and our foreheads.

'Thank you,' I say.

'For the cupcake?'

'For everything.'

'Are you busy?' he asks, and I know what he means.

So I tilt my head back and kiss him, run my hands up and down the skin beneath his T-shirt. Now that the heady early days are behind us, it's rare for us to have sex during the day. As he undresses me, I'm thinking about Isla, about the fact that I haven't seen her for a while, and I probably will now. It's that time between school ending and evening, that time that seems to be hers and mine. But, this time, when I jump into the future, she isn't there.

22

TEN YEARS FROM NOW (DECEMBER 2022)

I am alone in the future flat, oven gloves on my hands, my cheeks hot. I crouch down, look into the oven. I am making a pie. How do I know how to make a pie? Just then, I hear the door open and Oliver comes in, pulling his gloves off with his teeth, one finger at a time.

'Hey,' he says.

'Hey.'

'What are you making?'

'A pie,' I say, willing him not to ask me what kind. He doesn't.

'It feels quiet, doesn't it, when she's not here?'

I know, by now, that Isla isn't always with us, but I haven't worked out why. She seems too young for school trips or Brownie camp or anything like that. And then I see that this is probably the best opportunity I'm going to get, for asking this question I want to know the answer to. It's going to be clumsy, but it would always be clumsy. It's a chance, and I have to take it.

'Do you ever wonder about what our life would be like if we didn't have her?' I ask.

He looks at me, tilts his head to one side, not hurt, as I'd thought he might be. Just curious.

'I try not to,' he says.

'It's just, when we were first together, you said you didn't want to have children. Do you remember?'

He sinks into one of the chairs at the kitchen table, having shoved his gloves in his coat pockets and hung the coat up in the hall. 'Of course I remember. And god, I lie awake sometimes, thinking about how close I came to not having her, and it makes me want to throw up. When I'm in the park with her at the weekends, walking with a coffee while she scoots and tells me all the random things she's remembered from her week at school, I sometimes find myself wondering about what I'd be doing if I wasn't doing this. And it just freaks me out, partly because I don't know and partly because I don't want to know. This is it for me, Maddy. You, and her, and me. It's everything.'

There's a moment between him finishing this speech and me realising that there's a burning smell, and in it I am completely still and silent. And then it's over, and I am opening the oven door and wafting away the smoke and pulling the ruined pie from the oven.

23

NOW (DECEMBER 2012)

The next day, we go to see my parents and Henry. I'm finally letting Oliver all the way in. If it goes well, I'm going to invite him to come for Christmas. It's a lot, suggesting Christmas as his second time of meeting them, but I'm confident it won't freak him out. Oliver is all in. I don't doubt that.

On the drive there, Oliver at the wheel, we don't talk much, but I know that he understands this is a big deal for me. That he's the first man I've ever brought home. We've talked a lot about my family by this point, and I've told him about the ways in which my mum and Alan have changed since Henry's accident, as well as the ways in which Henry has changed, of course. I feel like my family is slightly broken, and he'll never see it whole, the way it was before, and I wish he could. But then, his family is broken too, so perhaps he doesn't expect too much.

Mum comes to the door as soon as we pull onto the drive, as if she's been waiting for us, which she probably has.

'This is Oliver,' I tell her, leaning to give her a hug.

'Hi,' Oliver says, putting up a hand, and then Alan comes out of the house onto the driveway, and there are a few moments of handshaking and hugging that feel sort of awkward, before we go inside.

In the kitchen, Mum makes tea and I ask where Henry is.

'He's in his room,' she says, her eyes flicking to the door of his new bedroom.

'Shall I go in and see him?' I ask.

'I think it's best to wait until he comes out. He's been having these moods, feeling angry and frustrated. He knows you're coming. He'll be out soon, I'm sure.'

We take our cups of tea through to the living room and I can hear Henry moving around in the room next door. Mum hasn't said anything about these moods on our phone calls. Could it just be a normal part of being ten? I have to remember, sometimes, that I can't tie everything to the accident. That some things are a normal part of being a kid and growing up.

'So, Oliver, Maddy tells us you're an actor,' Alan says.

'I am. And when there's nothing much going on, on that front, like right now, I teach swimming, too.'

'Any roles in the offing for you?' Mum asks me.

When my parents ask me about my acting prospects with that hopeful look on their faces, I hate having to tell them there's nothing almost as much as I hate the fact that there is nothing.

'I had a callback for this TV thing, but they went for someone else. I'm doing an advert for cheesecake next week, though.'

Oliver looks at me, gives me a supportive smile. He knows how much I wanted that *Summing Up* part. Not for the first time, I think how nice it is to be in a relationship with someone who understands this world. Understands how much rejection there is, and knows it doesn't necessarily mean you're no good, or that you'll never make it.

'And the writing work? Is there still plenty of that?'

'There's enough, yeah. We're surviving.'

Just then, the door opens wider and Henry comes through.

'Hey,' I say, going over to hug him. 'It's good to see you. This is my boyfriend, Oliver.'

Henry looks tired and pale, like he's been playing video games for days on end, which he quite possibly has.

'Henry,' Oliver says. 'It's good to meet you.'

Henry keeps his eyes lowered, but he mumbles a hello.

Mum announces that she's going to serve up lunch. 'It's a stroganoff,' she says. 'It's been in the slow cooker for hours.'

Now that Henry sleeps in what was once the dining room, we have to eat in the kitchen, which is fine on an ordinary day but always feels a bit strange when we have a guest.

'This is great,' Oliver says, taking big forkfuls of the food in front of him.

Mum thanks him and for a little while we all eat in silence. It's just getting to the point where I'm trying to think of something to say to break it when Oliver speaks again.

'Henry, I heard you're into football.'

'Yeah, I mean, I was.'

'What happened to coaching?' I ask.

'Nothing. I'm still doing that.'

'Who do you support?' Oliver asks.

'Chelsea,' Henry says.

'No way! Me too.'

Henry and Alan both break into smiles.

'It's Chelsea or nothing in this house,' Alan says. 'Maddy chose nothing, as I'm sure you know.'

'My dad wasn't into it,' Oliver says, 'and I just chose the team my best friend supported but they've done me pretty proud.'

'Do you play?' Henry asks, and I see that he's actually looking at Oliver now, for the first time.

'Sometimes, just for fun. Five a side. But when I was your age, I did.'

'I used to,' he says.

And I feel a crack opening up for him in my heart. He's so young to be dealing with this. It must be hard enough to find yourself in a wheelchair as an adult, but he's just a kid, and it's so unfair. I would swap with him, if I could.

'There's a match on TV this afternoon. Maybe we could watch it?' Oliver looks at me as if for approval. 'That is, unless we're in a hurry to get back?'

I'm in no hurry, and when I say so Henry looks secretly pleased, and when we've cleared the plates and eaten apple crumble for dessert, the two of them go through to the living room, and then Alan follows them, and it's just Mum and me.

'I like him,' she says, getting right to the point like she always does.

It's not until she says it that I realise how much it means to me, and I break into a grin.

'Is it serious?' she asks. 'It's just... there's never really been anyone before.'

She isn't disapproving. She just wants to know.

'I think it is.'

She has worried about me. Not so much since Henry's accident, as that has spread like a stain, taking up all of her capacity to worry. But in the past, I know she's wondered about my lack of boyfriends. She's hinted that they'd be fine with me bringing home a partner of any gender. And I've just avoided the topic, because what else can I do?

There's a roar from the living room and I wonder who's playing and why they're all so happy about the way it's going, but not enough to go in there and see. 'How are you?' I ask Mum. 'Really?'

'Up and down,' she says. She doesn't look at me while she's saying it, and I suspect there's been more down than up lately.

I'm about to speak again when Oliver puts his head round the door and we both turn to look at him.

'I was thinking, Saturday mornings at the pool where I work we have sessions for disabled people. It's a form of therapy. There might be something near here, or if Henry would like to try it with someone he knows, I could look into getting him access in London.'

Mum's expression is tight, full of worry, but I think this could be really good for him. I knew about these sessions and never really made the connection with Henry. If I'm honest, I thought they were for people with less severe injuries. Mum says something non-committal, and Oliver smiles and disappears back to the living room. And when we're leaving, giving hugs and being told to drive carefully, she pulls me in and whispers in my ear.

'Keep hold of him.'

And I tell her I will. Or that I'll try to.

24

NOW (JANUARY 2013)

Christmas comes and goes. Oliver spends it with my family and it feels like he's always been there. And then once we get back to London and back to normal, Oliver works on his plan to get Henry in the water. He has to talk to the people who run the sessions, has to get permission from Henry's doctor. And he manages to get everyone on board, so we end up seeing them all again just a couple of weeks into January. It's the first time any of them have seen the flat, since it's easier for me to go home than for them to come into London, and I like watching them look around it, like the way Oliver brings them cups of tea and the way Henry reaches down to pet Marjorie. Henry looks like he can't decide whether to be excited or scared, which I suppose is probably perfectly normal. When it's time to leave, we crowd in the hallway sorting out coats and shoes and umbrellas, and I feel Henry tug on my sleeve.

'What if I can't do it, when I get there?' he asks.

I look at Oliver and there is so much compassion in his eyes. 'No one is going to make you do it, Henry,' he says. 'Let's just go there and see.'

This reassurance seems to do the trick. Mum and Alan take Henry in their car and Oliver and I go on the bus because there isn't room for all of us and the wheelchair. We sit upstairs on the top deck, and I reach for Oliver's hand. 'I don't know how to thank you for all of this.'

He wrinkles his nose as if I've said something slightly distasteful. 'You don't have to thank me. He's a great kid, and I wanted to help. And, hey, we don't even know if he's going to do it yet.'

I think of Henry swimming. He used to have lessons, and a handful of times I went along to watch. I can picture him doing front crawl, turning his head to the side to breathe every three strokes. I think of him on holidays we've taken, doing somersaults and handstands, jumping in and splashing around.

'He'll do it.' I'm sure of this. He just wanted to know there was an escape route if he needed it, but he won't.

And I'm right, he doesn't. Mum and Alan and I sit on the small benches at the side of the pool and watch Oliver help Henry into the pool, watch him support Henry's torso so he can float on his back, and my brother looks so happy and free that I feel guilty that none of us thought of this before. There are only a handful of people in the session, so Henry has plenty of space to move around, and when it's over and we're heading back to the changing rooms to help him get dry and changed, he won't stop talking for a second. I remember that he used to be like this sometimes, after a football match or a friend's party. Bursting with enthusiasm and life. Sometimes you don't notice that something has been missing until it's back.

We have a late lunch together at the flat. I've bought quiches and a baguette and salad. Henry loads up his plate and talks without pausing while he eats, and I remember how swimming always used to make me really hungry when I was a kid.

'Can we do it again?' he asks Oliver.

Oliver nods. 'Of course, Henry. That session runs every Saturday, and you can come along whenever you like. Just say the word.'

I steal a glance at Mum, worried that she won't like Oliver making this promise when it involves quite a trek for them all, but she's never looked happier. And I know, then, that she'd bring him every single week if he asked her to. That seeing him like this, like he's been brought back to life, is worth everything to her.

After they go, I feel all churned up, emotionally.

'He's a great kid,' Oliver says.

'He is.'

We're sitting on the sofa, my head in his lap.

'You know,' he says, 'I hope you don't mind me saying this, but it seems a bit like you and your mum and Alan think him being in a wheelchair is the end of the world, and he's reacting to that. I've met a fair few disabled people at these swimming sessions, and they have challenges, of course, but it doesn't mean they don't have good, worthwhile lives. I feel like if you were a bit more positive about the whole situation, he might be, too.'

And in an instant, the whole atmosphere crumples. I sit up. 'What?'

'It's not a criticism. I haven't been through the same thing, but I'm just looking at it as an outsider, and it feels like—'

'No,' I cut in. 'I'm not listening to this. You're right, you haven't been through it. And you don't know them, not really.'

I'm standing, now, and there's a pounding in my head that wasn't there before. How dare he?

'Maddy, you've got it wrong. Maybe I sounded harsh, but I didn't mean to. Sit down, please.'

But I'm too keyed up to sit down. Five minutes ago, I was full of gratitude for what he'd done, and now I can't even look at him.

'I'm going out.' I go to the hallway, pull on my boots and coat.

'Maddy, it's freezing out there.' He's followed me out and he grips the tops of my arms. 'Please, let's talk about this.'

I look at him for a long moment. 'I can't be here,' I say.

I stomp down all the stairs and I reach into my pocket, planning to call Priya, but I've left my phone in the flat. I can't go back, not after such a dramatic exit, so I just walk over to her place, hoping she'll be there.

She isn't. I'm standing on the doorstep, shaking with cold, when I look at the buzzers and see that my name's been taken off and replaced with Nic's. If it wasn't for the argument I just had with Oliver, I wouldn't give it a second thought, but in that moment it feels like a betrayal, and I find that I'm crying, the tears coming fast and warm against my cold cheeks. And that's how Mrs Aziz finds me, when she comes home with her shopping, and she bundles me inside and doesn't let me carry a single bag up the stairs.

I water her spider plants for old time's sake. They're looking healthy. I wonder whether Priya or Nic help her with them.

'Do you know where they are?' I ask Mrs Aziz, pointing at the floor to indicate the downstairs flat.

'No idea,' she says. 'They are never there. So busy. Studying, working, exercising. They make me feel tired. Now, what's troubling you?'

Mrs Aziz knows about Henry, so I tell her about what Oliver did for him, with the swimming, and she looks puzzled, as well she might, about why I'm upset. Then I tell her what he said and she nods, understanding.

'Sometimes people don't think things through before they say them.'

I wait for her to offer more wisdom, but she leaves it at that and sweeps out to make tea. When she comes back, offering me a mug, she has a question for me.

'Do you love him, this Oliver?'

I do. Sometimes, when he slings an arm around me as we're walking or comes so close to my face that our eyelashes touch, I feel like surely this is love. Because if it isn't, then what is?

'Yes.'

'I thought so. If you didn't, you wouldn't be so upset about this. Here's what you need to do. You need to stay here until you feel a bit better, then go home and tell him that what he said hurt your feelings. Tell him calmly. Give him a chance to apologise, or elaborate. Because I don't think he meant to hurt you, Maddy. I think he's really trying hard to do the best he can for you.'

I don't say anything, just drink my tea and think about what she's saying.

'It sounds to me like being in the water did Henry a world of good. Try to focus on that, if you can.'

I think of the way he floated, his eyes shining. The way Oliver supported him, the way he was ready to help him if he needed it, and I know she's right. So I finish the tea and give Mrs Aziz a big hug and head back out into the freezing early evening.

When I let myself back into the flat, Oliver comes out to greet me, starts talking about how he didn't mean to upset me and I put a hand over his mouth, and then he sticks his tongue out through my fingers and we both laugh.

'I love you,' I say.

I hadn't planned it, but it's like now I've realised I can't keep it inside me. Oliver widens his eyes in surprise.

'You love me?'

'I do.'

'Well, Maddy, that's kind of great, because I love you too.'

We kiss, there in the hallway, and he runs his hands up and down the sides of my body, from hip to chest.

'What I said, about Henry...'

'You were right,' I tell him, only realising as I say it that it's true. 'Sometimes the truth is hard to hear.'

If Henry is in a wheelchair for the rest of his life, we'll deal with it. We'll have to. And it won't all be doom and gloom. Today has shown me that there are still amazing things he can do, still incredible experiences he can enjoy. Oliver has led us to all of this, and I'm so grateful, so I kiss him, and kiss him, his back against the hallway wall and my boots unzipped but not yet pulled off.

25

NOW (JANUARY 2013)

'So fill me in,' Priya says, shovelling popcorn into her mouth. 'Before the trailers start.'

Priya loves the trailers. I find them a bit depressing, sometimes. Because you pretty much know they've put all the best bits in the two-minute trailer and the two-hour film will be a disappointment in comparison. Priya doesn't see it like that. She likes to know what she's going to get.

'Well, he arranged for Henry to go swimming and Henry loved it and Mum cried and then I had a big fight with him and stormed out and then when I got back we said I love you.'

'That,' Priya says, 'is a lot. I'm so pleased, about the swimming.'

'Not about the love?'

'Of course about the love too. But if you ask me, that was pretty obvious.'

'How's doctoring?' I ask.

'Well, I'm making a list of specialisms I don't want to follow.'

'Any that you do?'

'Paediatrics.'

I think about Henry, about how hard it's been, watching him deal with this. 'Isn't working with sick kids heartbreaking?'

'I guess it can be, but the stakes are so high when it's the life of someone who's only had a few years in the world. Imagine how it must feel to help make a child better?'

I see what she means, but I'm stuck on the dying, on how you'd get through it. Kids with cancer, or other life-threatening illnesses, or who've had accidents. The unfairness of it all.

'What about you? Anything going on work-wise?'

I shake my head, and she doesn't push it.

'That audition I had after we had dinner at yours, I thought it went really well. I didn't say anything to Oliver, or to anyone, but I really thought I had it. Got a callback, and then my agent called to say it was between me and another girl, and they went with her. I felt like that could have been it, you know.'

'It?'

'The first step. A door, opening.'

She nudges me in the ribs. 'Shhhh, trailers.'

I sometimes wonder if she'd stop me talking for the trailers even if I was in the middle of telling her I was getting married, or I was pregnant, or I'd been cast as the lead in a film. I'm pretty sure she would. We're seeing a romcom called *Playing for Keeps*. Priya has a thing for Gerard Butler and I have a thing for films in general. I love to critique the actors, to cast myself in one of the leading roles and think about how I would have approached it. But perhaps more than that, I like studying the plot, what makes the film really work, or sometimes what doesn't.

In the brief gap between the trailers and the film starting, Priya turns to me, holding out her popcorn. I take a handful.

'Nic's got a job. The place where he's doing his training contract, they're keeping him on.'

I grab her hand. 'That's so brilliant. You've both worked really hard.'

She smiles but looks a bit empty, and I make a mental note to really ask her how things are with Nic after the film. And then it's starting and the sound is all around us and we sit back and let it wash over us. And it isn't until we've parted ways that I remember.

* * *

Back at the flat, Oliver asks how the film was.

'It was okay.'

'And is Priya alright?'

'Yeah.'

'So why do you seem all forlorn?'

He's in the kitchen, loading the dishwasher, and I go to him, circle his waist with my arms, pull him up to standing. 'I just feel a bit shitty, about work. How do you deal with all the rejection and the waiting?'

He kisses the top of my head, and I know he's composing his answer carefully. 'I just have to believe that it will happen, or I'd go crazy. Every bad audition, every time I get asked to perform for free, every play where there are three people in the audience. It's all a process, one step leading to another, and eventually it will lead somewhere good.'

I step away from him, pull a bottle of wine from the fridge, two glasses from the cupboard. 'But what if it doesn't? I know my parents think I should just call it a day, that I'll be doing my side hustle as my only hustle for the rest of my life, or end up training to do something completely different in my forties or something. I know that if I called them and said I was going to give it all up for a nine to five office job, they'd be absolutely delighted. It's hard to keep fighting against that.'

Oliver takes the glass I offer him and has a long drink. I love how serious he gets when I'm telling him things, how well he listens and responds. 'I don't know what that's like,' he says. 'You know it was just me and my dad, and we don't talk that often and I don't think he cares much one way or another what I do with my life. There's a weight to having people who love you that much. It's great, of course, but it does mean there's all this expectation and worry. With me, it's just me. I don't have to convince anyone else I'm doing the right thing. So I guess it's easier, in a way.'

I've never considered this, but he's right. 'So you just know, that you'll make it?'

'Yep. I have to believe it. Otherwise what am I doing? I'm a twenty-eight-year-old swimming teacher.'

This makes me think of Henry, of his face when he was in the water. 'That's not such a bad thing to be.'

'But you know what I mean. It's not the dream.'

'What is the dream?'

He looks puzzled. 'What do you mean?'

'I mean, I know it's acting. But what's the absolute dream? Hollywood films? West End plays?'

'I'd love to be part of a really great TV show. Films are amazing but if you're on TV you have the potential to be in every person's house, to be the thing that they choose to watch after a long day at work. That's such a privilege. What about you?'

'Something steady,' I say. 'Something that lets me act but makes me feel safe at the same time.'

'Soap opera,' he says.

And he's right. It isn't what I thought my dream was. I always thought I wanted to be on the big screen, because films are what I love watching the most, but they're not steady work.

'Yeah, maybe.'

When we've drained our glasses, we go to bed, and I don't think we're going to have sex, and I'm on the edge of sleep when Oliver kisses the back of my neck and snakes a warm arm around me, his hand on my belly. Just like that, I want him, and I turn, ready for kisses and touching. One minute I'm there, his tongue in my mouth and his hands everywhere, and the next I'm somewhere else entirely.

26

TEN YEARS FROM NOW (JANUARY 2023)

I'm with Priya, and I could weep with the relief of seeing her alive and well. Ever since I found out that I named my daughter Isla, I've been waiting for this moment. Waiting to see that she's okay. We're in a bar and her hair is different and it's so good to see her, to know that our friendship is intact in this future life I'm witnessing. It takes me a while to notice that she's sad. Drunk and sad. It strikes me that for the first time ever, I don't have to pretend. I could tell her what's happening. But would it freak her out?

'I just feel like I'm not doing any of it well. The kids at the hospital, the kids at home. I'm failing all of them in equal measure. And Josh. I can't remember the last time we had a conversation that didn't revolve around whose turn it was to get up in the night with them.'

Josh. I don't know a Josh. Not yet. I wonder what happened between her and Nic, whether they're still on speaking terms. It's a relief, to know he isn't the one she ends up with. And that she has children, like she always wanted. I have to force myself to stay composed, to not jump up and hug her.

'These are the hard years,' I say.

'How long do they go on for? I mean, I know you can't answer that. But seriously, I don't know how long I can carry on working twelve-hour shifts on three hours of sleep. And whose idea was it for me to work with kids? It was fine until I had the twins but now it's like I cannot cope with anything even remotely sad. Which isn't ideal when you're looking after kids who have cancer.'

Twins! Priya has twins. I focus on that for a moment, desperate to know what their names are, how old they are. Then I latch on to what she said about her work. I want to say that she told me she wanted to work with kids exactly ten years ago today, and then I realise that if I did, she'd probably understand what was happening here. That I was visiting from the past. Or visiting the future from the present. It's so tempting, to let her in on it, but I'm not sure it's the right thing to do. I'm not sure whether it would mess with the equilibrium in some way, bring something crashing down.

'It'll get easier,' I say, though I have no idea whether it will or not.

Priya rolls her eyes. 'That's enough moaning from me, anyway. How are Oliver and Isla?'

I really look at her, try to see whether saying my daughter's name costs her anything. It doesn't seem to. Could I ask her the things I want to ask Oliver, and can't? How I got him to change his mind about having a child. I don't know the answer to the question she's asked me, so I'm forced to be vague.

'Pretty good, you know.'

'Is Oliver still on set for a crazy number of hours?'

'Yes.' This seems like the safest bet.

'And don't you mind?'

This one I know. 'How could I mind, Priya? It's his dream. Not many of us get the exact thing we were working towards when we were just starting out. But he has, and I'm happy for him.'

'Do you ever wish you were still acting?'

Even though I knew I wasn't, have had enough future visions since being with Oliver that I was pretty sure, this is the first official confirmation, and it takes me a few seconds to let it settle. 'No,' I say, hoping it's true, not just for the sake of this conversation, but because I don't want to believe that the person I am in the future has such big regrets.

'Good, because when you gave it up, it seemed like it was breaking your heart. But now, I have to say, you seem so much happier.'

This makes me sit up and take notice. Because to my mind, giving up acting is failing, no matter when or how it happens. But if Priya thinks I'm genuinely happier, that makes all the difference. Maybe it was the right decision, for whatever reason. Maybe the person I am in my thirties is different enough to the one I am in my twenties that stepping out of that world is the right call for me. Maybe it doesn't have to be that Oliver has succeeded and I haven't. It's a new way of framing things, and I'm glad to have it.

27

NOW (APRIL 2013)

Though I only see Isla in glimpses, though I only get to spend brief pockets of time with her, there's no denying the fact that I'm head over heels in love. I remember Henry at this age, how much fun he was, how he was full of ideas and wanted to play endlessly. Isla is quieter, more thoughtful than he was. She writes stories, illustrates them, makes little books out of folded paper and staples them together and presents them to Oliver and me. She slips in and out of rooms, seeming quietly content on her own, with her Lego or a pile of books. I wonder how much of her personality is formed by her being an only child, and a girl, and how much is just inherent in her. I wonder, too, how happy this life is that we're giving her. Things between Oliver and me seem secure, and I know we both shower her with love, but is she lonely? I've heard her talk about friends but I haven't seen her interacting with other children, and sometimes she seems solemn and too grown-up for her age.

Perhaps this is what it is, to be a parent. Questioning every decision, every possibility. I feel the weight of holding her childhood in my hands, wanting to make it good enough.

And there's an idea that's been nagging at me. What if Oliver isn't her father? The more I see of her, the more it gnaws at me. I can't see him in her features. It isn't that their relationship is lacking, from what I can see. They adore each other. But she isn't always with us, and where else would she be than with an absent biological father? When I bring this up with Priya, sitting across from her in Ellen's café in early spring, flapjacks in front of us, she's not convinced.

'You're with Oliver now, right? And you're pretty serious. And if the future visions are correct, Isla is going to be conceived next year, so in that space of time, the two of you would have to break up and you'd have to meet someone else and get pregnant. And then you would have to split up with him and get back together with Oliver. What are the chances? Isn't it more likely that she belongs to the two of you?'

She's right, it is more likely. And yet, I just can't shake the thought.

'You know,' she goes on, 'when you're there, in the future, and she's not there, she could be with grandparents. Your parents, or Oliver's.'

It's a good point. 'Oliver only has a dad, and they're not close. I can't really imagine her being with him. But maybe my parents. It's just, sometimes she's not there and it's a school night. Why would my parents have her then?'

Priya shrugs and reaches for my cup of tea, takes a slug.

'Oy.'

'You never finish it. It's practically cold. How's Henry?'

This feels like safer ground. Between the football coaching and the swimming, Henry's come alive again. They come up once a month, and Oliver takes him into the pool. Sometimes my parents and I go along to watch and sometimes just the two of them go. It's changed something in Mum, too. I think it's reminded her that there are things we haven't thought of yet, that can make his life better. That we're not stuck at a dead end.

'He's good. More like the old Henry.'

'Well, that's great.'

I pause for just a moment too long. 'Yeah, it is.'

'But?'

Sometimes it's wonderful having a friend who knows you so well, and sometimes it's annoying. 'It's just... things with Oliver are great, but now he's involved with my family in this way, helping Henry in a way no one else has managed to, which is fantastic, but...'

'Ah, there it is.'

I smile. 'But what if it doesn't work out between us? What if he changes his mind, or I do? Where does that leave Henry?'

Priya drinks some more of my tea, puts the empty mug down between us. 'The way I see it, Oliver's a really good guy. He must know what this means to Henry – to all of you. He wouldn't take it away, out of spite, if something went wrong between the two of you.'

Do I believe this? He is a good man. He is. 'I hope you're right.'

Ellen appears at the side of the table, hands on hips. 'I just wondered whether you still work here? Because you're looking suspiciously like an unpaying customer at the moment.'

Priya pushes back her chair and scuttles over to the counter, and Ellen follows her there with her slow, hip-swinging gait.

I'm on the street outside when my phone rings, and it's my agent, Cora.

'Hello?'

'Maddy!'

She sounds a bit frantic. 'Have you got something for me?'

'I hope so. I've had Jennifer Waite on the phone. She's one of the casting directors for *Summing Up*.'

I stop walking, stop breathing. I move out of the crowd of people on the pavement, lean back against the window of Ellen's café. I put a hand over the ear I'm not holding the phone to. 'Yes?'

'They want to see you again. This afternoon. She said they're not convinced they made the right call and they want to be absolutely sure before they move forward with the production.'

This never happens. The cynic in me says something's happened with the girl they chose – she's ill or pregnant or she's refusing to play the character how they want her. But really, who cares? Once you're on a TV show, no one asks you about the circumstances around it, do they? No one cares if you nearly didn't get it, and then you did. It hits me that I need to give her an answer, that I can mull this all over to my heart's content later, but right now, I have to say yes.

'Maddy, are you there?'

'I'm here,' I say. 'Cora, that's brilliant. Can you send me the details?'

'Sending right now. Good luck, Maddy. I have a great feeling about this.'

And then she's gone, and I'm left holding the phone to my ear as people rush by me in both directions. I turn around and see that Priya is staring at me. She does an exaggerated shrug and I want to go back in there and tell her what's happened but I can't get sidetracked. I check the message that's just arrived from Cora, and I need to get going. They want to see me in an hour. I need to get there and impress them. I point to the phone in my hand, hoping she'll know I mean I'll call later, and I dash to the Tube.

But the trains are not behaving, and between a passenger

taken ill on the Northern line and a delay for no good reason I can see on the Central line, followed by a dash through the streets and up four flights of stairs, I arrive an hour and ten minutes later. Sweaty and unkempt. Damnit. If Tube delays cost me this role, I'll scream. Jennifer and two of her colleagues are clearly waiting for me, and I can't help but notice that there's no one else in the waiting area.

'I'm so sorry,' I say, bursting through the door in all my disarray. 'The Tube was a nightmare and I couldn't get here any faster.'

'If you're cast,' Jennifer says crisply, 'we'll expect punctuality.'

'Of course.'

'Now, we want to see you do something a bit different from last time. This scene is from the second episode this character is in.' She turns to the man beside her. 'Will, can you play Malcolm for it?'

'Sure.' He stands, walks over to me with two scripts in his hand, gives one to me.

'You look like a startled rodent,' he says. 'Can you lose the nerves?'

Lose the nerves. Like it's simple. But I give myself a bit of a talking to. This is a big chance, and I cannot get it wrong. I glance at the script, but the words blur and mingle on the page. Should I ask for five minutes? Go to the toilet, sort out my hair and my breathing? But no, I can't after already keeping them waiting.

I nod, and we run the scene. It's more emotional than the one from my previous audition, which was light and jokey. There's more to this character than I'd realised. I see how they're playing with the idea of extending her part. God, I want this.

'Great,' Jennifer says when we've finished, screwing up her

face as if she's just trodden dog shit into her new carpet. 'We'll be in touch.'

Out on the street, I walk away from the building and around a corner before stopping to take some deep breaths. What was that? Just another opportunity to dangle the thing I want most in the world in front of me before taking it away again? I'm almost at the Tube when my phone starts ringing, and I've barely said hello when she starts speaking.

'Maddy, it's Cora again. You got it! They want you to start next Monday, 9 a.m. prompt.'

'You... really?' I stutter.

'Yes, really. I'll email the script over as soon as they send it. Have a great weekend, Maddy.'

Before I can think better of it, I ask the question I'm dying to know the answer to. 'Do you know what happened to the girl they cast originally?'

'Pregnant.'

'Got it. Thanks, Cora.' I triple check that I've ended the call before doing a celebratory shout and fist pump in the middle of the street. No one seems to notice. This is London, after all. Everyone's world-weary or simply caught up in their own dramas.

All the way home, I think about telling Oliver, about how pleased he'll be for me. As I emerge from underground and make the short walk to the flat, I start to think about how I'll tell the story. How I'll frame it. I call in at our local Sainsbury's for a bottle of fizz.

'Guess what?' I call as I kick my shoes off.

'I have news!' he calls back.

We meet in the living room. I hold up the bottle I just bought, and he laughs, nodding in the direction of the kitchen. 'I've got one of those in the fridge too.'

'What's your news?' I ask, feeling a tiny bit disgruntled that this evening isn't going to be all about me.

'I got the part in that play, the one in Islington.'

'The one about the brothers, with the suicide?'

'Yep. What's yours?'

'I got the ditzy waitress job. *Summing Up*.'

'I thought that was off the table.'

'It was, but the girl they cast got knocked up.'

He grabs the tops of my arms and pulls me to him, and I feel like I'm being crushed, but in the best possible way. He takes the bottle out of my hand and disappears to the kitchen, and when he comes back he has two full glasses. He holds one out to me.

'To second chances,' he says. 'To strangers getting pregnant.'

'To success,' I say. 'To absolutely bloody smashing it.'

And we drink. First that glass, then the rest of the bottle, and then his. We talk non-stop about our roles, about our auditions, about the people we're going to be working with. At one point, several glasses in, Oliver gets a bit serious.

'This could be huge for you, Maddy. This could really be it.'

I think about the future I've seen, him a big star, me no longer acting. It taints things, a little.

'And for you,' I say.

It's midnight before we run out of things to say, and I realise I haven't eaten a thing since lunch. We eat toast with butter standing up in the kitchen, both grinning at each other madly whenever we remember our good fortunes. Before we've finished eating, I cross the room to him, unable to wait. We've been so busy talking and drinking that we haven't kissed once since I got home, and I feel, in that instant, like it would be impossible to wait another second. I press myself against him, kiss him hard, and he tangles my hair in his hands. There's a lot of pulling and tugging at clothes, and then we're back in the living room and I break the kissing to push him down on the sofa.

28

TEN YEARS FROM NOW (APRIL 2023)

I'm lying on my back in bed, the room dark. I turn on one side and there's just enough light to make out Oliver lying next to me, his breathing steady. As my eyes adjust to the dark, I take in the lines on his face that are new to me, the way his hair is slightly receding, and cut shorter. He seems sturdier, in a way, but he doesn't look like he's put weight on. It isn't a physical thing, maybe just something you acquire with age. I'm filled with so much love for him that I want to wake him up to tell him. To say I'm glad I chose to live these years of my life with him, that I hope we'll be side by side for many more. He stirs, seems like he's going to wake, and I roll back away as quietly as I can, but then he seems to settle again.

How have we held on to this for ten years? It feels like a small miracle, in a way, but also like something inevitable. His phone beeps, making me jump and lighting up his face from where it lies at the side of the bed. He doesn't wake. I don't know what makes me do it, but I slide out of bed and around to his side, where the screen is still lit up, the start of the message clear to read. It's from someone called Charlotte. And as I read it, I feel like everything is shattering around me. Walls falling, ceilings crashing down. And inside, my heart, cracking clean in two.

CHARLOTTE

See you and Isla tomorrow. Maddy's seeing her parents, right?

29

NOW (APRIL 2013)

Oliver is kissing my eyelids, wrapping his legs around mine, pulling me closer as if he cannot possibly be close enough. I feel lost, betrayed, devastated. And it isn't his fault, but it is, too. I pull away from him and get out of bed, and as I'm leaving the room, he calls my name and I turn back.

'Are you okay?'

I am not okay. But how can I tell him that? It's so simple for him. We just had an amazing night together, celebrating our career successes, ending in sex. Of course he can't understand why I feel like I've been broken apart.

'Fine, just going to the bathroom.'

I sit on the edge of the bath for a few minutes, and when I go back into the bedroom, he is asleep. I study him, the way I studied the older version of him so recently. He looks like a person who doesn't have any worries. I wonder what I look like. It takes me a long time to fall asleep, and I see those words imprinted on the insides of my eyelids. *See you and Isla tomorrow. Maddy's seeing her parents, right?* Is he having an affair? And if he is, how dare he involve Isla in it? I swing from thinking it's maybe one of those things that can seem suspicious but end up having a completely rational explanation to wondering who the hell I am to think this relationship will last forever without a single bump in the road. I wish I knew who Charlotte is. I wish I could talk to him about it.

When I wake the next morning at seven, I feel wrung out and sad. But Oliver kisses me, and I try to remind myself that I can't blame this Oliver for something the future Oliver may or may not have done. It isn't fair. Here, in the present, Oliver loves me, and I love him. So I let him nuzzle into my neck, let him run his hands over my back and around to my belly.

30

TEN YEARS FROM NOW (APRIL 2023)

Oliver is still asleep, and I lie there staring at him, willing him to wake up. When he does, he leans across and kisses me gently.

'Morning, Mads.'

'Morning.' I'm distracted, waiting for him to reach for his phone so I can watch his reaction. But instead, he gets out of bed and goes into the bathroom to shower, and I think about grabbing his phone, but there's no point. I don't know his passcode. I wait until he comes out, towel around his waist, hair dripping, and I see him pick it up. He scrolls and taps for a minute, and he must see it, he must, but his expression doesn't change. Not a flicker.

It's a Saturday, and I can hear Isla pottering about. Am I brave enough to bring it up? To simply ask him, outright, whether there's someone else? No, I don't think so.

'Do you want tea?' he asks.

I'm caught out by the simple kindness of the request. It's something he asks me in the present, his tone exactly the same, and I always says yes and then he makes it and brings it to me in bed because he knows I find it harder to get up than he does.

'What is it?' he asks. 'What's wrong?'

The concern in his voice is powerful, and it snaps me out of whatever daydream I'm in. I realise that I'm crying.

'It's nothing. I'm okay, really.'

He goes to make the tea, and I hear him chatting to Isla. I'm left wondering what happens if the same person makes you tea every morning for ten years, and then leaves you. Because he could be gearing up for that, couldn't he? I imagine me and Isla without him. Still a family, but a different-shaped one. It would take adjustments. Where would we live? Would my parents take us in, if I needed some time to get somewhere sorted? I'm sure they would.

I ache for my mum, then. I pick up my phone and search my contacts for home.

'Hello, love. Are we still seeing you later?'

Maddy's seeing her parents, right?

Her voice is a little quieter than I'm used to. 'Yes, later.'

'Are you alright? You sound a bit shaken.'

'I've woken up in a funny mood. Just wanted to hear a friendly voice.'

'Is Oliver with you?'

'He is. Making tea.'

'And Isla?'

'Yep.' *Where is she when she's not here?* I want to ask her. It's clear that she knows Isla is sometimes with us, sometimes away. There is a moment of flat silence, and I imagine filling it with all the things I want to ask. How is Alan? How is Henry? What have I made of my life, Mum? How am I doing with it all?

'Henry and Alan are going to the football this afternoon, so it will just be us.'

'Go Blues. How is he? Henry, I mean.'

'I'll find out, I suppose. I haven't seen him for a while.'

Does that mean he's living independently? It must, I think. I smile, thinking of my clever, strong brother, who must be twenty now, and who I barely know.

Oliver comes into the room, puts a mug of tea down on my bedside table and brushes my hair off my face in a gesture that's so gentle I feel suddenly fragile. 'Got to go, Mum. See you later.'

31

NOW (APRIL 2013)

Oliver is jumping out of bed and telling me he'll be late for his morning swimming classes and it's all my fault for being so irresistible. When he leaves, the flat feels painfully empty. I feed Marjorie and pick up a book, and she settles on my lap but I can't keep my eyes on the words in front of me. I keep drifting off and having to go back a page.

I decide to go for a walk. I don't have a destination in mind but I find myself heading in the direction of Priya and Nic's. But it isn't them I want to see. It's Mrs Aziz. I press her buzzer, see her peer out of her front window, and then her face breaks into a big smile and she gestures that's she's coming down to let me in.

As I follow her up the stairs, I notice that she's slower than she used to be. At the top, she pauses for breath before going inside her flat.

'How's Maddy?' she asks, going to the cupboard to get the small watering can out for me.

'I got a part in a TV show,' I say.

She claps her hands in delight, a look of genuine joy on her face. 'TV! That's incredible. Tell me all about it.'

So I do, and she reacts as if I'm telling her I'm going to be the lead in a multi-million-pound film.

'Why are you unhappy?' she asks.

I'm reaching up to water the plant on top of the bookshelf, and I wait until I've done it to answer her. 'I'm not unhappy.'

'Yes, you are. You've got that same look you had when you came to tell me you were moving out.'

I know I've been smiling and animated, but it turns out Mrs Aziz can see beyond that.

'What's your view on infidelity?' I ask.

Mrs Aziz narrows her eyes. 'Not that lovely Oliver, surely?'

How to answer that? 'It's sort of a hypothetical. You know, some people move past it, and others can't. I just wondered what you thought.'

'Well, I think we might need tea for this conversation.'

She goes off to the kitchen and I finish watering and try to formulate what I want to say, to ask.

'You never met my husband,' she says on her return, placing our drinks on the coffee table. 'May Allah bless him.'

'No.'

'If he was ever unfaithful to me, I didn't know about it. And I'm thankful for that. My youngest sister, she found out her husband was cheating with her best friend, and it ruined the marriage and the friendship. And her husband said the only thing he regretted was her discovering the affair, because it had been going on for years and not doing anyone any harm.'

Wow. I'm not sure what to take from that. I'm trying to decide whether I'm required to speak when it becomes clear that I'm not.

'I think it's straightforward, my dear. If you love someone, you love only them. I don't accept any of this nonsense about needing different people for different things, or about growing apart from the person you chose to spend your life with. My husband and me, we got married and we worked hard at it and we stayed together. It's as simple and as complicated as that.'

I nod. This is more like what I thought she'd say. We drink our tea in contented silence. I think she's finished, until she speaks again.

'You are a wonderful girl, Maddy. Oliver, or any other boy you choose, is lucky to have you. Don't forget that. Don't think of yourself as less than you are.'

'I won't,' I say. 'Thank you, Mrs Aziz.'

'Now, are you staying for lunch? Because I have some dahl I was going to reheat and I'm sure there's enough for two.'

'I think I need to go home,' I say. 'Oliver's teaching this morning but he gets back for lunch and he always brings food with him.'

At the door, I thank her for her kindness.

'I don't know what's happening with you and this Oliver,' she says, her eyes serious and her slight hand on my wrist, 'but I worry about you. Don't stop coming over, will you?'

'I won't.' Downstairs, I push through the door and into the April air. It's one of the first days this year to really feel like spring and I breathe it all in. The scent of daffodils, and sunshine. When I get back to the flat, Oliver's just returned and is unloading the bread and cheese and salad he bought at a street market after his lessons.

'Have you ever cheated?' I ask him before I can chicken out.

He spins around. 'On you? Maddy, no.'

'Ever?'

'Oh.' He shuffles a bit on his feet, takes a knife and a chopping board out. 'Once, yes. It was when I was at school, though. I'm not even sure it was a proper relationship. But that's no excuse. I did cheat, and I felt terrible about it, and I've never done it again. Why do you ask?'

'I don't know,' I say, and I must look forlorn because he comes over to me in the doorway and takes me in his arms.

'Where's this all come from? I won't hurt you,' he says.

I ignore the first part of what he said. 'You can't promise that.'

'No, I can't. You have to trust me.'

I kiss him then, and start to pull at his clothes, and lunch is temporarily forgotten. Our sex life has slowed down a bit lately, which Priya assures me is perfectly normal when you've been together for a while, but this weekend is like going back in time to when we first got together and couldn't keep our hands to ourselves. I lead him into the bedroom, trying to push out the voice in my head that is asking what I'll find out this time, and whether it will be something I want to know.

32

TEN YEARS FROM NOW (APRIL 2023)

Oliver's cutting bread and I see the paper bag on the counter with the name of our favourite local bakery on it. It makes me feel grounded, like there are aspects of this future life that are still familiar to me. His phone rings and he looks at it, makes a face at me and says 'Charlotte' before picking up.

Charlotte. The name from the message.

I'm making a salad, and I turn the tap off in the hope of listening in.

'Do you want to put her on?' Oliver asks. And then, after a pause, 'But if she's missing us...' His face is tight, and he's pacing up and down the tiny room.

'You know, we never asked her to call Maddy that. It's totally her choice.'

I'm not quite there yet but I know this is something seismic. Not in this day, in the future. Here, it seems like it's just another disgruntled phone call. But for me, when I get back to the present, this is huge.

'I know you're her mother, Charlotte. How could we ever forget?'

And that's when the bottom drops out of my world, and I have to stand there at the sink, a colander of salad leaves and chopped peppers in my hand, pretending it hasn't. Charlotte, the woman who sent that message, is Isla's mother. I am not Isla's mother. I feel like I might fall, like I might physically collapse, so I lean forward, let the kitchen counter take my weight. I won't cry. Later, I can cry. But here, now, I have to pretend this is knowledge I've always had. That this isn't the hardest thing I've ever had to hear.

33

NOW (AUGUST 2013)

'So this Charlotte,' Priya says, her voice gentle, 'do you know who she is?'

We're at the cinema, waiting for the trailers to start. It's summer, and the cool cinema is a wonderful contrast to the sticky air outside. I've had a few months to get used to the Charlotte bombshell, but I've only just told Priya about it. It felt too raw, initially. Too humiliating. 'Not a clue. But Oliver's going to, in the near future. He's either going to cheat on me with her or we're going to split up and then get back together at a later date.' I take a handful of popcorn and chew on it, one piece after another, trying to work out the impossible.

'Have you asked him if he knows a Charlotte?'

'No.' It's a good idea, and I know I'll do it next time I see him. It should be pretty easy to come up with a reason for asking. 'Let's talk about something else. How's Nic?'

Priya beams and I try to push aside the knowledge that Nic is not the man she ends up having her children with.

'Things have been good lately. You know we've always been a bit volatile?'

I almost choke on my bottle of water. 'A bit?'

'What? It's not that bad. But what I was going to say is, I thought it might get worse when we were living together. I thought we'd piss each other off. But we haven't, we don't. It's the best it's ever been.'

I'm tempted to remind her of the time she called me to say it was over, a few months into them living together, but I don't. Because friends don't, do they? She's happy. There's an advert on the huge screen in front of us, for some kind of family holiday resort. I glance at it. There are kids laughing, parents relaxing. It all looks so simple. 'That's great.'

'Maddy, is there something you're not telling me?'

I jolt my head around to look at her. 'Like what?'

'I don't know. Something about my future, maybe. You just seem a bit funny, that's all.'

Damn her and her ability to sense everything I'm thinking. I go on the defensive. 'Priya, I just told you that I'm not my daughter's mother. Maybe that's why I'm a bit funny.'

I think about what I just said, how nonsensical it would sound to an outsider. To anyone, really.

'Yeah, sorry. But you know, there's something wonderful about being a stepparent too.'

I consider this. Think of Alan, the way he's been steady and supportive for me across the years. Much more a dad than my actual dad, who I haven't seen for years. Priya is right. I'm not what I thought I was to Isla, biologically, but it doesn't mean I'm not important.

When I get home, it's gone eleven, and Oliver is in bed.

'What was it tonight?' he asks.

'*Grown Ups 2*.'

'Any good?'

'Pretty dire. I kept rewriting the lines in my head to make it funnier. Or even just funny.' I start taking my clothes off, pull on my pyjamas.

'I don't get it. Why is it always cinema, even if there's nothing much on that you haven't seen?'

I think about this. 'I've just always loved it, the cinema. When I was a kid we only did it now and again. And as an adult I just realised that I could go as often as I wanted to. It's cheaper than dinner or drinks. When we started, Priya said that one day we'd be watching a film with me in it. Obviously that hasn't happened but I think neither of us wants to admit that it never will. So we just keep going. Plus I really like seeing what's out there. The good and the bad. I like to keep my hand in with it, even if I'm not in that world.'

'Speaking of work, are you all ready for tomorrow?'

Tomorrow's my first day filming for *Summing Up*. We've had a couple of days of rehearsals, but tomorrow is the big day. I know my lines inside out and back to front, but I know I'll wake up with a feeling of nausea and a dull ache in my belly. If I manage to sleep at all. 'I'm ready. How were rehearsals today?'

'You know that guy I told you about, the one who's crazily talented?'

'Do you mean you?'

He laughs as I slide into bed beside him. 'Er, no. The one who's playing my brother. Anyway, he got a call from his agent today while we were eating lunch and he's got a part in a film with Bradley Cooper.'

'Wow. How big a part?'

'Pretty big, I think. So, one for Tuesday cinema night in a couple of years' time.'

'Remind me nearer the time. Do you hate him a little bit?'

Oliver turns to look at me. 'Hate him?'

'Yeah, for getting a massive break.'

'No. I've told you, I believe it's coming for me. And you. There's no point wishing I had what someone else has.'

I mull this over for a moment. 'So do you believe everything is pre-ordained? That it doesn't matter what you do because it will all turn out the same way in the end anyway?'

'I mean, I wouldn't go quite that far, no. But I sort of feel like things are following a basic plan of some kind.'

'Whose plan?' We haven't talked about this. I don't know whether he believes in god or what his take is on any of those big life and death questions.

Oliver shrugs. 'I don't know, really. I just have to believe there's some sort of order to life. It's so big and sprawling. But I don't know the details. What do you believe?'

I am on my back, looking at the ceiling. I think about the visions, about how they've impacted my understanding of how life is arranged, how the world works. 'I think I believe that it's all random. You know, if I'd turned left instead of right on some walk I took at the age of thirteen, I would be in a completely different place now.' What I'm saying is true, but the visions don't fit with it. I've never been able to make them fit. However much I believe in them.

'Doesn't that terrify you?'

'No, I think it's empowering. How my life turns out is down to me and no one else.'

'Huh. I guess I can see that.'

We are quiet for a minute or so and I think perhaps he's on the edge of sleep. But then he speaks again. 'I forgot to say, Charlotte wants us all in this weekend.'

The name jumps out of the darkness at me. Charlotte. 'Charlotte?' Can he sense the tremor in my voice?

'The director. Is that okay, because I know you wanted to do something with Priya and Nic? Maybe the three of you could get together.'

'It's fine.'

A couple of minutes after that, he's definitely asleep and I feel like I'm a million miles away from rest. The director. Could she be the one, the Charlotte he's going to have Isla with? It's not exactly an uncommon name, but it feels like too much of a coincidence. There are a hundred questions I want to ask him. What she looks like, whether he likes her, how she makes him feel. Can I meet her? Can you drop out of the play? Can you just stay here with me, forever? And I can't ask any of them. And even if I could, would I really do anything to jeopardize that little girl's existence?

I wouldn't. Of course I wouldn't.

34

TEN YEARS FROM NOW (AUGUST 2023)

I'm with Isla. Since I found out, I look at her differently, try to work out how I thought I could see myself in her features. It's so clear to me now that she *doesn't* have my eyes, or my nose or mouth. Perhaps I just saw similarities because I assumed it was true. Because I wanted it to be.

'Why are you looking at me like that, Mum?' she asks.

I don't know how I'm looking at her. With longing? With abject terror that I won't always be in her life? Because I've been thinking, about the whole cheating thing. When I believed Isla was mine, I could consider the breakdown of my relationship with Oliver, could see it as a possibility. But now I know that if I left him, or he left me, the bond I have with his daughter would be torn apart. I would have no hold over her.

'Sorry,' I say, shaking my head as if to disperse the thoughts. 'What shall we do?'

'That game where I'm the mum and you're the child and I get to tell you what to do,' she says.

'Okay.' I just want to gaze at her, but this will do. She makes me choose a teddy from her bed and gives me breadsticks for my snack. Then she tells me I have to play quietly while she makes the lunch. I sit on the floor with a one-hundred-piece jigsaw of a family of cats in front of me, watching her while she plays at a toy kitchen. Stirring something on the hob. Taking something out of the oven.

'You need to start with the edges,' she says, looking over.

I start to sort the pieces, edges and middles. Anything to stop myself from grabbing hold of her and never letting go.

35

NOW (SEPTEMBER 2013)

'It's a shame Oliver couldn't make it,' Nic says.

I smile tightly. 'I know, I'm sorry. He has to work. Rehearsals, for this play he's in.'

We're at Priya and Nic's flat, and Priya has cooked a roast chicken, and we're all in the kitchen, helping her get everything ready to serve.

'Can you get the drinks?' she asks me, looking hot and a bit frantic. 'There's wine, beer and soft drinks in the fridge.'

I spring into action, happy to have a job. When I lived here, Priya would do these roast dinners every now and again, and I would be in charge of the Yorkshire puddings or the gravy or the vegetables, but things are different, now. I pour generous glasses of wine and Priya carves the chicken and Nic gets the cutlery from the drawer.

'We have something to tell you,' Nic says. He turns to Priya. 'Right?'

'Babe, give us a minute to catch our breath.'

'I'm just excited.' Nic reaches across the table and takes hold of her hand, and I glance from him to Priya. Whatever this is, she's not fully on board with it.

Priya goes to lift her wine glass and then stops. 'I'm pregnant,' she says.

I don't know how to react. She's always said she won't have a baby until she's finished medical school. Plus, I know how this will land with her family. There was an older cousin who was unmarried and having a baby when we were teens, and it was all Priya's parents could talk about. The shame she'd brought on the family, the way she'd turned her back on them.

In that vision I had with her in it, she had twin babies with another man, and there was no mention of an older child. Or did I just assume the twins were her only children? But it strikes me that if they weren't sure, if they hadn't talked about this and decided what they were going to do, they wouldn't be presenting it to me like this, over roast chicken. If Priya was thinking about ending this pregnancy, wouldn't she be telling me when we were on our own?

'Wow,' I say, realising I've taken an awkwardly long time to speak. 'Wow, that's... I'm shocked.'

'You and me both,' Priya says.

Nic flashes her a look I can't quite interpret. 'It wasn't planned, but not everything has to be, right? I have a good job lined up at the end of my training contract.'

'What about Priya's career?' I ask.

Priya looks at me and there is gratitude in her eyes. And I know I need to talk to her alone about this as soon as possible.

'She'll take some time out,' Nic says. 'Go back in a year or two.'

A year or two. He makes it sound like nothing.

'It sounds like you have it worked out,' I say. But when I look over at Priya, she won't meet my eye. 'Congratulations!'

As if by mutual agreement, we all start to eat. When Priya reaches for her wine for a second time, and then stops herself, Nic offers to swap it for something soft for her and I wish the kitchen was a separate room because I'm desperate to ask her what the hell is going on.

'Will you stay here?' I ask after Nic has returned and I've tried and failed to think of anything meaningful to say. 'In the flat?'

'We'll have to at first,' Nic says. 'But hopefully we'll be able to buy a place in the next couple of years.'

'Right.' I remember so many conversations with Priya where we talked about our future plans. None of them involved breaking off near the end of her studying to have a child.

Nic's the first to finish his dinner. Priya looks like she's barely touched hers. He raises his glass. 'Compliments to the chef.'

Priya stands up, pushing back her chair, and leaves the room, and I hear her pull the bathroom door closed behind her. I'd wanted to get Priya on her own, but this will have to do.

'What's going on, Nic?' I ask. 'Neither of you seem like yourselves today. Have you talked this through properly? Is it what you both want?'

His eyes look stormy. 'What do you mean, is it what we both want? It's a human life, and that life starts at conception. You can't always pick and choose.'

I want to say that you can, of course you can. How did I not know that Priya was in a relationship with a pro-lifer? I suppose it's not the kind of thing that's ever come up in casual conversation.

'I just know how hard she's worked to get where she is,' I try. 'She's wanted to be a doctor for so long.'

'And she will be a doctor. This isn't the 1950s. Women can work and be mothers.'

'I know that, I just never thought she'd do it this way. And what if you have this baby and then you decide you want another one? What happens to her studies then? And what about her family? They won't exactly be thrilled about this.'

Nic stands up, folds his arms. There's a splash of gravy on his grey T-shirt. 'Maddy, you're her best friend, and we've just told you we're having a baby. Why aren't you happy for us?'

I stay seated, but I put down my knife and fork. I've lost my appetite. 'If this is what you both want, I will be delighted for you. I'll arrange the baby shower, I'll bring tiny shoes to the hospital, I'll babysit so you can eat a hot meal. But it doesn't look like Priya is in the same place you are, and until I know more about that, I'm reserving judgement.'

Nic doesn't say anything, but his face is full of fury. He storms out of the room and then I hear the flat door open and bang shut. He's gone. And I'm glad. I'm just about to go and speak to Priya through the bathroom door when she emerges, her face streaked with tears.

'Are you okay?' I ask, and she falls into my arms.

'It's like I don't know who he is,' she says. 'We've talked about having children in the future, but never what would happen if we got pregnant now. I just didn't know he'd be so adamant that we had to go ahead with it.'

'Is it a religious thing?' I ask. Nic's a Catholic, though not a practising one.

'No, it's not that. I didn't know this, but his parents had several miscarriages before they had him. They were trying to conceive for almost a decade.'

I nod, waiting for her to go on.

'I think he just can't tally all those years of heartache with deciding not to go ahead with an unplanned pregnancy.'

'Priya,' I say, holding her at arm's length and looking straight into her eyes, 'what do you want to do?'

She lowers her eyes, won't make contact. 'I don't know, Maddy. This isn't what I wanted. You know that. I'm terrified that I'll drop out of medical school and never go back. That there won't be the time or the money for me to finish it, and I'll end up doing some job I hate that fits in with school hours or whatever. And there's my family. They'll hate this.' She pauses, and her eyes have a faraway look. 'It isn't who I thought I'd be. If anything, I thought I'd be the woman who was stressed about leaving it too late to have kids.'

'If you decide not to have this baby, I will be fully supportive of that, regardless of whether or not Nic is. And if you decide to have this baby, I will be fully supportive of that, too. I just want you to know that. Okay?'

She starts crying again then, and looks more hopeless than I've ever seen her.

'We'll work this out,' I tell her. 'We will. Together. Okay?'

'What about Nic?'

I take a deep breath before answering, because honestly I want to tell her that I don't give a shit what Nic thinks or wants, that it's her body we're talking about, her child. 'Nic will come around,' I say, hoping I'm right. 'You'll make your decision, and you'll tell Nic, and he'll get it. He will, Priya. I'm sure of it.'

Shortly after, I walk back through drizzling rain to my flat. Nic had returned and it was clear they needed to talk, so I made my exit but made sure Priya knew she could call me anytime. When I get home, Oliver is there.

'Hey, I was just about to call you to see if it was worth me coming round. I thought you'd be at Priya and Nic's all afternoon.'

I lean forward and kiss him. 'Well, it was a bit of a bust actually. Priya's pregnant.'

'Shit,' he says.

I laugh, because it's such an honest response. 'Yeah, Nic doesn't think so, though. He's adamant that they'll have the baby and it will all be fine.'

'What about Priya's medical degree?'

'I know, right?'

I've taken off my coat and Oliver takes it from me and goes to hang it somewhere to dry. I like that he does little things like this. I feel taken care of. Like I'm in a partnership.

'So what does Priya think?'

'She doesn't know what to think. It wasn't planned. She doesn't want to give up on her career dreams.'

'What would you do, if it was us?'

I'm not expecting this, and I spin around from my position in the kitchen doorway to look at him. He returns the look, refusing to back down or retract the question.

'I don't know,' I say. 'What would you want to do?'

Oliver considers this. He has his hands in his pockets and his hair is a bit dishevelled from the wind and rain, and I think about how much I like him, how much I want this to work. 'You know I've said I don't want to have children,' he starts.

'I know that. And Priya and Nic both do – at least, eventually – so I guess that makes it different.'

He nods. 'But if it happened, we'd just have to decide based on how we felt, right? I think there'd be a hell of a lot of talking to do, and we'd just find a way through.'

It's not exactly a cop-out, but it's not him coming down on one side or the other either. Still, I'm placated by the idea that we would reach a decision together, which doesn't seem to be what Priya and Nic have done. I think, as I so often do, of Isla. Of the way her hair curls when it's wet, just like Oliver's is doing now. Of the way she tells jokes, really fast because she can't keep the punchline in. Of the way it feels when she holds my hand, or curls her body up against mine in bed. I can't tell Oliver about any of it, and I don't think I can tell Priya, either.

Just then, my phone rings, and I see Priya's name on the screen. Oliver sees it, too, and goes to the living room to give me some privacy. Her voice is slightly wild and breathless, and she doesn't bother with any of the formalities.

'You have to find out whether I have this child, and whether I stay with Nic,' she says.

I close my eyes. How did I not see this coming? 'What about believing these visions are just what might happen, rather than what will?'

She is quiet. Then, in a tiny voice, she speaks. 'It's all I have.'

'Priya, I don't know, I...'

'I need to know, Maddy. I can't make this decision on my own. Nic's so certain, and I'm all over the place, and I don't want to go along with what he wants just because I haven't formulated my thoughts as well as he has.'

I sit down heavily at the kitchen table. 'You know,' I say, keeping my voice low, 'when all this started it seemed relatively harmless, but now...'

'Now what?'

'Well, since I found out that I'm not Isla's mum, it feels a bit like I'm messing with all of our lives.'

She is silent.

'I saw something,' I say. 'I know something.'

Her voice is thick. 'What?'

'You're not with Nic, in ten years.'

36

NOW (SEPTEMBER 2013)

'Henry's got something to show you,' Mum says.

She looks nervous. We're all gathered in the living room of my flat, our eyes shifting from Mum to Henry and back again.

'Don't make a big thing out of it,' Henry says.

And I can see him, suddenly, as a teenager. There's a mix of embarrassment and pride on his face.

'Hold on, I need to get the thing,' Alan says, disappearing without another word.

I raise my eyebrows at Henry. 'So?'

'I sort of need to wait for Dad to get back. Could I have a drink?'

'Drinks!' I go into the kitchen and start lining up mugs on the side.

Oliver follows me in. 'This is mysterious,' he says. 'What do you think it's about?'

'Some kind of physio progress, I hope.' Could Henry have learned to get up out of his chair? It's what they've been working towards, I know, but I don't want to get my hopes up and be disappointed. Some nights, I have dreams with Henry in them, and he's always mobile. Like nothing ever happened. I remember shortly after the accident, Mum told me that he was throwing up the day before it and she nearly kept him at home, but he begged to go out on his bike, and Alan said the fresh air would do him some good. I wonder how often she thinks about that.

Oliver and I take the drinks from the kitchen to the living room and put them all down on the coffee table. Alan's back, slightly out of breath, and he's carrying a walking frame, which he puts down in front of Henry.

'Don't all stare at me,' Henry says, shuffling forward as Alan unstraps his feet from the rest they sit on.

Oliver whistles, makes a big show of looking all around the room, and Mum laughs a little too loudly. And we all watch, as slowly, slowly, Henry lifts himself out of the chair and takes hold of the walking frame. He's a bit wobbly, and I can see that Alan is in position, ready to catch him if he falls, but he maintains his balance for a few seconds and then sinks back into the wheelchair, clearly wiped out.

I clap my hands. 'Henry, that's just amazing!'

His skin reddens, and it reminds me of the way he's always reacted to praise from me. When he started walking, when he made the football team, when he got his swimming badges. I've never been as proud of him as I am in this moment. The courage and perseverance with which he's faced this huge challenge are astonishing. I look at Mum, see that there are tears in her eyes. Oliver goes over to Henry and gives him a high five.

'Okay, you can all talk again now, you know?' Henry says.

He's never been one for the spotlight. At least, not on his own. He's perfectly happy to shine as part of a football team, but he's not so keen when he's alone there at the centre of everyone's attention.

There are so many things I want to ask – whether the physios think this bodes well for walking again, in time. What the next step is. But I don't want to belittle his achievement. I want to let him sit for a while, feeling good about what he's managed.

'So who's coming swimming today?' Oliver asks.

'We'd like to come, and then we were thinking maybe we could all go out for lunch after?' Mum says.

The session goes well. Henry does a lot of splashing around and is somehow transformed, the way he always is. Afterwards, as we're walking to a nearby pub, he tells us all about how different his legs feel when they're underwater. How it almost feels like he has control of them again. Oliver and I hold hands and I keep sneaking looks at him, wondering whether all this time with my family is getting to be too much, but if he's thinking that, he's hiding it well.

We go into a pub where Oliver and I have eaten before, and there's a table with plenty of space and at the right height for the wheelchair. We order comfort food. A roast for my parents, sausage and mash for the rest of us. Oliver makes jokes that Henry finds hilarious and Mum and Alan exchange sweet smiles, and I see, then, that Oliver's really a part of this family. And that's been more his doing than anyone else's.

'How's Priya?' Mum asks.

I look down at the table. Mum doesn't know about Priya's pregnancy. I haven't told anyone other than Oliver, in case she decides not to go ahead with it. But the truth is that Priya's not doing great. And I hate lying to Mum.

'She's okay,' I say, noncommittal. 'Busy, you know.'

Every day, Priya and I text back and forth. Nic's finally listening to what she has to say about the situation, and some days she feels quite positive and like she can actually manage this, and other days she's so scared that she just pushes it out of her mind entirely. Focuses on work, and studying.

'How are the new acting jobs going?' Henry asks, and I'm grateful to him for changing the subject.

Oliver reaches for my hand under the table. 'Maddy's role just got extended,' he says.

'You didn't tell me that!' Mum says.

'I was waiting to tell you today.'

Oliver covers his mouth with his hand. 'Sorry, I should have let you say it.'

'No, it's okay. It's just another couple of episodes, so far,' I say, meeting Mum's eyes.

I don't tell them that the director said they were thinking about making it a permanent role. That they've been so pleased with how I've brought the character to life and slotted in with the rest of the cast that they're hoping to keep me on for a lot longer.

'When will we be able to see it?' Henry asks.

'The first episode is on in a couple of weeks. But I only have a few lines in that one. And then it's on weekly, and I'm in and out. I'm the love interest of one of the main characters.'

'Which one?' Henry asks. 'Colin or Malcolm?'

'You've watched *Summing Up*?' I ask.

'Of course I've watched it. My sister's going to be in it.'

I feel warm, content. Like I'm safe and protected, with my family and Oliver around me.

'It's not inappropriate, is it?' Mum asks. 'I don't know what he's watching half the time.'

'It's fine. No swearing, no nudity, no violence,' I assure her.

A waitress brings our food over and we all go quiet as we start eating. And then Mum speaks again.

'What about your play, Oliver?'

He swallows what he's chewing and puts his hands on the

edge of the table. 'I'm excited about it; it's a good play. It starts next month.'

'I can get us all tickets,' I say. 'If you'd like to come. Although, this one probably isn't ideal for Henry.'

Oliver's play tackles suicide and I know from running lines with him that there's a lot of swearing.

'Maybe I'll come,' Mum says. 'We can make it a girls' day.'

By the time they are ready to head home, my face aches from smiling so much, and as Oliver and I walk back to the flat through rain-soaked streets, I tell him I feel like I'm in a romcom. Oliver laughs, and neither of us acknowledge the fact that when everything's going well in a romcom, you can bet that something's about to go very wrong.

'You know,' Oliver says, 'Henry's pretty amazing just the way he is. I know I didn't know him before the accident, and it must be devastating for you to think about what he's lost, but if this is as far as he goes with his mobility, I think he'll still have a great life.'

I stop in the middle of the street. We're five minutes from home, and I'm already imagining getting in my pyjamas and curling up with him on the sofa with wine and blankets. My immediate response to what he's said is to get angry, like I did the last time he said something similar. To say that he doesn't know Henry properly, that he doesn't know what he's talking about. But I know that he's being kind. And beyond that, I know now that he's right. Things don't always look how you thought they might. It doesn't have to be a tragedy.

'What you're doing with him, with the swimming,' I say, not sure what exactly it is I'm trying to get across. 'Nobody's done anything like that for us before. It makes me scared, sometimes, because if anything goes wrong between you and me, that's it. It's going to negatively impact him, and all of them, and that's on me.'

'Maddy, you don't need to catastrophise like that. Maybe nothing bad is going to happen. Maybe we're just going to be happy.'

Yeah, right. I think of Isla, of the fact that I'm not her mum. Of Priya, carrying a baby I'm pretty sure she isn't going to have. He's wrong, about nothing bad happening, but I think it's probably fair to say that there is more good than bad in this future of ours.

37

TEN YEARS FROM NOW (SEPTEMBER 2023)

'Hey.' I hear Henry before I see him. 'Hey, Maddy.'

I'm in a crowded bar, and I turn and there he is, pushing himself through the crowd towards me. For a moment, my heart sinks. I know that if he's still in a wheelchair now, he always will be. He's a few feet away and he asks what I want to drink and I tell him red wine and then I watch as he queues, the mere sight of him as an adult man enough to floor me. When he turns and comes over to where I'm standing, I find a chair and sit so we're face to face. I look in his eyes and see Henry the kid, but when he removes his coat, I notice the tattoos on his muscled arms and have to stop myself from saying that Mum will kill him. This man in front of me is twenty-one years old.

I wonder why we're meeting. Does he live in London now? Is this just a casual thing we do, every now and again?

'How are you?' he asks. 'How's Oliver? And Isla?'

I'm guessing when I tell him we're all fine, because of course I have no idea, and when I ask about him, he grins. 'Good. A bit stressed. Final year, you know.'

University? 'You'll be fine,' I say, hoping it's true.

'I was ready to get back to it. There are only so many weeks you can spend eating everything in your parents' house and staying in bed until two in the afternoon.'

We both drink, and I take in our surroundings. The bar is packed. Henry is one of the youngest people here and I'm one of the oldest. The music is loud and has a repetitive beat, and I notice Henry's shoulders are moving in time with it, just slightly.

'So what else is going on?' I ask. I'm torn, desperate to spend as much time as possible with him but wary of tripping myself up with something I should know, and don't.

'I've got some big matches coming up,' he says. 'You should come to see one. Bring Isla. And Oliver, of course.'

I think about football, how he loved to play. And then how he helped Pete with coaching the team. Is that what he's talking about now? 'Tell me where and when and I'll be there.'

He gets out his phone and starts going through photos, clearly looking for something to show me. And then he passes it over, and it's an action shot of him on a basketball court, the ball somewhere between his hands and the net – a triumphant arc. The expression on his face is childlike and I know instantly where I've seen it before. At those long-ago football matches, every time he scored.

'I'm so proud of you,' I tell him. 'How you adjusted after the accident, all of it.'

He bows his head, embarrassed. 'You know, Oliver really turned things around for me.'

'Really? Not your physios or your doctors? Oliver?'

He laughs. 'That swimming, it changed everything. It made me realise that there was still joy to be had and it made me feel like I could do anything. I think I pushed harder with everything after that.'

'So you're saying that if I hadn't met and got together with

Oliver at that time, your life might be totally different?' I want him to say no, to say of course not, and I'm not sure why.

'I mean, I don't know, things could be the same. You just don't know, do you? But what I do know is that Oliver was the right person at the right time.'

'To Priya throwing me out of our shared flat and making me find somewhere else to live,' I say, raising my glass and smiling at him. He chinks his chunky pint glass against my more delicate one.

'Annabelle's going to be here in a few minutes,' he says.

I don't know an Annabelle. Is she a friend, a girlfriend? His face changes when he says her name, so I know she's important. And I will myself to stick around to meet her, but it isn't like that, this thing. I don't have control.

38

NOW (OCTOBER 2013)

Opening night. This morning, Oliver looked sick with nerves. He's told me that that's how it is, for him. He often throws up seconds before going on stage or starting a scene. But I've seen some of his TV stuff, and you'd never know. He's able to give his very best performance despite those nerves, or perhaps even because of them.

I get to the theatre half an hour early and grab a glass of wine, then message him to say I'm here. I make it clear that he can come out and see me if he wants to, but I'm perfectly happy to sit here and wait if he doesn't. I know that the last thing he needs is to feel any kind of pressure. But he asks me to come up, so I do.

I find the door that leads to the backstage area, and there's Oliver, his skin so pale it's almost white, beads of sweat on his forehead. He'll be like this every night, but tonight is probably the worst. That's why I'm the only person we know who's coming to this performance. Priya and Nic have tickets for next week, my Mum and I for the week after. But tonight, it's just me.

'I don't think I can do it.' It's the first thing he says to me. He's already in his costume, though it's hard to tell because it's just old jeans with his own trainers and a badly buttoned shirt.

'You can,' I say. 'You absolutely can. You know the lines so well, you could probably play any part. Don't let the fear win.'

We're talking low, because there are other people moving around. A woman with a clothes rail and another who's rooting through a huge bag of makeup. Oliver reaches for my hand and I give it to him to hold in both of his. He's clammy.

'Why do we do this?' he asks. 'When we could just stay at home and eat Chinese food? Get a normal nine to five job at an office and go there and do our thing and come home and not think about it again until the next day.'

He raises a good point. At these moments, and I've had a number of them myself, it's so hard to see why you'd choose to put yourself through this kind of agony. But these moments tend to come before some of the most incredible highs, when you know you wouldn't give this up for anything. Or so I've always thought.

'You're going to be great,' I tell him. 'You're going to blow the roof off.'

'It hasn't sold out,' he says.

I shrug. 'So what? Have I told you I once performed in front of three people? And my director at the time told me something I've never forgotten. He said, "You just have to give it everything, as if the place was packed out, because you never know who those three people are."'

Oliver nods, swallows thickly.

'I'll buy you a drink, after,' I say, 'and we'll sit in the bar and talk about how great you were, and we'll keep getting interrupted by people saying, "Sorry to bother you, but are you Oliver Swanson? THE Oliver Swanson?"'

He manages a smile, and I breathe deeply, encouraging him to do the same.

Twenty minutes later, I'm sitting on the third row and he's on the stage. Magnificent. The place isn't full, he was right about that, but it almost is. It's a respectable crowd for an opening night. Oliver is talking about the family who don't love him, and the woman playing his friend is gripping his wrist, trying to get him to focus on what he has rather than what he doesn't. And even though I live with this man, even though I see him every day, I'm completely invested in him as this depressed and worrisome character. That's how good he is. There's no interval and I'm shocked when it's over, even though I know the rough arc of the story. It's been an hour and a half, and it felt like ten minutes. I applaud, looking around at the other audience members to gauge their reactions. Everyone is clapping, but no one is on their feet. I catch Oliver's eye, and he gives me a look that says a hundred things. *I did it. Thank you. How was I?*

Back downstairs in the bar, I find a table in the corner, order us both a drink and wait for him to emerge. I haven't done much theatre, but when I have I've always loved this bit where everyone is on a massive high from a performance that's gone well but is also, crucially, over. He comes down with a huge smile on his face, and it's infectious. I hand him a drink.

'You were brilliant,' I say.

He leans across the table and kisses me, and it's like he's electric. 'Thank you for talking me down.'

I wave a hand. 'Remembered why we do it now? Not going home to look for that normal office job?'

He laughs. 'I remember. You know, Maddy, there was this moment, just after my character had had that fight with his dad, when I looked up and saw you in the audience, and I was terrified of slipping out of character but it just felt so damn good to have you there supporting me on opening night. Gemma never did that for me.'

He hasn't mentioned Gemma for a long time. 'No?'

'She always came to see me but she said she liked to go towards the end of a run, once any problems had had a chance to be smoothed out.'

'I think I just get it, because I do the same thing,' I say.

'Yeah, it's that but it's more than that, too. I feel like you really care about me, about what's best for me. I feel like you've got my back.'

I feel high, like nothing could tear me down. But I'm so wrong about that.

'You know, Charlotte said earlier that she'd like to take this thing on tour.'

I swallow, and my throat feels the way it feels before I cry. I cannot cry, not over this mention of a woman who may or may not temporarily come between us. 'Where? For how long?'

He shrugs, drains his glass. 'I don't know, she didn't go into any details. But I'd love to keep doing this for longer, if the opportunity is there.'

What about me? I can't say it, but I can't stop thinking it, either. Just then, a petite woman with a neat blonde bob approaches the table. She's wearing jeans and a black T-shirt, ankle boots. I'd say she's five years or so older than us. Early thirties. She puts a hand on Oliver's shoulder.

'Oh, Charlotte! I was hoping I'd see you before you left. This is my girlfriend, Maddy.'

Charlotte looks at me then, and I see it straightaway. She has Isla's eyes. I know it's the other way around, that really Isla has hers, but I knew Isla first.

'Hi, Maddy,' she says, and her tone is friendly, and anyone looking on would never predict that the three of us are going to end up in a messed-up love triangle. 'He was great, wasn't he?'

'I've just been telling him,' I say.

'Well, same again tomorrow, please,' she says, giving his hair a playful ruffle and then turning away and walking towards the door.

He turns, watches her go. And I see, in that instant, that there's something between them. Some spark that could turn to a flame.

'She seems nice,' I say, for want of anything better. I want to know what he thinks about her, what it is that will make her turn his head.

'She's very intense,' he says, 'in rehearsals, I mean. She makes us go over and over stuff, and she gets angry if we change a single word. But I think she's very good at it.'

'What's her situation?' I ask.

'What do you mean?'

'I mean does she live alone? Or is she married? Does she have kids?'

'I don't know any of that. She's really focused on the work. Do you want another?' He raises his glass and his eyebrows.

'No, I have an early start. Let's go home.'

He holds my hand as we walk, and on the Tube, he gestures for me to take the only free seat in the carriage and stands in front of me, holding onto the bar, his T-shirt rising to show a strip of his abdomen. He talks incessantly, using his free hand to make gestures, and I know that he's basking in the success of all the work he's put in. He won't be able to go to sleep for hours, and he'll wake up tired and jittery, and he'll be terrified just before the next night's performance. This is all part of it. It's how we live.

And it doesn't feel fair, or right, to pick a fight about the way he looked at his director. Not tonight. So I don't.

'I haven't even asked about your day,' he says as we climb the stairs up to the flat.

'My contract was extended,' I say. 'Ten more episodes.'

'Maddy!' He stops on the stair above me and turns to look at me. 'Why didn't you say?'

'Because tonight was about you,' I say. 'I knew there'd be plenty of time to tell you afterwards.'

He comes down a step and we start walking up again, together. He links my arm with his. 'This is the start of it all,' he says.

'Of what?'

'The glittering careers. It's all starting to fall into place.'

I don't say that it's a few episodes of a TV show that most people haven't heard of and a part in a good but relatively unknown play. Because maybe it is the start of it all, for him. Maybe this run will be where he's spotted by someone who has something bigger to offer, and one thing will lead to another like so many dominoes. One way or another, he's going to get to the top. It's only me who isn't. I take my key out of my bag and let us into the flat.

'Glittering,' I say, a laugh in my throat. 'I feel like there's a distinct lack of glitter so far.'

'Stick with me,' he says, taking hold of my hands and spinning me down the hallway like a ballroom dancer. 'I promise there'll be glitter.'

39

NOW (OCTOBER 2013)

'I think we'll call it a day there. Good work, everyone.' Jon, the producer, does a solitary round of applause, like he always does when we're done for the day.

My co-star, Gavin, looks at me and smiles his big, easy smile. 'Any plans?'

'No, I'm just going to go home and curl up. This kind of weather makes me want to hibernate.' It's freezing outside, blowing a gale. It's October but feels more like February.

'Got it. I just wondered whether you'd like to get a drink sometime?'

I'm thrown. Gavin is one of the stars of the show. He's been on it for the two years it's been running and he played a lot of small roles and did a lot of ads before that. He's bordering on famous. We've been working together for a couple of months now and I've never noticed any kind of vibe between us. I realise I've probably been silent for an awkwardly long time.

'Oh, that's... I mean, thank you, but I have a boyfriend.' As soon as I've said it, I feel sure he's going to laugh and say he didn't mean it 'like that', but he doesn't.

'Of course you have. Why wouldn't you?' His tone is light but he looks pissed off, and I see that he's the kind of man who gets what he wants, who hates it when anything gets in the way of that.

I flash him an apologetic look, even though I know I have nothing to apologise for. And I go to the room where we've stashed our bags and coats, and I see that I have a string of missed calls. Priya. For a second, I can't work out how to call her back, and my fingers aren't working properly. She's not the kind to call over and over, especially when she knows I'm at work and won't have my phone on me. There must be something wrong.

Priya's voice sounds thick with emotion when she answers. 'Maddy, can you come?'

'I'm coming right now. Do you need me to bring anything?'

There's a pause, as if she's thinking or checking, but then she comes back, slightly clearer. 'No, just come.'

When she lets me into the flat, she looks like she's been crying for days. She pulls me inside, leads me to her bedroom. Out of the corner of my eye, I see Nic in the kitchen, leaning against the worktop and looking like he doesn't know what to do.

'What is it?' I ask her, once the door's closed. 'Is it Nic?'

'Kind of.' She climbs into bed, fully clothed, and pulls the covers up to her chin. After a moment's pause, I get in next to her. 'It's the baby. I'm losing it.'

All the way here in the taxi, I didn't think of this, but now she says it, it seems so obvious. 'Oh, Priya,' I say, taking her in my arms and holding her tight. I know this will be destroying her, to be losing a baby she wasn't sure whether or not she wanted to have. I rock her a bit, gently, and she cries, and the tears soak through my top and I don't care. I just want her to be okay, or to see a sign that she will be okay, in time. She hadn't made a decision, as far as I know. She was still wavering, trying to find a path that suited both herself and Nic.

'What has Nic said?' I ask. Please, god, let him have been sensitive.

'He doesn't know what to say. I started bleeding in the night, and we went to the hospital first thing, and they did a scan and said there was no heartbeat. There was nothing they could do. They told us to go home and just let it happen.'

I take a sharp breath. Surely, when you're losing a baby, they could let you stay in the hospital and keep an eye on you. It seems medieval to send you away. 'Are you in pain?'

'Yes, but it comes and goes. It's not so bad at the moment.'

Nic puts his head around the door, then. 'Tea?' he asks.

Priya doesn't look at him, so I answer for us both. 'Yes please.'

When he brings the mugs in, on a tray with a plate of biscuits, he leaves it on the top of the chest of drawers. Then he looks at Priya, and I know she can feel his eyes on her, but she doesn't meet them. 'I'll be out there, if you need anything.'

I get out of bed and put the mugs of tea on the bedside tables, the biscuits between us, and then climb back in.

'He told his mum,' Priya says.

'What? About the baby?'

'Yes. She's the only person who knew, other than you. And we didn't agree to it, he just told her. So now he's going to have to tell her it's not happening.'

'So no one in your family knows?'

'No. Because of this. This is why they tell you not to tell anyone until you've had your three-month scan.'

I think about this for a moment, take a chocolate digestive and cup my hand into a makeshift bowl for crumbs. 'The thing is, if no one knows, and this happens, you have to go through it without anyone else knowing there's anything wrong. So it makes sense to tell those you're closest to, in a way. So they can help you get through it, if things go wrong.'

I'm watching Priya, and her face goes pale and she clutches at her stomach. 'Fuck.'

'Pain? Did they give you anything to take?'

She shakes her head. 'They just said to use paracetamol.' I watch as the grip on her stomach loosens slightly. 'It's going off again.'

I realise that Oliver's probably wondering where I am, so I go out into the living area to call him. I talk quietly, and I don't go into what's happened. I just say that I'm with Priya, that she needed me and I don't know when I'll be back.

'I'm ordering pizza,' he says. 'I'll save you some.'

'No pineapple.'

'I can't promise anything.' I'm about to end the call when he says my name. 'I'm glad you're looking after Priya, Maddy. And when you get home I'll look after you.'

It's the sweetest thing he could have said, and there are tears in my eyes as I end the call and slip my phone back in my pocket. When I look up, Nic's standing in the kitchen doorway. He beckons for me to go to him and he shuts us in. I see that his eyes are wild and pleading.

'She won't talk to me,' he says. 'I don't know how to help her.'

I look at him and I see the Nic I saw when we had that dinner, the one who was so unequivocal about them having the baby regardless of what Priya wanted. But I see the Nic I've known for three years, too, the one who isn't always perfect but who loves my best friend.

'I think she just has to go through it,' I say. And I feel like I'm betraying him in some strange way, because of the vision I had, of her in the future, without him. I have to remind myself that I don't control those. That I'm not pulling the strings. Who is pulling the strings?

'You should go back in there. I mean, if you're okay to stay a bit longer?'

I nod and reach to touch his arm before going back to Priya. She has her eyes closed and I get in beside her as quietly as possible so she can sleep. Twenty minutes later, she wakes with a jolt and I know she's in pain again.

Nic and I get her the things she needs. A hot water bottle, painkillers, a blanket, chocolate. None of it feels like it's enough, but it's all we have. Much later, my phone rings and I see that Oliver's calling and notice, at the same time, that it's dark outside. It's almost eleven. It must have gone dark hours ago.

'I'm coming to get you,' Oliver says. 'I don't want you to walk home on your own this late.'

I want to say that I don't know whether Priya is ready for me to go, but she's right next to me and I don't know how to word it. So I just say okay, and fifteen minutes later there's a quiet knock on the door.

'Is it okay to tell him?' I ask Priya. 'I don't have to.'

'No, you can.'

I hug her tight, tell her I can come back tomorrow if she wants me to.

'Tomorrow it will be over. Like I was never pregnant at all.'

I want to say I hope so, but I don't, because I know it could seem callous. On the walk home, Oliver holds my hand and doesn't ask me any questions. He hasn't had a show tonight, and he only had swimming lessons with toddlers this morning, so he's been free most of the day.

'What have you done today?' I ask.

'I had lunch with Charlotte.'

I feel my insides turn to ice. 'Oh.'

'Yeah, she wanted to talk about this plan to take the play on tour.'

'Is it happening?' I ask. In one way, I'm glad I've met Charlotte, that I can picture her, but in another, I wish I had no idea what she looks like.

'Seems like it might. We went to this burger place in Soho and the chicken burger was insane. I'll take you there.'

I want to snap at him but I know he hasn't done anything wrong. It's so hard to feel like a jealous girlfriend when you don't yet have any reason to be jealous. Or do I? There's no way of knowing.

'So, Priya's losing the baby,' I say, after a pause.

'Shit, I wondered whether it might be something like that. How is she?'

'Messed up. I don't think she knows how to feel. She hadn't decided whether or not to have it, so...'

'I get it.'

'I'm not sure Nic does. Or maybe he does, but it's like something's changed between them. They're both hurting and they're not really talking to each other.'

'They'll work it out,' Oliver says. 'They've been together a long time, right?'

'Three years.' I want to ask him how he can be so sure.

There's pizza left but I don't have any appetite. So we go to bed and Oliver holds me, buries his face in my hair.

40

───────

TEN YEARS FROM NOW (OCTOBER 2023)

Oliver lets himself into the flat, and I can tell he's drunk before I see him. I'm in the kitchen with Isla, eating fish fingers and peas.

'My favourite girls!' He holds his arms out wide.

'Daddy!' Isla gets out of her chair and goes to him.

'Where have you been?' My voice is steel.

'We wrapped up early and went out for lunch,' he says, not yet noticing my tone.

'You and who?'

'The whole cast, pretty much.' He goes to the cupboard for a glass and turns on the tap, runs the water until it's cold.

'Daddy, there was a fire at school...'

I see his face change and know that mine is changing too. But she's here, in front of us. She's fine. 'Do you mean a fire alarm?' I ask.

'Yes, that's what I said. A fire alarm. And we had to stand in the playground with our coats on the whole time we were supposed to be doing maths.' She is gleeful, knowing she's got away with something. And him?

Oliver ruffles her hair and picks up a stray fish finger from the baking tray on the kitchen side. I think about the fact that I've been here, with Isla, making tea, while he's been drinking with his celebrity friends. And it's so hard to know whether I'm happy in this life, whether this is something he does a lot or a one-off.

'Can I talk to you for a minute?' I ask him.

We go into the living area while Isla carries on eating, oblivious.

'You're really drunk,' I say.

He grins. 'I know, it's ages since I got this drunk. It was just so fun. We went to this really exclusive cocktail bar...'

'I thought you went for lunch.'

'After lunch, I mean. Is something wrong?'

It takes me a moment to decide how to answer that. 'I don't like Isla seeing you like this.' Is that really it? It's true, but I think perhaps it's more about the fact that he lives this totally different life now, that he is rubbing shoulders with people I've been watching on TV since I was a kid, and I'm stuck at home.

'Christ, Maddy. It's not like it's every day. We finished early, had a long lunch. What's the big deal?'

It's so hard to navigate this, when I don't know how kindly or unkindly he treats me. I look at him hard, trying to see the man I fell in love with, the man I've so recently fallen in love with, and he's there. He is.

'It's just... sometimes it's hard, that you're still acting and doing so well and I'm not doing it any more.'

'Oh.' He hangs his head and seems instantly sober. 'But Maddy, I thought you loved the writing work. If you don't, you could start again. You were so good in those *Summing Up* episodes.'

The fact that it's this show he brings up gives me a pretty clear indication that it was the height of my career. There's a pain in my chest, to think of that. How long did I keep chasing the dream after it was obviously over? And why does he think I love the writing? It was only ever a means to an end.

We look at each other, neither of us speaking, and I feel so tired.

'Can I have pudding?' Isla shouts.

'No,' I say, just as Oliver says, 'Yes.'

I give him a look. 'Can you sort it? Can you make sure it's fruit at least?' And I go into the bathroom and lock the door, let the tears that have been threatening start to fall. Am I happy, in this life? And if I am, is it him who makes me happy or is it her? When I've pulled myself together, I go out, and they are in the kitchen together. Oliver's sitting opposite her and pretending his hand is a spider getting closer and closer to her plate and she's laughing uproariously. They're both eating bananas. It's a sweet scene. And they are mine, I remind myself. Not in every sense, but in the sense that they are my family. They live here, with me. We are a unit. Oliver must sense me standing there, watching them, because he turns his head and gives me a huge smile and I know I'll forgive him because he makes me feel so warm and wanted.

41

NOW (NOVEMBER 2013)

It's Tuesday, and Priya and I are at the cinema. The first Tuesday after her miscarriage, I sent her a message reminding her that it was okay if she wanted to cancel, and she replied with a shocked face emoji and our time of meeting, even though it's pretty much the same every week. So we've carried on as usual. Now, a handful of weeks have passed. She looks better than she has the last few times I've seen her, and when she crosses the road and comes to me, we hug for slightly longer than usual.

'How are you doing?' I ask.

She shrugs, and I want to tell her how brave I think she is, but it's not bravery when you're forced to go through something, I suppose. It's just surviving.

'Wine?' I ask.

'Definitely wine.' We go inside with our arms linked and queue at the bar.

I want to know how things are with Nic, but I know I should wait for her to bring it up. I feel like I'm floundering around in the dark, with conversational obstacles I don't want to trip over. I'm used to saying anything and everything to Priya, but we've never dealt with anything like this. Anything quite so big and terrifying. In the end, she mentions him when we're sitting in the dark. Perhaps it's easier that way.

'I'm not sure Nic and I are going to get through this.'

I turn to her. She's dead serious. In the pale glow of the lights that help people to find their seats, I can see her expression is grim. 'Is he being a dick?'

'No, it's not that. He hasn't said it's my fault or anything like that.'

'Well, good. I feel like that's the least you should expect.'

'I think we're both grieving but in different ways. He wanted to have the baby, and now it's gone. And I didn't know what I wanted, and the decision has been taken out of our hands. But it's like we don't know how to comfort each other, you know? When his dad died, I knew what to do, and I helped him through it. But with this? It's like it's highlighted all the weak spots in our relationship.'

I think about what I saw in that vision. What I know, or think I know, about her future. The fact that I've only told her the bit about not being with Nic. But then the trailers come on. I reach across the armrest and hold her hand. We stay like that through the whole film, and when we come out, I don't think I could tell you the first thing about it. Priya has this rule that when we have drinks after the film, we have to spend at least the first twenty minutes talking about it. But that falls by the wayside tonight. She finds us a table and I queue at the bar.

'So tell me more about how things are with Nic?'

Priya shakes her head, and I can see in her eyes how sad she is. 'We're just coexisting. I feel like I've forgotten all the reasons we're together.'

'Do you want to remember?'

'I don't know. No, I don't think so. I mean, I've known him for three years and I saw a whole different side to him the last few weeks.'

'He loves you,' I say, and I'm not sure why. I do believe it's true, though.

'I know he does. And I love him. But maybe we've just learned that we want really different things. Better to find out now than in another five years, right?'

The way she's talking, it's like she's already made the decision. So I decide to risk it. 'There's something I haven't told you.'

She flicks her eyes up to mine and fixes me with a stare. Because we tell each other everything. Always have. 'What?'

Where to start? With the truth, I suppose. 'The vision I had, with you in it. I know more than I told you. You're not with Nic, but there's more.'

She claps a hand to her mouth. 'What? Why haven't you told me?'

'Because you might not want to know. *I* don't want to know. I just want to go about my life and find things out as they happen, not ten years in advance.'

'Not me. Tell me.'

Is it fair to tell her? Is it fair not to?

'Come on, Maddy. I promise I'll never hold it against you. I just want to know whether I'm okay, whether I'm happy.'

I pick at one of my nails, think about all the times she's called my belief in these visions into question. It's irresistible, I realise, when it's about you. 'When I saw you, you weren't particularly happy. We were out having drinks, and you were talking about how tired you were. The shifts, you know, and...'

'So I'm a doctor?'

'Of course you're a doctor. I mean, you didn't actually say so, but we know that's what you're going to do, right? You definitely mentioned twelve-hour shifts.'

'Okay, and?'

'And?'

'You said the shifts and...'

I take a deep breath. 'The children.'

I see her light up inside. 'I have children?'

'Twins.'

She widens her eyes. There are no twins in her family, as far as I know. 'Twins,' she repeats, as if she's getting herself used to the ideas. 'But not with Nic?'

'Not with Nic.'

'Who with?'

This is the one piece of information I feel like I have to hold back. Because I don't want her to wonder, any time she meets someone called Josh, whether he's the one she's going to be with. It might send her off down the wrong track. It would be a kind of torment, I think.

'I don't know,' I say.

She blows her cheeks out. 'Wow. That's a lot. Thank you.'

I'm still unsure about whether I've done the right thing, but she's known about the visions from the very start, and she wanted to know. She's an adult. Still, I'm glad I didn't tell her the name of her future partner. 'I just wish,' I say, formulating the thought even as I speak it, 'that something would happen in the here and now to make me know whether the visions are true or not.'

'You've always believed they are,' she says.

'I still do, but sometimes you need a little something to prop your belief up on, you know?'

'So what do you need? What would be enough?'

This is something I've thought about, over the years. 'I don't know,' I say. But I do. There are things that could happen which would give me a good idea, but nothing hugely solid. Apart from one thing. If someone died, someone who I've seen in one of my visions of the future, that would discredit the whole thing. But everyone I've seen in them is someone I love, so I don't want it to happen. I don't even want to say it.

'How long until Isla is conceived?' she asks.

I do a quick calculation in my head. 'Shit. Seven months.'

'Wow, soon. That will go some way to proving it, right?'

And she's right. If Oliver cheats on me and gets Charlotte pregnant, then that will be a pretty clear indicator that the visions are true.

'I can't piece it all together. How we'll either break up or he'll cheat on me and then we'll get back together and end up having Isla live with us, at least most of the time. It's so weird, knowing there's heartache ahead. Because it's going to hurt, however it plays out, right? I feel a bit like I'm bracing for it. All the time, when I'm with Oliver, I want to just enjoy our relationship while it's good, but I can't stop thinking about what's to come.'

'I can't even imagine,' Priya says. 'Although I still don't know if I quite trust in it all.'

I know it will always be like this. That Priya's intellect prevents her from believing wholeheartedly. I'm okay with that. I think I would be the same, if our roles were reversed.

We walk to the bus stop together, not saying much. There are a group of people bunched around the shelter, and it's starting to rain. Priya takes out an umbrella, turns away to open it, and then holds it over both our heads. We stand there, closer than we normally would.

'What are you going to do, about Nic?' I ask.

'I don't know.'

Part of me was worried she would say she's going to go home and end things right now. She can be impulsive. The fact that she doesn't say this is testament to how much she loves him.

'I guess I'll just carry on, see what happens. We're not unhappy. I mean, we weren't, before the whole baby thing.'

The bus comes and we get on, and there's no room to sit together so we stand in the pushchair space, holding on to bars to keep ourselves upright. It strikes me how tired I am, suddenly. I'm ready to stop thinking about all this stuff, to stop second-guessing. I want to be at home in my pyjamas chatting to Oliver about something that doesn't really matter.

And twenty minutes later, I am. When Oliver asks about the film, I tell him I don't remember anything, and he laughs. Then he asks how Priya is, his face serious. 'She's going to be okay,' I tell him. Because she is. She has to be. And now she has this hope that good things are coming, even if that means that things in her current life have to end.

'Shall we go to bed? I was falling asleep on the sofa before you got back.'

'Sure.' I know I won't sleep for a while. I never can when I've been out and feel stimulated. But Oliver and I try to always get into bed together, and we go over our days with our heads on the pillows, inches between our mouths, and sometimes it ends up in sex, and sometimes it doesn't, but it's pretty much always my favourite part of the day.

42

TEN YEARS FROM NOW (NOVEMBER 2023)

Oliver and I are watching TV. It's such an ordinary thing, but I can feel the tension radiating off him, where he sits beside me, his back ruler straight. And then I realise what this is. We're watching his show. Just then, he strides onto the screen. His hair is shorter and he's speaking with a Mancunian accent, and he's brilliant. I think about the play I saw him in, wish I knew which roles got him from there to here. Has it been a steady stream of success, or has this role come on the back of years and years of low-paid work?

Neither of us hear Isla coming into the room until she says: 'It's you, Daddy!'

Oliver grabs the remote and puts it on mute. It's in no way child friendly.

'Isla, it's so late, baby. Can't you sleep?' He's on his feet, lifting her into his arms, already taking her back to her room.

'I lost Smoky,' she says.

'Oh, well let's have a good look for him, shall we?'

I hear her squeal with laughter and know he's done something dramatic like pulled the covers off the bed and thrown them across the room. I'm relieved it was him who went with her and not me. I don't know which of her soft toys Smoky is. And it pains me, that I don't know. But I remind myself that when I get to this part of my life, I will know. I'm just not there yet.

When he returns, he nods towards the screen. 'What do you think?'

I can see in his eyes that my response means a lot to him. 'It's so good,' I tell him. Oliver's no longer on screen and he tells me he's not in it again until the next episode.

'I still want to watch it,' I say. 'I don't only want to watch it for you.'

He leans across and tickles my ribs, and I fold my body away from him, but then he moves and covers me and I'm lying beneath him and I'm not sure how it happened. 'You know how my character is reincarnated, over and over again, and has a different love in each life? I mean, of course you know.'

I just keep looking at him, our bodies aligned. Hip to hip, shoulder to shoulder.

'You are the love of all my lives,' he says. And then he starts to kiss me and I get that incredible feeling I get with him sometimes, where I'm not thinking, or deciding, or questioning. I'm just all skin, and I'm on fire.

He sits up, suddenly. 'The credits!'

I'm confused, but I watch him watching the screen, and then turn to look at it myself.

'There!' he says, pointing.

And it's my name. Written by Madeleine Hart.

43

NOW (DECEMBER 2013)

'Maddy, sorry to call so early.' Mum is speaking softly as if she doesn't want someone close to her to hear.

I'm in bed. Oliver's asleep. I hold the phone to my ear a bit tighter, slide out of bed as quietly as I can, and pad out into the living room. 'What is it, Mum?'

'It's Henry. You know we had that meeting yesterday, with his doctor and physio and everyone?'

'Yes.' I did know, and I'd made a note in my diary, intending to send a message about it yesterday morning. But I'd forgotten. I feel horrible.

'They seemed to be suggesting that the progress he's made so far could be as far as it will go.' The way she says it, I've never heard anyone sound more sad.

'Oh, Mum.' I'm torn, conflicted. Because I feel like I know that Henry won't fully regain his mobility, but I do know that he'll find his way. That he'll be happy. I wish I could tell her that I've had a drink with him at twenty-one, and he was fine. Perfect. 'How sure were they?'

'I don't know. They always say there's a chance, but...'

The rest of the sentence hangs in the air. 'And how is he taking it?'

There's a moment of quiet on the line and I find myself pacing. I realise Mum's crying, and I wish I was there with her, wish I could offer her some comfort.

'Mum, who's there with you? Just Henry?'

'No, love, Alan is here too. We're all just reeling a little bit. When we got home, Henry went straight to his room, didn't say a word. He didn't want to come out for dinner. I had to practically force him. He just seems to want to shut himself away and play video games.'

'Probably because that's the one thing that hasn't changed,' I say. 'He's still just as good as he always was at playing Minecraft. Whereas everything else...'

'Will you come for the weekend, try to cheer him up?'

She never asks me this. She never asks anything of me. I'm all ready to say yes when I remember that I'm working on Saturday. It's my last day on *Summing Up*. 'I can come Sunday, but I can't really stay. Is that okay?'

She doesn't ask what I'm busy with. 'That's fine, love. Bring Oliver, if he's free. I'll do a roast. I just feel like Alan and I keep saying the same things over and over, and none of it's getting through to him. Maybe you'll have a fresh perspective on it. He listens to you.'

I nod, even though I know she can't see me.

'It just feels so unfair,' she goes on. 'I wish I could swap places with him.'

She's said this numerous times, and every time I'm moved by how much she means it. She loves him more than she loves herself. That's motherhood. An image of Isla flashes in front of me, racing around the playground at the park, the tip of her nose red with cold, her body bundled up in a big coat. I miss her, I realise. When I'm here, in the present, I miss her.

'I'll come,' I say. 'Sunday. And in the meantime, tell him he can call me if he wants to talk.'

'Okay, love,' she says. She sounds old, in that moment. Defeated.

I end the call but I don't go back to bed. There's so much in my head. Henry, in his wheelchair, the way he is now, sombre and defeated. And then the grown-up Henry I met, confident and happy. Plus Isla and Oliver. Charlotte. Priya and Nic. It's all so complicated, and I didn't ask for any of it.

* * *

On Saturday, I'm up early to film my last scenes for *Summing Up*. We're filming on location in a café in Shoreditch. The role was stretched from three episodes to fifteen in the end, but now they've decided that my on-screen boyfriend is going to break up with me and I'm trying not to take it too personally. When I get there, Gavin's already there and in makeup. I grab a coffee and go over to wait my turn.

'So, last day,' he says.

'Yep.'

'We'll all be very sorry to see you go.' He turns to look at me and the makeup girl steps back and tuts. He ignores her, and flashes me a patronising smile.

There's something in the way he says it that makes me piece it together. He's engineered this, because I turned him down when he asked me out. Before I can say something I might regret, I turn and go in search of the producer. Jon is on his phone, pacing. When he sees that I want to speak to him, he holds one finger in the air to tell me to wait. I took my coat off when I went inside and now I'm shivering in the cold air, goosebumps raised on my arms. I find myself getting more and more worked up while I wait for Jon to wrap up his call. My heart feels like it's going to burst out of my chest.

'Maddy?' Jon asks at last. 'Did you want me? Shouldn't you be in makeup by now?'

'Gavin's in makeup,' I say. They're a similar age. Mates. They often leave the set together, heading for the pub.

'Well, make sure you don't miss your turn. We don't want you looking au natural on camera, do we?' He laughs, and I feel something pull tight and then snap inside me.

'Did Gavin ask for me to be written out of the show?' It's so direct, but it's the only way to ask it.

'What? Why would he do that?' He looks amused. He has what can only be described as a smirk on his face.

'I don't know. Did he?'

Jon looks down at his phone, starts scrolling through Instagram. The message is clear. He doesn't want to have this conversation, and he doesn't have to. 'Don't be that girl, Maddy.'

I'm still cold, but I feel the blood rush to my cheeks. 'What girl?'

'That girl. Blaming everyone else for anything that goes wrong in her life. Thinking men are the root of all evil.'

I have never felt closer to reaching out and hitting someone, so I turn and walk away, back to the makeup room. I need to find my costume. Tiff wears skinny jeans paired with a variety of high-heeled boots and pretty, floral tops. While I shut myself away and put them on, I go over my lines in my head. I go on a date with Gavin's character and he ends things with me. I spend most of the time in tears. When the makeup artist calls me over, Gavin smiles sweetly at me as I sit down.

'Got anything lined up?' he asks.

I don't know how to answer. I don't have anything lined up, not even an audition, but I don't want to give him the satisfaction of admitting that. 'A couple of things on the horizon,' I say, trying to keep my voice level. 'I need to talk to my agent.' I think about that vision, about my name on the credits of Oliver's hit show.

'Yeah, I remember those days, adverts and bit parts. It's so much less stressful when you find something longer-term.'

I don't say anything.

'Did you say your boyfriend's an actor, too? What's he doing?'

'He's in a play.'

'West End?'

The makeup girl, Annie, tilts my head to one side and starts applying foundation. If she's listening to the conversation we're having, she doesn't give any indication of it. I wonder whether she can tell how close I am to exploding.

'The Albert,' I say, naming the definitely-not-West-End venue.

'Oh, I saw there was some studenty-looking production on there.'

I've been telling myself I'm not going to say anything, that I'm just going to get through the scene and leave, and then I'll never have to see any of these people again, but in that moment, I find I can't do it.

'Does it make you feel important?' I ask. 'Taking things away from other people?'

He actually laughs then, but it's cold. 'Taking away? I'm not sure what you mean, Maddy.'

'I think you know exactly what I mean. I think you asked me out for a drink and I turned you down and so you went to your buddy Jon and the two of you decided I was out.'

'Oh, Maddy. That's not how things work, darling. But I'm flattered you would think I have so much influence.'

At the exact moment that I know I'm going to cry, that there's no stopping it, Annie passes me a tissue and asks Gavin if he could give us a minute. When we're alone, I expect she's going to say something about being put in an awkward position or messing up her work with my tears, but she surprises me.

'He's a bully,' she says. 'Always has been. I've been on the show since the beginning and lots of women have come and gone, and he's either slept with, or been a dick to, all of them. I know that knowing that probably doesn't help, but I wanted to tell you anyway.'

I swallow hard, blink away tears, and thank her. 'It does help. Honestly, it does. Did you know it's my last day today?'

'I knew. I'll be working on some other beautiful woman's face next week, knowing he's going to break her down too.'

A thought strikes me: I don't want to work in this industry. It's new, something I've never explored, but really, when it's unofficially run by men like that, who would want to be part of it?

We get the scene done in three takes, and when I've changed back into my own clothes and am about to leave for the last time, Gavin touches my arm. 'Some of us are going for drinks. Would you like to join us?'

I look at him, refusing to be the first to look away. I think about how Oliver's at home, waiting for me. How we'll eat dinner and maybe watch a film, and how Marjorie will curl up on one of our laps and the other one will be in charge of getting drink refills and snacks. I don't need this. I don't need any of it.

'No,' I say, and as I'm walking out I can hear Jon and Gavin laughing about something and I can't stop thinking about what Annie said to me.

Oliver's furious when I tell him the whole story. He's all for going to speak to Jon, but I tell him it won't do any good. I don't have any power. The scripts are written and the breakup scene has been filmed and it's over.

'For you, yes, but what about the next person who gets treated like that?'

He's right, but I just know anything we could do wouldn't help matters.

'It's all bullshit,' I say. 'The whole goddamned industry.'

Oliver always laughs when I swear, because I don't do it very often, but he's not laughing now. 'Maybe it's not right for you any more.' He's looking at me, steady, his eyes full of concern. 'Think about why you wanted to do it in the first place. Think about whether those reasons are still there, still true.'

I take a moment to think back to the girl I was. The girl who chose Drama for GCSE without much thought, but who surprised herself by falling in love with pretending to be someone else. 'It was about the feeling being on stage or in front of a camera gives me. When I know I've given the best performance I can. There's nothing like that.'

'So maybe you need to get back to that feeling,' he says. 'I know it. I'm feeling it at the moment. Maybe you should do some stage work. It's so immediate, you know, with the audience right there, reacting to your work in real time.'

'Maybe,' I say. But I do something else instead. I go to my room, telling Oliver I want to lie down and read for a bit, and I search on my laptop for screenwriting courses, sign up for the cheapest one before I can change my mind. Later, when I'm thinking about cancelling, I picture myself in my future visions, where I don't act and I seem content and fulfilled. Sometimes it isn't getting the things you thought you wanted that makes you happy.

44

NOW (JANUARY 2014)

It's the start of a new year, and Priya and Nic's relationship is over. I didn't know whether to be surprised when she told me. There have been so many arguments and walkouts over the years, but I know from the minute Priya tells me that this is really it. They've given up the flat and are both moving into flat shares with strangers, and today, Nic's gone out so I can help Priya pack up her things. It's the most melancholy of tasks, so I turn up laden with a bag of things to try to make it a bit easier.

Priya opens the door and pulls me in for a hug. I can tell she's been crying. 'What's this?' she asks, taking the bag I hold out to her.

'Have a look,' I say, and we go through to the kitchen where she flicks on the kettle, and it's such a familiar setup that I want to suggest we go back in time to when we lived here together and everything seemed a bit simpler. As if that might be possible.

Priya unpacks the bags and makes grateful noises as she discovers all her favourite snacks and drinks. Butterkist popcorn, Liquorice Allsorts, the saltiest salt and vinegar crisps, cans of Pepsi Max. 'Where shall we start?'

And I know she means with the packing, but I point to the popcorn and she opens the bag while I make the hot drinks. When we do venture out of the kitchen, I see there are boxes everywhere and they're mostly empty. 'Let's do your clothes,' I say, heading to her bedroom. I can see I'm going to have to take charge if this is ever going to get done. 'Find me a suitcase.'

It goes like that, her doing what I tell her to, and an hour later we've made good progress, but the more we do, the emptier the flat looks, and I can see that it's breaking her heart.

'Do you ever think you and I should have just both stayed here? Do you think we messed things up by changing them?'

I think about how I felt when they first told me I had to move out, and then about Oliver, and about the way their relationship has fallen apart. 'No,' I say. 'I think things are working out the way they should. I know it doesn't look like that to you right now, but it will.'

There's a silence and neither of us goes to fill it. She's filling a box with books, and I've told her not to add too many because we need to be able to lift it. I'm taking pictures down from the walls. Priya's new place is only a couple of streets away, and we have a man and van coming in an hour to take her things there.

'I'm so sick of my breakup. Tell me things about you and Oliver,' she says eventually.

Things are tricky there too, but in a different way. There are no arguments. Oliver is tirelessly supportive of me. He's kind, he's funny. And yet I can't lose sight of the knowledge that he's going to conceive Isla with another woman in the next few months. I tell Priya all of this, and I can hear how crazy it sounds, but she doesn't laugh or even acknowledge that the things I'm saying are unusual.

'Maybe he won't,' she says.

She's always been less sure than me that the visions are accurate. Is that what she's saying?

'What do you mean?'

'I mean, things are solid between you, and he just doesn't seem like someone who would cheat. Maybe if you keep going as you are, making sure nothing too dramatic happens, he won't do it.'

I shake my head. 'I can't explain it, but there's something between them. I've seen it. I feel like if it doesn't happen now it'll happen at some point. I feel like it's hanging over us.'

'Have you talked to him about it?'

I laugh. 'No.'

Priya has her doubts about the visions, and I don't blame her. If I hadn't seen them, been in them, I would too. I think about the tiny details I see, not just about the people I already know, like Oliver or Priya, but about Isla, too. I've noticed a patch of dry skin on her calf, a small cluster of freckles on her right shoulder. I can't possibly have imagined her, can I? She's a whole person, with quirks and dislikes and lots to say.

'But then,' I say, 'there'd be no Isla.'

'Yes, and I know how you feel about her, but don't you want to do everything to make it work with Oliver?'

And I know, in that moment, that I would give it all up for Isla to be born. This girl whose hand I've held, whose tears I've wiped, but who doesn't yet exist. I know that Priya does everything she can to understand, that she believes the things I tell her about this strange gift or curse that I have, but it isn't the same as being there. It isn't the same as being me, and living those moments. It's not like watching something, like a dream. It's like real life.

'No,' I say. 'I feel like I want to do everything I can to make sure she gets to live.'

'In that case,' Priya says, 'I think you know what you need to do.'

And as soon as she says it, I do, though I haven't considered it before. I need to end things with Oliver. I need to take a sledge-hammer to our happy life and happy home, for no good reason that I can share with him. Because that way, he can sleep with Charlotte without me being in the way. I don't want to do it, but I need to. And I need to do it soon.

We finish off the packing without speaking much, and I know we both have a lot to think through, a lot to process. When the knock at the door comes, it jolts me out of my thoughts, and for a moment I can't think who it could be.

'It's the guy with the van,' Priya says, as if she can read my thoughts.

She goes to let him in, and I hear muffled voices and then she brings him into the living room. 'Maddy, this is Josh.'

The name goes through me like a body through water, and I feel my insides start to churn. Josh. Could this man be the father of Priya's future children? He's good-looking, probably a few years older than us. He isn't obviously Priya's type, but she's looking at him as if she's curious and wants to find out more. I realise I've been looking at him for an uncomfortably long time.

'Hi, Josh,' I say. 'We're almost done.'

'Shall we all have a cup of tea?' Priya asks, and Josh says he would kill for a strong brew with half a teaspoon of sugar.

'Half?' I laugh. I'm not sure why half a sugar is funny, but it seems like something an older woman who was watching her weight might ask for.

'I'm weaning myself off it,' he explains. 'I've got a wicked sweet tooth.' And then he breaks into a smile that I imagine has made many a woman feel weak.

'Great,' Priya says, 'I'll put the kettle on.'

As soon as she's gone, I finish taping up the boxes and find I'm not sure what to do next.

'Are you two a couple? Sisters? Friends?' Josh asks me when I stand and stretch my back.

'Friends.'

'Gotcha.'

'How long have you been doing this?' I ask.

'This? The van stuff? Oh, I don't do it, not really. It's my dad's business, but I help him out sometimes, when I can.'

'And what do you do the rest of the time?'

'I'm sort of... in between things.'

I'm curious about this, especially if this man might come to feature in Priya's life, but I don't feel able to press him on it while we're standing here in her packed-up flat making small talk. He starts to pick up boxes and carry them to the front door, and I go around opening and closing drawers, trying to make sure we haven't forgotten anything important.

When Priya returns with the drinks on a tray, Josh is outside putting the first boxes in the van.

'He's cute,' I say, tilting my head in the direction of the door, because I want to get her reaction.

'Is he?' she asks.

And I see, at once, that she's not in the right headspace to think about possible future love interests. Of course she isn't. She's still cleaning up the pieces of her broken relationship. Does that mean I should step in, make sure we get his number or something, for when she is ready? I shake my head, annoyed with myself. No. If it's going to happen, it will happen. I don't need to interfere. I shouldn't interfere. And yet where does that leave me with ending things with Oliver? I'm so confused.

'Just these?' Josh asks, coming back into the room and gesturing at the boxes and suitcases we've piled up neatly.

'There's some furniture too,' Priya says. 'This armchair and a chest of drawers.'

'Got it.'

I watch him as he lifts things, the muscles in his back moving. Priya isn't looking. She's lost in her own world, probably saying her sad goodbyes to the flat she's lived in for so long.

'When does Nic move?' I ask.

'Tomorrow.'

And that will be it. They're not married and they don't have children, so no ties. I wonder whether they'll be friends, in time. I think probably not. It must be so hard, shifting a relationship from one context to another like that. I think Nic will probably leave our lives as if through a hidden door, and if we see him again it will be by mistake and in passing, in a pub we all like or going down the escalator into the Tube. I think about the time he fixed my laptop and the times when Priya and I still lived together that he'd come over and make bacon sandwiches for all of us on a hungover Sunday morning. He's not a bad man, he's just not the right man for her.

I leave shortly after that, hugging her for a long time on the doorstep. Josh is going to help her unload at the other end and I promise to visit her tomorrow and help her get settled. I'll bring her a plant, I think, and I also make a mental note to call in on Mrs Aziz soon.

'What are your plans for the evening?' she asks, and I tell her I have no idea but it will probably involve the sofa and a takeaway.

But when I get home, Oliver is getting ready to go out. 'Impromptu work drinks,' he says. 'Just some of the cast and crew. Do you want to come? I'm worried it will be boring for you.'

I ignore that last part and say I'd love to, even though I'm desperate to flop down and chill out. I can't miss an opportunity to meet Charlotte again. I want to try to understand what it is that exists between them, whether it's something I can fight. Whether I want to.

'Who's going? And what time do we need to leave?' I ask, going straight over to my wardrobe and flicking through my dresses.

'Not sure. Charlotte's organised it. But I'll make sure to introduce you to everyone. And we could do with leaving in about half an hour if that's doable?'

I tell him it is and disappear to the bathroom to have a quick wash and do my makeup. While I'm applying mascara and giving my hair a brush, her name repeats in my head, in his voice. *Charlotte's organised it. Charlotte's organised it.* I hope it's a small, intimate gathering rather than a huge party, because I want to spend some time with Charlotte, to try to understand who she is and what Oliver means to her.

45

NOW (JANUARY 2014)

It takes me a bit longer than half an hour to get ready, so when we get to the bar, the others are already there. We're in the basement of a slick bar near Chelsea. It's lit by candles and there's seating for about fifteen people. It feels intimate. There are nine other people there, and Oliver introduces me to all of them and I know I won't remember their names. But when it comes to Charlotte, I remind him that we've already met.

'That's right, opening night,' he says.

Charlotte is wearing a black dress with a plunging neckline, silver sparkly earrings that drop to her shoulders. Her hair is pinned back. She looks like the kind of woman you might worry about leaving your boyfriend with.

'Mandy?' Charlotte says.

'Maddy,' I say. Was it on purpose, to undermine me? Or an innocent mistake? She leans in to kiss my cheek and she smells of a fragrance that's sharp and citrussy.

'Maddy, of course. Oliver talks about you all the time.'

Oliver has his hand on the small of my back, but I notice a look passing between them that I can't quite interpret. After a bit of small talk, he goes off to talk to one of the other actors. Charlotte insists on taking me to the bar and buying me a drink. We order cocktails, clink glasses. And all the time, I'm trying to work her out. Does she have a thing for Oliver? Or will it be, when and if it happens, just a one-night thing? A drunken mistake or a masterplan? I noticed when Oliver was doing the introductions that there was no boyfriend or husband. If she has one, he isn't here.

'So Oliver tells me you're hoping to take the play on tour?' I say. The play's been a bigger success than anyone anticipated. It's transferred to a slightly larger theatre and now there's this.

She looks at me and there's something in it that I can't quite work out. Is it a challenge? 'It's all happening. We're still working out logistics. It won't be immediately after this run. We're looking at June.'

June. The month of Isla's conception. And I feel sick, because it's so obvious that it's going to happen, no matter what I do. I have to break up with him, for his sake and for mine. Not to mention Isla's.

'June,' I say, because I don't know what else to say, and it's hard to look at her, knowing what I know about the ways our lives are about to intertwine. I can't let her see how devastated I am, how something she hasn't yet done has broken my heart into sharp, spiky pieces, and it feels like they're lodged into the wall of my chest.

'Oliver tells me you're an actor too. Are you working at the moment?'

I tell her that I have an audition for a play tomorrow, but that otherwise I'm keeping myself busy (and keeping the rent paid) with copywriting work, and she nods sympathetically and says things are tough out there. Then she rests a hand on my arm and tells me she needs to speak to someone over in the corner, gestures over there, and he holds a hand up in an awkward greeting. Will I please excuse her?

I stay at the bar after she's gone. Oliver's in the middle of an animated conversation with two of his co-stars. There's a lot of laughing and hand gestures. I could go over there. I know he'd step back and invite me into the circle. I know he'd steer the conversation in such a way that I'd be involved, somehow, despite not being part of this production. He's good like that. But I'm happy watching him for a minute or two. Thinking about what comes next, and how hard it's going to be. One of the men he's standing with notices me, and then Oliver follows his eyes and sees me, alone at the bar, and gestures for me to come and join them. He isn't the type to bring his girlfriend to a work do and then leave her to fend for herself. I walk over, my heels starting to rub.

'Maddy!' He greets me like a long-lost friend, not a woman he came here with and was standing beside until mere minutes ago. 'Bri's just telling us about a play he did with Eddie Redmayne! Before he was huge.'

I know the name but I can't bring Eddie Redmayne's face to mind, but it doesn't matter because I know what's expected of me – to feign shock and delight.

'He was so nice to everyone, but you could just see he was going to make it big,' Bri goes on. 'It was like someone had turned a light on when he came in the room.'

It's a nice expression, and I wonder what it must feel like for people to think that about you. To have that ability to brighten someone's day. There's a brief silence and I see a way into the conversation.

'Charlotte says the tour is all set for June,' I say. I look at all three of them as I say it: Oliver, Bri, and a woman who I'd say is a few years older than me, and who plays Oliver's older sister.

'Seems to be,' Oliver says. And then he excuses us and steers me away from the group, into a slightly darkened corner. 'Is everything okay?' he asks. 'You seem... not quite yourself.'

I look into his eyes and see how he cares. How will he look at me, later or tomorrow, when I tell him it's over? That it has to be over, for all our sakes? 'I'm not feeling the best. I think I might leave you to it.'

'I'll come,' Oliver says. 'I don't want you going home on your own if you're not well.'

'It's nothing, really,' I say. 'Just the start of a headache. I'll be fine. I'll get a cab. Honestly, you go back and enjoy yourself. You've been working hard. You deserve this.'

He isn't sure, but I bustle him back over to the bar, picking up my jacket on the way, and before he knows what's going on, he's talking to Charlotte and a very small man whose name I've forgotten, and I'm outside, breathing deeply in the night air like I'm only just remembering how.

When I'm home, I get into pyjamas and curl up with Marjorie, watching a film I've definitely seen before, possibly on a Tuesday cinema trip with Priya, but which I don't remember much about. When it gets to eleven, I go to bed. Now that I'm decided, I want to do it tonight, to set something in motion, to begin the unpicking of this life we've so hastily put together. But it's too late, and he'll be drunk, and it isn't fair, so I will wait until morning. I can't help but cry as I lie there, alone and wondering what he's doing. Whether it's starting already, this thing with Charlotte. By the time I fall asleep, the pillow is wet with tears.

But the next thing I know, it's 3 a.m. and I'm getting up to use the bathroom and his side of the bed is still empty. I check my phone, and there's a series of messages. They're going for food. They're going to do karaoke. They're going back to Charlotte's to carry on the party. That last one was sent ten minutes ago. I reply:

MADDY

See you in the morning.

And I wait, sitting up in bed with my head uncomfortable against the wooden headrest, but he doesn't reply.

* * *

It's six when he comes in, and I can tell he's wasted but also trying not to wake me. Still, he crashes about, almost toppling over when he takes his jeans off, and part of me wants to sit up and shout at him to go in the spare room. When he slips in next to me, he places a kiss on the back of my neck but I don't let him know I'm awake, at least partially. I wake up properly for the day at eight, and leave him sleeping, the stench of stale alcohol coming off him in waves. And then I wait, because there's a conversation we need to have and I know I won't get anything much done until we've had it.

At ten, he comes out of the bedroom, his eyes bloodshot and one hand to his head like he's having to hold it on. 'Is there coffee?' he asks.

I make him one and we sit at the kitchen table. There's sunlight trickling in through the window, making patterns on the walls. It's a gorgeous day, and if it wasn't for this thing I have to do, and his obvious hangover, I'd be suggesting a long walk somewhere.

'I think we did karaoke,' Oliver says, and I hold up the phone to show him his messages. 'So we did. And then we went back to Charlotte's – yes, I remember that.'

'A group of you or... just you and her?'

He looks at me, curious. Does he know that I know? Even if nothing's happened, there are feelings there. Is he wondering how I've detected them? 'All of us,' he says.

'Oliver,' I say, and there must be something in the way I say it, kind and gentle as I can manage, because his head snaps up and he puts his coffee down like he knows this is going to be a moment of great significance.

'Are you okay?' he asks. 'Last night, you weren't feeling good...'

'I'm fine. But this – us – we're not fine.'

If it's possible, he goes a shade paler. 'What? Maddy, what? I thought everything was going so well. Is this about Charlotte?'

'Partly. I've seen the way you look at each other. There's something there, Oliver. It's obvious.'

I wish I could tell him that I'm doing this now so we can be together later. That I'm doing it for his daughter, who he will adore the second she arrives, so he doesn't need to be scared of the fact that he doesn't actively want her. But I can't say those things, so I have to lie and just hope that he'll forgive me. 'And I think we just went into it too fast, got too serious too quickly.'

Oliver lurches forward suddenly and then puts a hand to his head and sits back. 'We can slow down. It's crazy, that we were living together from day one. We can get separate places, if you want, go back to just dating. And I promise you that nothing has happened with Charlotte.'

'But you can't promise me that nothing will.'

He looks down at the floor, his jaw set. And I know he's torn, wanting this to work with me but feeling something for her too.

It's so hard, when you can see a person's heart breaking in front of you, and yours is doing the same thing inside you, and you are as sure as you can be that it's for the best, but it doesn't feel like it. 'Oliver, you are kind and patient and wonderful, and I think maybe things would work between us in another time, but right now, there's just something off and I can't pretend it's not any more. It's not fair.'

Oliver stands up and walks over to where I'm standing, leaning back against the kitchen counter. He's at his worst, pale and reeking of alcohol, and yet I still want to tell him I'm being silly, that of course I'm not going anywhere, that I love him. Because I do love him. And that's precisely why I need to let him go.

'Maddy.' There's a plea in his voice. He takes both my hands in his and threads his fingers through mine. 'Is this real? This feels like a bad dream.'

'I'm sorry. Honestly, Oliver, you don't know how sorry I am. Maybe I just need a bit of time…' As soon as I say this, I realise I'll have to retract it. If he thinks we're just taking time apart, he might not let anything happen with Charlotte. And he has to. 'No, that's not right, it's not fair. I don't know what will happen in the future, but I know I have to put an end to this now. I'd do anything to change it.'

'Change it,' Oliver says, and it's little more than a whisper. 'It's in your power to change it.'

I shake my head, carefully unlace my fingers. 'I'll start looking for somewhere to live. But you should advertise the room straight away. I can go to my parents' if I need to.'

As I go into my room and close the door behind me, I hear him say one more thing. 'I don't understand what just happened.'

And then I let myself cry, for the pain of hurting this man I love, for the pain of having to walk away. I think of Isla, see her throw her head back in laughter, then look up at me as if I have all the answers, then pick her nose while she's watching TV and thinks I'm not watching. It's all for her. It's possible that she would happen either way, that everything is pre-determined and she is coming into all of our lives regardless of how we conduct ourselves. But this is the neatest, cleanest way. This way Oliver doesn't have to cheat, or lie.

I pick my phone up off my bedside table and send a message to Mum.

MADDY

Can I come to stay for a bit?

46

NOW (JANUARY 2014)

Mum lets me walk into her arms and strokes one hand down the back of my hair in the way she used to when I'd tripped and scraped my knee or fallen out with a friend or found out I didn't get the part I wanted in the school play. It's instantly soothing, and I feel my breath slow and deepen and realise how tense my body is.

'It's over, with Oliver,' I say. I step back to see how she's taken this, because I know it's not only about me. Oliver and Henry have built up a special relationship, and the work they've been doing together, the swimming, has had a huge impact on Henry's wellbeing. But she's my mum, and she can see I'm heartbroken, so she keeps any feelings about that locked away for the time being and just tells me she's sorry and holds me. Henry and Alan are out, at football training, and I'm glad, because I'm not up to telling everyone at once, and I know this way Mum will tell them for me. Mum makes tea and gets out some chocolate digestives, and we go into the lounge and she asks if I want to talk about it. I shake my head.

'I will, but not now. It all feels a bit too...'

'Raw?' she suggests.

'Definitely raw.'

'So when you asked about coming to stay for a bit, did you mean moving back in?'

I shrug. 'Most of my stuff is still there, and I'm looking for a new place, but if he finds someone new to move in before I get one, I might stay here until I do. If that's okay.'

I know it's okay. Mum's always been very clear about the fact that Henry and I will always have somewhere to live, that this will always be our home. But it feels like good manners to check.

'I love having you home, whether it's for a night or a few months or whatever, you know that. It's been a long time since all four of us were living together. I just wish it could happen without you being hurt.'

There have been moments, over the years, when I've thought about telling Mum what happens to me when I have sex. It's not the kind of thing you want to go into in any great detail with a parent, but it's a big part of my life and it's the reason why I haven't had boyfriends before now and why I've ended things with this one. I think back to the very first time it happened, when I went straight to Priya's and told her. I didn't know then that I was making such a huge decision in sharing that with her. It's bonded us together, in a way. Back then, the thought of discussing sex with my mum was unthinkable, and it's not much better now, but I know it would help her to understand me. And I know she would believe me, because she's my mum.

'Can I ask how Oliver is?' she asks then.

'Of course you can. He's pretty much the same as me.'

I see it in her eyes, the question. If you're both so broken and devastated, why have you split up? And I want to answer it, but I can't. It's too involved, too complicated. And I don't want her to worry about me having this to deal with. She has enough to worry about, with Henry.

'I think I'll go up to my room,' I say, finishing off my drink. 'I promised Priya I'd call.'

Mum nods, and I take the cups through to the kitchen and then head upstairs to the sanctity of my childhood bedroom. It was a lie, that I said I'd call Priya, but I do owe her a call. I haven't told her about any of this. When I do, she gasps, and I almost laugh because it's a proper pantomime reaction.

'Where are you now?' she asks.

'At Mum's. I'm sorry I didn't tell you ahead of it happening, I just, I made the decision and then I had to go through with it as quickly and cleanly as I could, before I changed my mind.'

'Christ. I wish I could give you a hug.'

That almost sets me off again. There's something about the fact that Priya knows the full story – that she actually understands why I'm doing this – that makes me feel somehow protected by her.

'So this Charlotte woman. What's she like?'

I think about Charlotte, who I'm leaning towards disliking, but is that only because of the circumstances? If I'd met her in a different way, like if she was a friend of Priya's, would I get on with her? But no, that's not fair, because casting her as a friend of Priya's already suggests she's someone I would like. I close my eyes, picture Charlotte. Do all I can to be neutral. 'She's a monster,' I say.

Priya laughs and then I do too, and it feels good, like when you're out walking in the cold and the sun breaks through the cloud for just a moment.

'A monster, huh? Lucky Oliver.'

'I know, but—'

'Isla,' she says. 'I know. At least we know she has good taste in baby names, right?'

'I guess that's something.'

'So who'd have thought, a few months ago, that we'd both be single again so soon? I guess we could look for a place together, although...'

She doesn't finish that thought, but I know exactly what it is. We don't know how long Oliver and I are going to be apart. I could rent a place with her, get settled, and then it could be time for things to get back on track, and I'd have to leave her in the lurch. 'I think I might just stay here,' I say, realising as I say it that it's the simplest thing. 'It will be nice, to spend some time with Mum and Alan, and with Henry.'

'What about auditions, though?' she asks. 'What about Tuesday cinema?' I can picture her face. Her forehead is all crumpled, and she looks the way her mum used to when she was telling us off for shrieking too loudly in Priya's bedroom.

'I can travel in for auditions. And it's hardly like I'm inundated. We might have to put Tuesday cinema on hold for a bit, though.'

'Just, don't give up, all right? Don't curl up in a ball and play dead. This is a means to an end. It's not *the* end.'

Priya always knows the right thing to say.

* * *

Later, while Mum's preparing a roast dinner, Henry and I go for a walk. He's got an electric wheelchair now, so he doesn't need to be pushed. I know the information about my split with Oliver will be a blow to Henry, so I get it out of the way. Short and sharp. At first, he doesn't react, and I have this fear that he's about to have a full-blown tantrum, here in the street, and I won't know what to do. But he doesn't, of course. He's not such a little kid any more. He says he's sorry for me.

'Do you think he'll still do the swimming with me?' he asks.

'I don't know, Henry. I think we'll have to wait for him to get in touch. I was the one who ended things, so I don't think it would be right to call him and ask if he can still do this big favour for my brother.'

Henry nods, and I can see he understands but he's disappointed, too. Aren't we all?

'I thought it was the real thing. That you'd be together in five years. Ten years.'

'Me too,' I say. And I feel like I owe him more than that, more of an explanation, but I don't have one. At least not one I can share. 'How's it going at football?'

'I think we're going to move up a level at the end of the season.'

I'm so pleased that he says 'we' and not 'they'. That this help he's giving the coach truly makes him feel part of the team. 'That's great, Henry. Well done.'

When you're walking side by side, and you're at different levels because one of you is in a wheelchair, there's no real chance for eye contact. Sometimes that's a good thing, and sometimes it isn't. I want to know how Henry feels, about Oliver, about football, about his injury. Everything. He used to be so open as a little kid. He'd tell you exactly how he felt about the lunch you'd made him, or the book you'd chosen. No feelings spared. But now he's older, and he's learned to hide things, the way we all do.

'How long are you staying?' he asks when we're nearly back at the house.

'I don't know. A while, I think. I'm sort of taking stock, deciding what comes next.'

'Because of Oliver?'

Because of Oliver? Not just because of him. How can I explain it in a way that will make sense to Henry? 'Kind of. When you're really young, and you have relationships, it's just fun and you don't think too much about the future. But then there comes a point where you're thinking about the kind of person you might want to marry, or have children with. It all feels a lot more serious. Plus I'm thinking about my career. I don't know whether I want to be chasing acting jobs like this my whole life. And if I don't, and I want to get myself set up in something else, then I should really start thinking about that. The younger you are when you make a big change, the better, I think. Sorry, this is probably boring you to death.'

Henry laughs. 'No. I think I get it. You're young enough to start again. With your career and your relationship.'

He's wiser than he has any right to be, at his age.

'So what kind of job would you want to do?' he asks.

I think about the visions I've had, what I've managed to piece together about my working life. I assumed I was copywriting, like I do to fill in the gaps now, but now I know that I'm screenwriting. I think about the online course I've been doing, how enjoyable it is and how well people have reacted to the work I've shared. But I don't think I'm ready to tell anyone about it yet.

'I don't know.'

'You'll work it out,' he says.

It means a lot, this faith. Henry doesn't say things he doesn't mean. We're heading back home now, and I'm looking forward to going in and being able to smell the beef Mum's cooking. Henry's challenged me to a game of Monopoly after lunch, and Mum says she's steering well clear because I used to get really cross if I didn't win when I was a child. It's just the kind of day I need: time with these people I love, with nothing much to do.

Henry sees him first. He's standing on the doorstep, nothing in his hands. Oliver. It's so unexpected that when Henry says it, I'm sure he must have made a mistake. But no, there he is, his clothes all crumpled from the drive, and he's rotating his neck the way he does after sitting in the same position for a while. Before we get there, the door opens and he steps inside.

'What do you want to do?' Henry asks. 'We could turn around. He didn't see us.'

It's tempting. But he's come all this way and I owe it to him to listen to whatever it is he has to say. 'I need to face him,' I say. 'But thanks.'

We let ourselves in and Oliver's still in the hallway, taking off his shoes, and Mum flashes me a look that says she didn't know what to do for the best, and I ask Oliver if he wants to come up to my room because there are too many people in this confined space. Now I can see him properly, I see that his eyes look a bit hollow, his skin dull. He follows me up the stairs.

47

NOW (JANUARY 2014)

'I should have brought flowers,' Oliver says.

We're in my bedroom and I've closed the door. 'No, there's no need.'

'Do you know why I'm here?'

I suspect it's because he wants to try to talk me round. 'No.'

'Because I don't give up without a fight. What we've got, Maddy, what we had, it's really special. I think we both know that. It's not something you can just throw away.'

We're standing inches from each other, both of us refusing to look away. 'I didn't throw it away, Oliver.'

'What would you call it?'

'I changed my mind. I thought it was right and then I realised it wasn't. And that's my decision. You can't just come here and force me to rethink. It doesn't work like that.'

For a moment, we stare at each other. We're both angry, and I sense how easily it could tip over into passion. If I stepped forward, leaned in, we'd be kissing. And there's a part of me that wants to. It's the biggest part. But I have to remember the big picture. I have to remember Isla.

'I just don't get it,' he says, his voice pleading now. 'It was so good. I know you felt the same way. I've just been sitting around at the flat, trying to work out what went wrong. When it went wrong. And your stuff is everywhere, and it's so hard to stop thinking about you for a single second when I can smell your stilton every time I open the fridge and see your shampoo when I have a shower.'

I'm so sorry I've hurt him like this. If there was a way to undo it, without jeopardising the future, I would jump at it. 'I'll come for my stuff, Oliver.'

'No, I don't want you to do that. Because then it will feel like it's properly over.'

'It is properly over.' I say this as gently as I can, and then I reach for his hand and hold it in both of mine. It's cold, despite the warmth of the room. It's like his heart's given up. 'Look,' I say, and I know I should just stop talking but somehow I can't help myself. He just looks so sad. 'Maybe one day I'll be able to explain this to you better, but for now I need you to trust me. It's the only way. I'm so, so sorry.'

I watch him take this new information in. His expression passing through confusion and into hope. And I hate myself for not being strong enough to just hold my position.

'I'll wait until then,' he says.

'No,' I'm firm. 'No, you can't wait. You have to live your life, Oliver. You have to try to forget about me, about this, and find a way to be happy.'

I see an image of Charlotte from that drunken night out. Wonder whether it's started already. Whether she whispered something in his ear after I went home, set the ball rolling. I'll never know, and that's okay. There are things he can't know, and things I can't.

'I should go,' he says, and I nod. 'But before I do, can I talk to Henry, do you think?'

My breath catches at the thought of Henry being hurt by my actions. 'To tell him you won't be able to do the swimming thing any more?'

Oliver shakes his head. 'No, no, to say we'll keep doing that, if he wants to.'

I should have known to expect this. He's a good man. He wouldn't let Henry suffer as a result of whatever is or isn't happening between him and me. 'Are you sure? I've been so worried about how he'll take it.'

Oliver takes a step closer to me, and I can feel the warmth of his breath. 'I like Henry,' he says. 'I like helping him. I wasn't only doing it because I was with you.'

It would be so easy to kiss him. And it would complicate things monumentally, so I force myself to stand still, to hold his eye contact but not let it progress to anything else. 'Let's go and find him,' I say.

Henry is playing FIFA in his bedroom when I knock. He pauses the game and asks us to come in the room, and there's a wariness about his expression. He thinks exactly what I thought. That we're coming to break bad news.

'Hey, Henry,' Oliver says. 'Sorry, I didn't get to say hello properly when you got back with Maddy. I just wanted to check that we're on for Saturday?'

Henry raises his eyebrows. 'Really?'

'Look, things are a bit complicated between me and your sister right now, but as far as I'm concerned, they're pretty straightforward between you and me. So if you want to carry on with the swimming, we can do that.'

Henry beams. It's the expression of a much younger child. It's a 'Santa's been' kind of smile. It's so good to see it that I almost waver. 'I want to carry on.'

'Good. I'll be in touch with your mum about it.'

Henry doesn't say anything, doesn't move, and I can tell he's trying to decide something. And then something must tip the balance, because he starts to come over, and when he reaches Oliver, he holds his arms out for a hug, and Oliver leans down into it, and I have to look away. Because this man is everything I want, and I'm letting him go.

At the door, Oliver tries one last time. 'If you change your mind...'

'I'll be in touch,' I say, 'about collecting my stuff. But please just get on with things. Don't wait around.'

He nods, but I don't think it's an agreement. It's just what you do, when there's nothing left to say. I stand and watch him get in his car and drive away, and I can imagine myself on the other side of it. In the car, beside him, driving away from this house after a visit. But that isn't what's happening.

When I turn around, Mum is standing a few feet behind me and there's an expression on her face I can't quite pin down.

'Come on,' she says. 'We're going out for a coffee. You and me.'

I don't argue. There's no point when Mum's decided something. I'm just surprised it's this. She and I used to go out a fair bit, shopping or to get our nails done or for lunch. But since Henry's accident, she's shrunk inwards on herself, stopped doing anything for fun. She ploughs all her energy into looking after her boy. But it looks like she has some left, after all, for her girl.

We walk into town and she leads us to her preferred café, where we order lattes and brownies. It isn't until we're seated on an almost threadbare floral sofa in a dimly lit corner that she goes in. 'Something isn't right about this breakup with Oliver.'

'Breakups always feel wrong, don't they?'

She fixes me with a stare. 'That's not what I mean. It's clearly not what he wants, and I don't think it's what you want either. Which begs the question – why is it happening?'

She's sharp, my mum. Intuitive. When Priya and I were about thirteen, we started hanging out with this girl called Tara who wasn't very nice to us. She used to play us off against each other, pairing up with one at the other's expense. Mum saw straight through it. She sat us both down and said she'd dealt with people like that in the past, and she basically coached us through the termination of the friendship group.

Over the years, I know she's had questions about why I haven't had boyfriends. Why there was Mark, when I was sixteen, and then no one until Oliver. And I know she had high hopes of Oliver being the one.

'The timing's wrong,' I say. 'I can't really explain it, but there might be a chance in the future. Just not right now.'

She sips her latte, never taking her eyes off my face. When she takes a bite of her brownie, she rolls her eyes back in her head to show how good it is. 'When people don't want to say the real reason why they're breaking up, there are all these excuses they use. They say vague things about timing or gut feelings or being on different paths. When really it's usually about something much more concrete, like someone cheating or not seeing eye to eye on important issues. I mean, that's what I've observed, anyway.'

I smile at her. It's a kind of 'you're good but I'm still not going to tell you' smile. We eat our brownies in silence, and I think about what I could tell her, what I could reveal without revealing the entire, sorry story. 'If you're worried about Henry, you don't need to be. Oliver said today that he's going to carry on swimming with him.'

Mum takes both my hands in hers and holds them as if they're the most precious thing she's ever seen. 'I'm worried about *you*.'

'Well, you don't need to worry about me either. Promise. I know what I'm doing.'

'Every twenty-seven-year-old in the history of the world believed they knew what they were doing. Fun fact: only approximately 0.00001 per cent actually did.'

I look down at my hands. My nail polish, applied before I came home, is chipped on my right thumb. I can't touch it up, because my nail colours are at Oliver's. It feels hard, suddenly, all of it. Mum is still holding my hands, and I see her notice the shift in me, and she pulls me into her for a hug.

'There's this woman,' I say.

Mum nods for me to go on, and there's fury in her eyes. And suddenly it doesn't matter how much she likes Oliver, how grateful she is for what he's been doing for her disabled son, because he's hurt her daughter, or she thinks he has, and there's no greater transgression.

'It's not like that,' I say. 'Nothing's happened. I don't think anything would happen. But I'm just stepping back, because I think they need to get it out of their system.'

She furrows her brow. 'Let me get this right. You've ended the relationship, even though you still love him, because there's another girl that he hasn't cheated with but you think there's something there between them.'

It isn't even about her, I want to say. It's about the person they're going to create together.

'Kind of,' I say. 'I know it sounds crazy but I promise you, I've thought it all through.'

Mum doesn't look convinced, but what can she do? I drain my coffee.

'We should get back soon,' she says, and I feel myself deflate a little. It's been so nice to see her outside of her home or mine, not at a physio session or by the pool where Henry swims. It's felt like old times, like the mum I had before. But she's snapped back, and that's okay too. She has enough love for everyone.

Henry's in his room when we get back. Alan's in the shed, no doubt fixing something. I want to say 'See? They're okay. We could have taken longer. You could take some time, for yourself, more often.' But I know from experience that you can't tell her what to do. The best you can do is make suggestions and then stand back in case she hates them.

'I'll put the kettle on,' Mum says, even though we've just had a coffee, because she has to always be doing something. Because if she stopped, she might never start again.

48

NOW (JUNE 2014)

Winter tips into spring and spring into early summer, and before I know it the days are long and sunny, and I've been at home for almost six months. I spend most of my time with my laptop in Mum's garden, sunglasses on against the glare. Writing house descriptions, and product descriptions for a fashion website, which is my latest thing. They send me email attachments with photos of items of clothing, reams of them, and information about what they're made of and how they should be washed, and I churn out one hundred-word descriptions and paste them onto the back end of the site, linking together products that have been styled together in the photos. It's boring and thankless, but it's easy, too. And the money isn't too bad. Evenings, I shut myself up in my bedroom and work on a screenplay I'm writing. The course is over and I'm feeling determined.

My days take on a sort of loose shape. I get up at seven and have breakfast with Henry before he goes to school, and if Mum and Alan have busy days I walk there with him and pick up a paper on the way back. Then I write for a few hours, breaking off for a salad or sandwich for lunch, before writing again until

Henry finishes school. Mum or I meet him and I've usually done enough by that point to take an hour to talk to him about his day over a game of FIFA or sometimes Monopoly or cards. He's good company. He's grown up a lot these last few years. He's had to. But he's turning into such a great person, and I love hearing what he thinks about things.

One evening, I've stayed downstairs and Henry turns on the TV and *Summing Up* is on. It's one of the episodes I'm in. I'd forgotten it was coming up. Henry insists on watching but I have to watch my scenes from behind a cushion. There's truly nothing worse than seeing yourself act.

'You're good,' Henry says. 'If I didn't know you, I'd totally believe you were like that in real life.'

'Like what?'

'You know, kind of silly and clumsy.'

I see Gavin lean in to kiss me on the screen, and Henry makes a gagging sound and I push him gently and we're laughing.

'What was he like?'

'You want to know the truth?'

He nods eagerly.

'He was horrible. Not at first, but towards the end. It was him who made sure I didn't get to stay on the show for longer.'

He's horrified. 'Why would he do that?'

'Because he asked me to go for a drink with him, and I turned him down.'

'Because of Oliver?'

'Because of Oliver.'

We don't talk about Oliver much, but he's always there. Not physically there, just in the air, ready to be brought up in conversation. The swimming's still going well, by all accounts. And I can believe it, looking at Henry. It's like he's transformed.

'He sounds like an idiot,' Henry says, and I have forgotten that we were talking about Gavin and think for a second that he means Oliver. But when I get it straightened out, I laugh.

'Big idiot.'

'Why haven't you done any acting work since you moved in?' Henry asks. 'Is it because it's too far from London?'

It would be so easy to say that was why. 'Nothing much has come up,' I say instead. 'I've done a few auditions but none of them have led to anything.'

'Is it hard, to have a job like that? Mum and Dad, they just go to their jobs and get paid, and I know they don't love them but at least they know where they stand.'

I think about this. It is hard, to keep putting yourself out there and inviting approval or rejection. It's hard to read a part you think you'd be perfect for and then see someone else doing it months down the line, when you'd almost forgotten. 'When I was younger, I thought it would be hard for a few years and then I'd have a big break and I'd get loads of amazing parts without really trying, and get rich and famous. But that's not how it works out for most people. So yes, it's hard. I feel like I'm moving away from it, really. I don't think it's what I'll do forever.'

'What will you do instead? The writing?'

I could fill my days with copywriting. It wouldn't be the worst way to earn a living. But I need some form of creativity. 'I'm still thinking about that,' I say.

'Well, you'd better think fast. You're twenty-eight, that's almost thirty.'

I don't reply, just throw a cushion at the side of his face. Twenty-eight must seem like a lifetime away for him, at twelve. But to me, it feels like I'm only just starting out.

Oliver sends messages often, and I leave them all unanswered. I would miss it if he stopped, though. I like to hear about the minutiae of his days. There's going to be no swimming for a while, because he's off on his tour, and some days I feel like I can't breathe because I know that if it's going to happen, with Charlotte, this will be when it does. I know when Isla's birthday is, so although I can't know her exact conception date, I do know it's around now. And it's while I'm sitting with Henry, watching *Summing Up*, that I get it. The message I've been dreading and hoping for.

OLIVER

I messed up, Maddy. Got drunk and slept with someone. Feel shitty about it.

Someone. He didn't say it was her. But I know. I wait a full five minutes before messaging back.

MADDY

That's not messing up, Oliver. You're free to do that.

He replies immediately:

OLIVER

I don't want to, though. And I told you I wouldn't. I'm just so lonely, away from home and you and Marjorie. But it won't happen again. I just wanted to be upfront with you, because I still hope we'll get back together and I don't want there to be any secrets.

I tell Henry I'm going to use the bathroom, but I go to my room instead, and I cry, hard and silent. I picture him, hating himself for this thing that had to happen, and I picture her, unaware that her entire life is about to change. Has changed, already. This is it. The next step.

Another message from Oliver, and I know it will have taken a lot for him to ask this:

OLIVER

Has there been anyone else for you?

Would it be kinder to say there has? But I can't do it. I've never been a good liar. Perhaps I'd be a better actress, if I was better at lying.

MADDY

No.

It's the simple truth, and I think of him, in his room, absorbing it. And then another message comes in and I'm confused for a moment, but it's from Mum, and she's asking if I can take Henry to his physio appointment tomorrow because she has a meeting at work she can't get out of. I tell her I can. I haven't been to one of these sessions, despite offering my services as driver and sidekick. I go down and tell Henry I'll be taking him, and he raises his eyebrows and turns back to the TV.

* * *

Henry's physio is a woman in her thirties called Hannah. She's good with him, giving him high fives and talking to him at just the right level, about football and school.

'Shall we get you standing?' she asks.

Henry looks over at me. I haven't seen him get out of his chair, other than to transfer to a car, since that day in mine and Oliver's flat. I ask him, often, whether there's any progress, but he's always glum and says there isn't and I never want to push it. But now, at the prospect of seeing him stand, I am filled with glee. I give him a big smile and a thumbs up, and he rolls his eyes in a way that is supposed to suggest I'm embarrassing, but which I know means he's pleased I'm here.

Slowly, slowly, Henry gets up out of the chair with Hannah's support, stands holding on to a walking frame. I wonder whether she'll try to get him to take a step, but she doesn't, and it's clear soon enough that just standing is taking a huge effort. But each time he looks like he's going to go back down to sitting, Hannah encourages him to just manage for a few more seconds.

'You are such a cry-baby, sis,' Henry says.

I hadn't even realised I was crying. It's just so hard to see how much this is taking out of him. He sinks back down to sitting, and Hannah says she'll give him a couple of minutes to rest and then they'll try it again.

I think about the vision again. Henry as a man, still in a chair. If I told him, if he believed me, it would drag him down. But I know that sometime over the next decade, he will make peace with his limited mobility and find his rhythm. Find his joy.

By the time the session is over, Henry's exhausted. I offer to call in for a McDonald's on the way home, knowing that Mum will be planning to cook something, but knowing, too, that she won't mind. Henry's face lights up.

'Can I have nine chicken nuggets?' he asks.

I shrug. 'I don't see why not.'

'Really? Mum and Dad never let me.'

'Well, let's make it our secret, then.'

When I let him dip his fries in his vanilla milkshake too, my position as best sister in the world is officially secured.

'You know you said you don't know whether you'll always be an actor?' he asks.

'I do.'

'Does it make you sad?'

I like to always answer Henry's questions truthfully, which

was a challenge when he was in his 'why?' phase as a three-year-old, but now it's just a case of taking my time and thinking properly about what he's asking me. 'I suppose it does, because it's what I've always wanted to do, so stopping feels a bit like failing. But if what I want has changed, there's no point clinging on to the thing I thought I would always want, is there?'

Henry shakes his head, and I lean forward and ruffle his hair. 'What are you thinking about?'

'How I'll never be a footballer.'

It's honest, direct. And it takes my breath away. I'm tempted to challenge him on it, to say he doesn't know that for sure, but that would be patronising. Most kids who want to be professional footballers don't make it, and those are the ones who don't have accidents that paralyse them.

'Does that make you sad?' I ask instead.

'I don't know. Yeah, I suppose so. But maybe if all this hadn't happened, I wouldn't have got there anyway. Or maybe I would, and I'd be like you in my twenties, changing my mind.'

I take a fry and dip it in ketchup, remember a time years ago when I bopped him on the nose with a ketchup-smeared fry, probably in this very same branch of McDonald's, and he didn't know whether to laugh or cry. 'Maybe,' I say, 'you just never know. Are there other things you've thought about doing?'

'Sport, you mean? Alan's found a wheelchair basketball team that I might try.'

I can't help but grin. 'And what about as a job?'

I don't expect him to have an answer for this, but he does. 'Maybe physio. You know, helping kids like me.'

It's such an honourable thing, this desire to pay it forward by going into a profession that has helped him. I reach out and take his hand across the table, and he doesn't shake me off. 'I think you'd be really good at that,' I say.

49

NOW (JULY 2014)

It's Priya who says it first. She's visiting her mum for the weekend and has called in at mine. So my mum has made her tea and grilled her about her life, and now we're up in my bedroom and it's like old times.

'So it's happened, this thing with Charlotte?' she asks.

We're sitting side by side on my bed, propped up with pillows. 'Yes, I mean, I think so. He told me he got drunk and slept with someone.'

'And you're just assuming it was her?'

'Yes. Wouldn't you? The dates work, for Isla's conception.'

'I think I'd want to be absolutely sure. Because then, if it has, there's nothing to stop you getting back together, is there?'

It stops me in my tracks, this. Because I'd just told myself this story about how he would be with her once they found out about the baby, and it would either explode or fizzle out at some point in the next couple of years, and then he and I would find our way back to each other. But it doesn't have to be like that, does it? Perhaps I've prepared myself unnecessarily for a year or two of this heartache. Like Priya says, we could get back together now. I think of Charlotte, finding out she's pregnant and knowing the father is in a relationship with someone else. Is that cruel?

'Ask him,' Priya says, picking up my phone and handing it to me, and it's like when we were teenagers and she'd threaten to call the boy I liked if I didn't just get on with it.

I find my WhatsApp conversation with Oliver. Like usual, it's a string of messages from him. Telling me what he's been doing, who he's seen. The auditions he's been on, how they went. I have to scroll back a long way to find a message from me, and it's the ones I sent after his confession about sleeping with someone. The ones where I told him it was okay. I type.

MADDY

Oliver?

The ticks turn blue absurdly fast and he's typing a reply:

OLIVER

Yes.

MADDY

The woman you slept with. Who was it?

A longer pause, this time. He starts typing, stops. Starts again.

OLIVER

Charlotte. My director.

Even though I knew, it still feels a bit like a knitting needle being plunged into my chest.

MADDY

And was it just a one-off, or is there still something there? I need you to be honest with me.

I'm waiting for a reply when my phone rings and Priya lets out a small scream.

'Who just calls?' she asks.

'Oliver,' I say, and then I answer.

'I thought this was more of a phone call conversation than a WhatsApp one,' he says.

And he's right. I know he's right. 'So?'

'It was a one-off,' he says. But it's clear there's more, so I wait. 'I think she wants it to be something more, but it just isn't, for me. She knows how I feel about you.'

'Must make things pretty awkward at work.'

'Yeah, well, not too bad. You know what acting's like. There are always people sleeping with each other, or not doing that but wanting to.'

He's right, it is like that. An image comes to me, unbidden, of Gavin. That smile he gave me when I left. 'But couldn't she make life difficult for you?'

'She could, but we've nearly finished the run, and besides, I don't think she will. She's not a bad person. She's just a lonely person, I think. And I was lonely too, and we're on tour, and it was a bad combination. Sorry, it's probably not great to hear this.'

I take a deep breath. 'I think I need to hear it,' I say. I turn to look at Priya, and she's sitting perfectly still. Not looking at me. Picking at a small scab on one of her fingers. 'I want...' I say, and then I break off because I don't know what I want. Or I do but I'm scared to say it.

'What?' Oliver asks.

'I want to come back, to London.'

'To the flat?' He sounds elated.

'I don't know yet. But maybe I could come back to London, live somewhere else for a while, and we could see how things go.'

'Yes,' Oliver says. 'Yes, I want to do that.'

I want to tell him it won't be straightforward. That at some point Charlotte is going to come to him and tell him that she's having his baby. That that won't scare me away. But it's impossible, of course. So I choke out something between a laugh and a sob and I tell him I'll start looking for rooms.

'I hope you find somewhere really shitty,' he says, and I laugh, and it feels a bit like how it used to feel between us.

But Priya's tugging on my sleeve, and I know she's going to tell me I can share her room for a few weeks. It feels good, to have a friend who would offer that.

'How's Henry?' Oliver asks before we end the call.

'Amazing. I saw him standing today. He's coming on so well.'

'That's great to hear. Tell him I'm looking forward to getting back to our swimming routine.'

'I will.' I finish the call and I know I have a stupid, goofy smile on my face and I know Priya will tease me about it.

'You look like you booked a holiday at Butlins and they upgraded you to the Maldives,' she says.

And that's a pretty accurate description of how I feel.

Later, over dinner, I tell Mum and Alan and Henry, and they all do that thing where they say they're happy for me but will be sorry to see me go. I'm careful not to say too much about Oliver, to not suggest we'll be getting back together, because I just don't know. Still, they're not stupid and they know that my feelings for him are sitting beneath this change, and they are pleased.

'Where will you live?' Mum asks.

'I think I'm going to share with Priya, while I find somewhere.'

'Isn't she in a house share? There won't be much room.'

'It won't be forever.' Sharing with Priya again makes me think about our old flat and I picture Mrs Aziz, and realise I haven't seen her for months, and I hope her spider plants are surviving. And that she is, too.

And then it's two days later and I'm on a train to London with as many of my things as I could carry. Mum said she'd bring the rest at the weekend, but I told her to wait until she was bringing Henry for swimming again. I have enough with me to get by, and it's not like I can take up a lot of space in Priya's room.

'Ta da,' Priya says, spreading her arms wide to show me the room that I've seen before, but not for a long time.

It's going to be cramped, but it's only temporary. I thank her for letting me share her bed and her room while my life is a mess. And she slaps my arm gently and says that both our lives are a mess, thank you very much. What I don't say, to her or anyone else, is that I'm hoping I'll go back to Oliver's as soon as possible. When Priya goes to make us some tea, I call him. I've lost track of where in the country he is, but I do know the tour is nearly over. When he answers, he sounds groggy.

'Sorry, did I wake you?'

'Hey, Maddy. Kind of. I'm on a train.'

'Where are you going?'

'I'm coming home. You're back in London, right?'

I hold my breath for a few seconds. 'I don't understand. Have the shows been cancelled?'

He laughs. 'No, we just have a night off, so I wanted to come to see you. I was only in Oxford. So, are you free tonight?'

Priya has talked about having a movie night. But I know she won't mind if we put it off until tomorrow, if Oliver's only back in town for one night. 'I'm free,' I say. 'Shall I come to the flat?'

By the time Priya brings the tea in, I've pulled half of my clothes out of my suitcase and I'm in a panic about what to wear. I try to tell myself it's Oliver, that he's seen me in my pyjamas and no makeup, in my gym clothes, in nothing at all.

'What's going on?'

'Oliver's coming back, just tonight. I said I'd go to the flat. And now I'm stressing.'

Priya rubs her hands together. She loves this kind of challenge. 'I'll do your nails while we decide what you're going to wear.'

We're halfway through my manicure when I ask about Nic. She hasn't mentioned him for a long time, and I'm painfully aware that her relationship was a lot longer than mine. That it's her breakup we should be focusing on. But she doesn't see it like that, because of the visions. Something's changed in her and she believes in them fully, now. So we both think we know that Oliver will be in my life in ten years' time, and Nic won't be in hers. She's surprisingly pragmatic, sometimes.

'We talk occasionally,' she says. 'It's hard to get out of the habit of wanting to tell each other everything, after so long. But it's morphed into friendship, mutual support. It's happened so quickly it makes me wonder why we were ever together in the first place.'

'Is he seeing anyone?' I ask.

'I think he's dating.'

'And are you?'

Priya pulls a face. 'It's so exhausting. I'm hoping to meet someone in real life, you know, like in the old days.'

I think about Josh, the guy who helped her move. Is he the one? Time will tell. 'I met Oliver in real life,' I remind her.

'So you did. And dressed as an elf to boot. What a meet cute. What time are you going over there?'

I look at my phone, realise that we've been sitting and talking for longer than I thought. 'Pretty much now.'

She leans in and kisses my cheek. 'Go get him back,' she says.

50

NOW (JULY 2014)

I don't use my key. It feels wrong. The lift's out of action so at the top of all the stairs, I take a minute to catch my breath, leaning against the wall, the way I did the first time I came here. And then I knock. Two knocks, one after another. No indication of the hesitancy I feel. I hear muffled footsteps and I can picture him walking down the hall, his phone or a mug of coffee in one hand.

'Hi,' he says.

'Hi.'

I follow him in and it feels immediately like coming home. And I want to just say, *Let's dispense with all the formalities. I'm back and I'm ready to move back in, and by the way, when the woman you slept with tells you she's pregnant, don't worry, that doesn't need to come between us.* What I say instead is: 'I could murder a glass of wine.'

Oliver smiles and his face creases in all the usual places, around his mouth and his eyes, and I think of the older Oliver, how I haven't seen him for a long time, how I've missed him.

'So how's touring?' I ask once we're settled on the sofa. Marjorie is ignoring me, presumably because I left, so she's curled in Oliver's lap and I'm at the other end of the sofa, and our feet are about an inch from touching.

'Tiring,' he says. 'You know when you hear rock stars talking about how they just go from plane to hotel to stadium and lose track of what day it is and what country they're in? It's just like that but with cheap coach travel and Premier Inns.'

I laugh. He's easy to laugh with. 'This thing with Charlotte...'

Oliver holds a hand up to stop me. 'It's nothing. It's done. I'm so sorry it happened, Maddy.'

But I shake my head. 'You don't have to keep apologising, Oliver. In fact, I'm the one who should be apologising, for leaving like that. I got scared.'

'And now? Are you scared now?'

I shake my head. 'No. I feel like maybe this was supposed to happen. Maybe we were supposed to have this time apart and it will mean we appreciate each other more in the future. I think it took you being with someone else to make me realise I can't bear for you to be with someone else.'

'I wish I could be more like you.'

'No. Really, you don't.' I pause for a moment before asking my next question. 'Does Charlotte know that I'm coming back? That I'm here with you now?'

'Absolutely,' he says. 'Total honesty from here on out, Maddy. She knows that I'm going to do everything in my power to get you back. And after this tour is finished, she'll be out of our lives forever. I promise you that.'

Ha. If only he knew. Charlotte will never be out of our lives, but that's okay because she's going to bring someone else into them. Someone wonderful.

'I've missed you,' I say. And I lean forward, move onto my knees, put my hands at either side of his body and move closer to him while being careful not to squash Marjorie. I kiss his cheek.

And when I move back, he puts a hand on the back of my neck and brings me closer again. Marjorie makes a disgruntled noise and jumps off his lap, and then there is nothing between us and he's pulling me onto him and kissing me properly, and there's a tiny part of me that is thinking about how it was with the two of them, with Charlotte, but I have to push it to one side. I have to. If this is going to work, if I'm going to get the life I've seen with this man, the life I want, I have to get past it. So in my mind, I push Charlotte out of the way, because I'm back. I'm what he wants, and we are both here, with an empty flat and hours and hours to fill.

51

TEN YEARS FROM NOW (JULY 2024)

Oliver's standing in front of me, miming opening a book.

'Book!' Isla shouts.

I turn to her, and she looks like she has new freckles, and her hair is half an inch longer, and she's wearing pyjamas that I haven't seen before. I feel tears prick my eyes at the sight of her, because I missed her. I missed her so much.

'Come on!' Oliver says, looking at me. He's holding up three fingers.

'Three words,' I say. 'First word... the?'

'Mum, you said you'd let me do the guessing and only help if I needed you to,' Isla says.

'Sorry, Isla.' I sit back, let her do the rest. It's *The Worst Witch*, and Isla punches the air when she guesses it and Oliver picks her up and spins her around.

'Your turn,' Oliver says, looking at me.

'Okay, let me think.' I stand up, turn so I'm facing them. They're on the sofa now, and they both have their elbows resting on their knees and their chins in their hands. I'm struck by how similar they are. Why couldn't I see it before? Or did I just not want to? Isla has Oliver's face shape, Charlotte's hair. Oliver's nose and eyebrows, Charlotte's eyes. There's nothing of me in there, and that's okay. Because she isn't mine in that biological way. But she's mine – as well as theirs – in every way that matters. She's a mix of all of us. She uses my phrases, she joins in with my hobbies. She's my girl. I draw a square in the air.

'TV!' Isla shouts. 'One word.'

I make an oinking noise, and Isla shouts: '*Peppa Pig!*'

'Ah, *Peppa*,' Oliver says. 'A classic of our time.'

'Shall we watch *Peppa*?' Isla asks, hopeful.

'No,' Oliver says. 'Because I'm going to run a bath, and then I'm going to dunk you in it headfirst, and then we'll wash your hair.'

Isla squeals and jumps up, runs away in the direction of her bedroom. He'll chase her while she removes her clothes, and when the bath is finished there'll be bubbles everywhere and at least three towels will be soaking wet. And I'll do my best not to moan, because it's all part of this happy childhood we're hopefully giving her. Three parents, though Oliver and I seem to be the ones she spends most of her time with. No siblings (yet), and a whole heap of love.

52

NOW (JULY 2014)

'I won't keep asking you to come back, because I know that would be annoying,' Oliver says. 'But please know that that's what I want.'

'Have you found anyone else for the room, in the meantime?' I ask.

He shakes his head. 'I've got some savings, so I'm going to just keep it open for now. But you should not consider that pressure.'

'Oliver,' I say.

'What?'

'Ask me to come back.'

He turns and our eyes meet, and he raises his eyebrows and I raise mine back in response. 'Will you come back, Maddy?'

'Yes,' I say. Sod waiting. Sod being sensible. This is where I want to be.

Oliver punches the air, and it's so similar to the gesture I just saw Isla make while playing charades that I can't help laughing.

'What will Priya say?' he asks.

'She'll probably be pleased that she doesn't have to share her tiny room with me and all my things.'

'Let's get dressed and go over there now, and bring your stuff back here.'

It isn't late. We could do that. But there's no need. It will all still be there, waiting to be transported, tomorrow. 'Or we could just stay in bed and I could bring a bottle of wine in and we could do that tomorrow.'

'Oh yes, yours is better. But can we have crisps, too?'

I get out of bed, pull his T-shirt on. 'Crisps coming up.'

I'm in the kitchen getting a bowl out of the cupboard when I hear him coming up behind me, and then his arms are around me and he's holding me so tightly I feel like it's hard to breathe.

'You won't leave again, will you?'

I see it from his perspective, then. He thinks I left him for no reason, probably sees me as a flight risk. How can I reassure him? Just by showing him, I suppose. By staying.

'I won't leave again,' I say, hoping he can trust me.

I bury my face in his neck, catch his familiar scent. There were nights, at Mum's, when I lay in bed trying to imagine this smell. It made me feel lonelier than I've ever been before. And now I'm here, and he's here, and I want to stay with him forever, and I might just be able to.

'It feels so right, being back here,' I say.

We go back to bed and Oliver puts on some music and we fill each other in on what we've missed of one another's lives. He's been messaging me throughout, of course, but he's still full of stories about the play and about an audition he has lined up for a drama series, and I tell him about Henry and the progress he's making, and little stories from my time at Mum's that make him smile.

'I wish we never had to leave this bed,' he says.

And I know what he means. It's warm and cosy and we're on our second bottle of wine and our second bowl of crisps and I know he's going to kiss me soon, and I'll take off his T-shirt and lose myself in his body, and in the future, for a while.

'I've been thinking about something,' I say.

He is propped up on one elbow, looking at me intently. All ears.

'I think it might be over for me. The acting.'

His face runs through a range of emotions. Shock, confusion, sadness. 'Why?'

'It isn't making me happy. When I first started, when I was doing drama at school as a teenager, I loved that rush I got from being up on stage and knowing people were listening to what I was going to say. It made me feel powerful, and there was something so satisfying about interpreting people's stories, giving them a voice. I remember going home and saying to Mum that I never wanted to do anything else my whole life. And at some point, I've lost touch with that. Now it's all about money, and whether something will pay the rent, and it's really sucked all the joy out of it, for me.'

He nods, and I can see that he's listening but that the words I'm saying make no sense to him.

'I think it's different for you,' I say. 'I think you love it in a different way. And I think you'll stick with it as a career and make it work, but me? I think I might be happier if I concentrated on doing something else to make the money and just joined an am-dram group to get that kick I get from performing.'

'You're too good for that,' Oliver says, reaching across the distance between us and tapping the fingers of one hand on my hip. It feels good. Reminds me that I'm here, that I'm a solid thing.

'I don't think it's about being good, I think it's about doing the thing that will make you most happy.'

He considers this. 'Have you thought about what you'll do instead?'

I have. Of course I have. But I haven't said it out loud yet, to anyone. And I haven't worked out whether it's come to me because it's what I've seen in the visions, or whether it's just the right thing. 'I want to write,' I say. 'Not copywriting, though I'll do that to pay the bills, of course. I want to write scripts. TV shows.'

'I could see you being really good at that,' Oliver says. 'I couldn't imagine you doing a nine to five in an office.'

I shudder. 'No, me neither.' And I'm grateful that he doesn't say anything about how competitive that world must be, how I'm talking about potentially moving from one impossible dream to another.

'You know, when you were away, I watched your *Summing Up* episodes. You really inhabited that character and commanded attention. I was looking at you and no one else every time you were on the screen.'

'That's just because you like me,' I say, but I'm secretly pleased.

He lets his tapping fingers come to rest and then he pulls me towards him until there's no gap between our naked bodies. 'I do like you,' he says. He moves his mouth to my ear. 'I like you very much.'

53

TEN YEARS FROM NOW (JULY 2024)

My phone rings and I see Henry's name on the screen and feel so pleased. That glimpse I caught of my grown-up brother has stayed with me, and I'm excited to talk to him again.

'Hey, Maddy,' he says, and his voice is steady but there's something in the tone that makes me sit up, something that tells me this isn't going to be a carefree chat between siblings.

'Is everything okay, Henry?'

'How do you do that? How do you always know?'

I feel a coldness, like a sliver of ice tracking down my throat and into my intestines. I feel like I've swallowed snow. But I know it isn't something really terrible, because if it was, he would have said it by now. There would be no talking around the subject. 'What is it?'

Oliver looks over. He's muted the TV and he can hear in my voice that this is one of those calls.

'I'm staying with Mum and Dad for a few days and I'm kind of worried about Mum,' Henry says. 'Dad thinks I'm being overly protective or some shit but she's been having these headaches and she's kind of different in really tiny ways. I'm not explaining this well.'

'Has she been to see the GP?' I ask, because I have to get as far as I can with this before I disappear back into my present.

'Yes, and they're sending her for some tests.'

'For what? What do they think it might be?'

He says nothing and I imagine him, there in our mother's house, in his old bedroom with the door closed so they can't hear what he's saying. Does he feel lonely? Should I go to him? And how can I, when I have no control over how long I'll be here in this future? 'If she knows, she hasn't said anything.'

'So what about Alan? Isn't he worried?'

'You know what he's like. He thinks it will be nothing and we'll all have been worrying for no reason. He's always so optimistic.'

Henry's right. It's one of the things we both love about Alan. His ability to always find a bright side.

'I have to go,' he says, and I want to say no, to beg him to stay on the phone. Not to sever this weak connection between the two of us.

'Will you keep me updated?' I ask. 'Text or call or whatever. Anytime.'

'You know I will,' he says, and then he's gone, without a proper goodbye, and it feels ominous.

'What?' Oliver asks, his eyes full of worry.

'I'm not sure. It's Mum. Headaches and... I don't know what else. Henry just thinks she's not quite right.'

'Do you want to go there? In the morning?'

Do I? She hasn't had the tests yet and she might be cross with Henry for involving me. 'No, but I might go with Isla at the weekend. You too, if you want to.'

'Isla's with Charlotte this weekend, remember? We can't mess with it. She hasn't seen her for weeks.'

'Of course. I'm all over the place. Anyway, it might be nothing. Alan thinks it's nothing.'

Oliver nods but doesn't speak. And I feel like, somehow, we both know that it isn't nothing. That it's very much something.

54

'So I'm guessing things went pretty well with Oliver,' Priya says.

I realise I didn't message her to say I wasn't coming back to hers last night. 'I'm sorry. You didn't wait up?'

'All night like a worried mother,' she says, before bursting into laughter. 'Don't worry, I knew I wouldn't see you again until the morning.'

'Even though I was adamant you would?'

'Sometimes I know you better than you know yourself. So tell me, are you back together?'

I look down at my feet, then back up and she's peering at me intently, eager and hopeful. We've talked about being single at the same time, about how great it will be, how much time we'll have for each other, but she doesn't want that for me. She wants this. 'Yes. And – I know it's quick, but I'm going to move back in.'

'Thank god.'

I sit down on her bed and look around. There isn't much to pack, since I didn't really unpack, but still, the thought of gathering my things and getting them over to Oliver's flat – our flat –

is daunting. I should be feeling light, but I can't stop thinking about that vision, that phone call with Henry.

'Can I tell you something?' I ask.

Priya looks at me, confused. Because I tell her everything. Always have. 'Er, yes please.'

'I had this vision last night, and it really scared me. I got a call from Henry, and he was worried about Mum, about her health.'

'Why? Had something happened?'

'He said she was having headaches and that she just wasn't quite herself. It sounds like nothing, I know. But the fact that he called me about it. And he just sounded so scared, like he knew it was going to be something serious.'

Priya looks at a loss, and I don't blame her. How do you comfort your friend who has just heard that there might be something wrong with her mum ten years in the future? 'How old will she be, in ten years?'

'Sixty-four. Not so old, right?'

'I mean, it could be anything, Maddy. Or it could be nothing. I guess you'll find out.'

'Through the visions?'

'Yes, or failing that, when the time comes.'

'I've been wishing for so long that I didn't have them, that this didn't happen to me. But now, I feel like I need to know what's coming.'

'None of the rest of us know what's coming,' she says. And she's right. Of course she's right. Other people cope with not knowing how things are going to pan out.

We are quiet, thinking.

'Do you know what I think?' Priya asks after a long pause.

'What do you think?'

'I think you need to tell someone else about the visions. Maybe Oliver. It's been so many years that only we've known, and we haven't really got anywhere in terms of working out whether it's real or whether it's possible to stop it from happening.'

I feel like I'm standing on sand, and it's shifting. 'I don't want to tell Oliver.' I can't explain it, but I feel sure it would change things between us. I don't know whether he'd believe it, for a start. And I don't want him to be worrying, every time we have sex, about what I'm seeing. But there's something in this suggestion about telling someone else. And I have an idea, then. I stand up and go to the door.

'Where are you going? Aren't you supposed to be getting your stuff together?'

'I need to go and see someone. I'll be back in an hour or two. Is that okay?'

'Of course.' Priya doesn't ask who I'm going to see and I wonder whether she knows. I doubt it. I think she just respects my privacy, knows that I'll tell her when I'm ready.

Outside, the air is a little chilly for the first time in days. I walk the unfamiliar path from Priya's new flat back to our old one, and then I press on Mrs Aziz's buzzer for a good five seconds, willing her to be there.

She is. 'Maddy who?' she asks through the crackly buzzer. Then she laughs. 'Just joking, dear. Come on up.'

At the door, she hands me her little watering can. 'The spider plants have missed you.'

The plants all look to be in good health, which suggests that she manages to water them just fine when I'm not around. 'I'm sorry it's been so long. I went back to live with my mum for a while.'

'Oh?'

'Bump in the road, with Oliver.'

'And how are things now?'

'Back on track.'

She smiles, but it fades quickly. 'So why are you anxious, if things are good?'

I put down the plant pot I'm holding, turn to face her. 'How can you tell?'

'The way you're holding yourself. Lots of tension in your shoulders. What's happening? Shall I make tea?'

I finish watering the plants while she makes the drinks, and then we sit down on her soft sofa, the one I always wonder how I'm going to get back up from. 'There's this thing that happens to me, that's been happening to me for years now, and I don't know what to do about it.'

While I tell her, she doesn't say a word. I'm hoping she'll step in when I'm fumbling over the mechanics of it all, trying to avoid saying the word 'sex', but she doesn't, and I'm forced to say it, and her face doesn't change one bit. I keep it simple, not going into the whole saga with Isla and Charlotte. And when I've finished, she does a couple of quick nods and it's clear that she's thinking it all through. I'm relieved that she hasn't dismissed me out of hand or accused me of lying.

'Do you believe me?' I ask.

She tilts her head slightly to one side. 'Believe you? But of course. Why would you make something like this up?'

'It's just so outlandish. I'm not sure I'd believe it if it wasn't me it was happening to.'

'My dear,' she says, reaching out and covering my hand with her smaller one. 'I have lived on this earth for eighty-one years, and do you know what I've learned?'

I shake my head.

'That there is more going on than we could possibly know or see in our lifetime. This thing you've described, these visions, I've never heard of anything like it, but that doesn't mean I doubt that it's true. You have to keep your mind open' – she taps the side of her head with one finger – 'if you want to keep up with this world.'

It's quite the speech, and I mull it all over. I'm more the type to believe something when I've seen evidence of it, but I like the sound of her approach. I make a mental note to try being more open-minded about things. 'Thank you,' I say, realising that it means a lot to me, to be believed. I've shared this extraordinary thing with two people in my life, and both of them have taken me at my word.

'So the question is, why are you telling me? What are you hoping to achieve?'

'I want to stop it,' I say. 'Or I did. But then last night, in a vision, my brother called and said he was worried about our mum, about some headaches she'd been having. And now I feel like I need to know what's happening with that. So I'm not so sure any more. Not that I know how to stop it, even if I was.'

We both reach for our mugs and drink our tea.

'There must be an answer,' Mrs Aziz says. 'But I don't know what it is.'

'That's okay, I wasn't expecting you to. It just feels good to talk about it to someone else. Priya is the only other person I've ever told, and sometimes I feel like it's a lot for her to carry, you know? I hope you don't mind me burdening you.'

'Being let into someone's confidence is never a burden,' she says.

And I think, not for the first time, that I could imagine some of the things she says printed on signs and tea towels. She's so effortlessly wise.

'It seems to me,' she goes on, 'that all of this has made you believe you can keep a tight rein on love, and in my experience, that's not possible.'

'What do you mean?'

'Well, my husband and I, we loved each other very much, and we wanted to have children, but that wasn't on the cards for us, and then he died when he was still quite young. I couldn't control any of that, but I don't regret any of the choices I made. It might be that if I'd married someone else, I'd have been able to be a mother, and I might have had a companion with me in my old age, but that isn't how it worked out. These visions you have of the future, they give you an element of control, or at least an illusion of it. But that only stretches so far, I believe, and that's something you have to come to terms with.'

I leave soon after that, thanking her for both the tea and the company. For listening. And on the walk back to Priya's, I think hard about everything she said. I have felt like I'm in control of my future, to an extent. The thought of letting go of that is terrifying, but it's appealing, too.

'I'm making soup,' Priya says. 'And then I need to go to the hospital. Are you going to tell me where you've been?'

'I had to tell someone,' I say, pulling off my shoes in the hallway.

'About the visions? Who?'

'Mrs Aziz.'

Priya gives me a puzzled look. 'And did she have any words of wisdom?'

'Lots, actually, but I still don't know what I need to do.'

'Maybe you don't need to do anything. Maybe it will always happen, and you'll just learn to live with it. You've lived with it so far.'

This is true, but only because I avoided romantic love for so long. Now that Oliver and I are back together and I hope and believe it's for good, I feel like it's getting on top of me. I feel like I need to find a way to make it stop.

We eat tomato soup and I keep mulling it over, getting nowhere. Afterwards, Priya dashes off and I pack up my things and call Oliver, who's offered to bring the car over to transport them back to the flat.

'Is this everything?' he asks, gesturing to the case and the bags cluttering the hallway.

'That's it,' I say.

He comes to where I'm standing, kisses the top of my head. 'Then let's get you home.'

We're in the car when it comes to me. An idea, one I haven't had before. One that might stop the visions. I just have to work up the courage to try it.

55

TEN YEARS FROM NOW (AUGUST 2024)

'Hi, love.'

Mum's voice sounds normal, but I wish I was in the same room with her, and could see her face. I don't know what I was expecting. I can't tell her that Henry called me, that he's worried about her. So I just ask her how she is and hope for the best.

'Everything's okay here. How are you three?'

I like that Oliver and Isla and I are an 'us three'. I don't like that I can't answer the question in any detail. 'We're good.'

'Come to see us soon, won't you? I've missed my girls.'

It strikes me for the first time that Isla not being mine means she's not really Mum's, either. But it doesn't sound like it matters to Mum. She sounds like a proud grandmother.

'Thanks for everything you do for all of us,' I say.

'Where did that come from?'

'I just don't say it enough. We love you. Now, you're sure you're all right? Nothing to report?'

She goes quiet for a moment, and then her voice is back and it's different, a little tighter. 'Have you been talking to Henry?'

'No.' I wait a beat. 'I mean yes. I'm sorry, Mum. He was worried. Did he have a reason to be?'

There's a pause that feels unending. 'I need to have some tests. I've been having a lot of headaches, and my memory's not been great.'

I feel like my heart is plummeting from my chest to my gut. 'Mum,' I say.

Because we both know what this kind of thing means, don't we?

'Let's just wait and see what happens,' she says. 'Try not to worry. Okay?'

'Will you tell me what's going on from now?'

'I will. I promise.'

And I'm gone before we say goodbye.

56

TEN YEARS FROM NOW (SEPTEMBER 2024)

Isla and I are snuggled up on the sofa, and she's giggling because Marjorie is lying on her arm and it's gone numb.

'Pins and needles?' I ask.

'Pens and noodles,' she says between laughs.

It must be something we say. I'm glad that we have in-jokes, that we are bonded that way. I look at the clock, and it's coming up for nine. It's a weekend, but it's definitely time this one was going to bed. I don't want her to, though. Because any of these times could be the last time. I lean in towards her and smell the top of her head, and it's so intoxicating I feel like I could live off that scent alone for years and years in the wilderness.

'Why are you sniffing me?' she asks, finally pulling her arm free.

Marjorie makes her grumpy noise, the one she makes when we're moving or otherwise disturbing her. She stands up, turns around and sits back down again.

'It's one of my favourite things to do.'

'Sniffing me? You're so weird.'

There's the sound of a flush and Oliver comes into the room. 'I think it's time for bed for someone.'

'You?' Isla asks, and then she starts laughing as he lunges for her and tickles her ribs.

'Do you want a bath?' I ask.

'Isn't it a bit late?' Oliver checks his watch.

And it is. It is late but I can't let go of her. I can't say goodbye.

'Bath,' Isla says, seizing on this chance to put bedtime off for another twenty minutes. Oliver shrugs and I go into the bathroom and turn the taps on and watch her fling her clothes around, study her perfect body. Her skin, milky and unblemished.

'Come here.' I hold out my arms and she barrels into them, and then I'm gone.

57

TEN YEARS FROM NOW (OCTOBER 2024)

'Another glass?' Oliver asks, gesturing to my wine glass with his head.

'Why not?' We're in a restaurant, and I think it's the Greek one just down the street from mine and Priya's old flat. She and I used to come here a lot, sometimes with Nic. I wonder whether it was me who suggested it, whether it's somewhere Oliver and I have been before. I remember how good the spanakopita is here and my mouth instantly fills with saliva. I hope that's what I've ordered.

'Anyway, I think she'd be fine on a long flight now, don't you?'

Isla. A long flight. 'Yes, I'm sure she would.'

'So shall we start looking?'

Where is he proposing we take her? Asia, Africa, America? I don't really care, as long as it's me and him and her. 'Let's do it.'

I could tell him now. I could put an end to this, or at least I think I could. Ever since I realised what I needed to do, I haven't been able to. Because in my visions I haven't been on my own with Oliver. But now, he's here and I'm here and there's no one else around and I could just say it. Whisper it in his ear or stand up and shout it across the restaurant. I really don't think it would matter, because I think it's just the admitting of it that will make it stop. But I don't, because it isn't only Isla I'll miss, and the grownup version of Henry. It's this version of Oliver too. This older, more confident man, who knows what he wants and has mostly got it. The one who doesn't have to teach kids to swim any more to pay the rent, but probably would, if anyone asked him to. I want to soak him up for another few minutes. It's like when you're wrapped up in your duvet when the alarm goes off on a frosty winter morning, and you keep telling yourself you'll get up in another minute, or another five. And then the decision's taken out of my hands, because I'm gone.

58

NOW (NOVEMBER 2014)

'How do you know?' Priya asks. She looks unconvinced.

'I don't know. It just sort of came to me a few months ago and I feel like I know it's going to work.'

'A few months ago? So why haven't you done it already?'

There's no good answer to this. 'I'm scared to. I know I want it to stop but it's terrifying, too. I won't see that version of Isla again for years. But I think I'm ready now.'

'So you're just going to tell Oliver that you're visiting the future while it's happening. That's it?'

'That's it.'

A woman in the row in front of us turns around and glares. She might as well have shushed us. We're at Oliver's final show. The tour's done and they've come back to the theatre where they started for three last shows. Priya was supposed to see it ages ago, with Nic, but he had the tickets and there was no way she was going to ask him for them. Oliver's shattered, and I'll be glad to properly have him back when tonight is over. When the woman's turned back to face the front, I cross my eyes at Priya and she smiles but manages not to laugh out loud. And then Oliver shuffles onto the stage, and it begins.

Afterwards, we're standing at the bar downstairs, waiting for the cast to appear. Most nights, they stop for a drink after the show but tonight is likely to be a big one. There's an area reserved, and Priya and I are on the guest list, but for now we're waiting.

'Don't take this the wrong way, but I didn't realise he'd be so good,' Priya says.

And I know what she means. Oliver lifts this whole production, and each time I've seen it, it's become more and more clear that he's going to make it, that this will be one of those things he talks about doing in the early days. The other cast members will dine out on the fact that they played opposite Oliver Swanson before he was famous. 'I know,' I say. 'He's just got it, hasn't he?'

'You have too,' she says, but it isn't true. I don't pick her up on it. She's just being a friend. 'So, are you going to do it tonight?'

'I think so.' I consider not seeing the future versions of Oliver or Priya or Henry again, not until we get to that part of our lives. It doesn't feel real.

In less than a year, I'll meet Isla for the first time. I'll get to meet all the other iterations of her. Baby Isla, toddler Isla, first day of school Isla. I can't wait.

'Yes. Tonight,' I say, and I don't know whether I'm trying to convince her or myself.

It's then that Oliver appears, throws his arms wide and puts one around each of us.

'I was just telling Maddy that I thought you were a bit shit,' Priya says, and Oliver grins. He knows it was a triumph.

'I told her you're doing your best,' I say.

'All anyone can do,' he says.

And then I hug him properly and whisper in his ear that he

was brilliant, the best I've ever seen him, and he squeezes me tightly in response. We go into the area that's been sectioned off, and the drinks start flowing. Everyone from the cast and crew is on a high, and they're all offering to do rounds, coming over with trays of shots, refusing to take no for an answer. We're several drinks deep when Charlotte comes over to where Oliver, Priya and I are standing. I can just about make out a bump, but I don't think you'd notice if you weren't looking for it. I've been wondering for a while when she's going to come out with it.

'I have something to tell you,' she says to Oliver, not acknowledging Priya and me.

'Okay,' Oliver says.

And, my god, is she going to do it here? Like this? Priya and I exchange slightly frantic looks and I think about taking her off somewhere and letting them have this moment in private, but I can't do it. I need to know.

'I'm pregnant,' Charlotte says. No messing around, no easing in.

Oliver doesn't connect the dots at first. It only happened once, after all. And he's told me she's seeing someone now. Some guy who does lighting. Oliver's expression runs through surprise and confusion and then he settles on happy. 'Wow, that's... wow. Congratulations.'

Does he wonder why she's telling him? They are not friends. Charlotte is enjoying her moment. She thinks she's about to break us apart. I have to wonder why. Does she want him for herself or does she just want to drop a bomb on our relationship and see what happens? Either way, it says a lot about the kind of person she is. If I had a say in any of this, I wouldn't choose her to be Isla's mother. I'd choose me, wouldn't I? But I don't, so I wait, holding Oliver's hand, ready for her next move.

'The baby's yours,' Charlotte says, and then she just stands there, her arms folded across her chest, and I don't want to hate her, but I sort of do.

I feel Oliver's fingers go limp but I don't let go of his hand. I want him to know from the very outset that this isn't a disaster.

'Mine?'

'Yours.'

Priya mutters something about going to the loo and disappears, and I can't blame her. There are only two people who should be in on this conversation, and neither of them are her or me. But I do have slightly more reason to be invested. I look at Oliver, and I can see he is totally at a loss.

'Why are you telling me this now?' he asks.

Charlotte shrugs, looks from him to me. 'Good a time as any. Sorry if I've spoiled your night.'

'You haven't,' I say, because I want to do something to support him. 'I know about what happened between you. Obviously this is unexpected, but we're all adults. We'll sort it out.'

'I'm not getting rid of it,' Charlotte says, 'if that's what you mean by sorting it out.'

It's me and her now, Oliver just watching on. 'It isn't.'

'Jesus Christ, Charlotte,' Oliver says, rubbing the back of his neck. 'How could you think this was an appropriate time to tell me this?'

'I waited until the last show was over,' she says. 'And then I didn't want to wait any more.'

She turns and walks off in the direction of the bar, leaving Oliver and me standing in the same place we were in ten minutes ago, but also in a different world. I remind myself that I've had time to adjust to this, and he hasn't. I remind myself that he's currently convinced he doesn't want to be a dad.

'I mean it,' I say. 'We'll work this out.'

He sets his jaw in a grim line, and when he speaks again, he sounds completely sober. 'Let's go home.'

I find Priya and tell her we're going, and she gives me a quick hug and wishes me luck. On our way out, I make sure to grab hold of Oliver's hand. I don't know where she is, but I know Charlotte will be watching us.

Back at the flat, I make cups of tea for something to do. I feel sure it's going to be a long night and we won't be going to bed anytime soon. When I take them through, Oliver's pacing the living room.

'I slept with her *once*,' he says, as if he's trying to convince himself. 'You believe that, right?'

'I do,' I say.

He looks at me, confused. 'Why aren't you freaking out about this? This isn't anyone's dream situation, is it? We've literally just got back together and now another woman is having my baby. What will we tell people?'

Frankly, I don't care what we tell people. I don't care what people think. But that's because I've had the benefit of seeing how it all pans out. Seeing how wonderful our lives are with Isla in them. 'I think that life doesn't always go the way you thought it might. Take Henry. One day – one moment – and his whole life changed. And now we're looking at a different situation to the one we thought we were looking at earlier today. Now there's going to be a baby. But I don't think we should assume that's going to be a bad thing.'

'I've never wanted this. You know that. And if I did want it, it would be with you.'

My heart cracks the tiniest amount when he says that. And I decide, there and then, to try for a baby with him in the future, when he suggests it. 'Things happen.'

Oliver comes over to me, where I'm sitting on the sofa, and sits down beside me, gathers me up in his arms. 'How did I get to be with you, Maddy? How did I get so lucky?'

I don't answer that, because I don't really know. I'm just glad we've ended up here, even if we've taken quite a circuitous route and have a lot of bumpy road ahead. Marjorie comes over to us and nudges my foot with her nose, which means she's hungry. 'I'll feed her. Do you want anything?'

'To go back in time?' Oliver says.

To go back in time. If only he knew, that I've been going forward in time. That I know what's coming. I'll have to paint him a picture, I think, as I empty a pouch of salmon food into Marjorie's bowl. Through the kitchen window, I can see the moon, full and round. No stars. That's London for you. At Mum's, the sky was always sprinkled with them. I think Oliver might be asleep when I go back to him. He's curled in on himself, his eyes almost closed. I know what I need to say to him, but not how.

'You know,' I start, and he looks up, his face pale and handsome, 'this doesn't have to be a bad thing. I know you think you don't want to have a child, but you might feel entirely differently in a year. You might wonder what you ever did without her.'

His head snaps up. 'Her?'

'Or him, of course.' I feel like my heartbeat is sounding out her name, and he'll hear it. Is-la, Is-la, Is-la. 'I'll be here. We'll manage. And as for what we tell people, let's just let them talk. We'll explain it to our parents and our closest friends, and everyone else can just piece it together.'

'They'll think I'm the worst guy in the world.'

I shrug. 'Let them. I know you're not.'

'I think I need to go to bed,' he says. 'The show and this news, it's exhausted me. Can we go to bed?'

I remember saying to Priya earlier that I would tell him

tonight. The thought of us having sex now is laughable. But perhaps in the morning. It will be Saturday, and we don't have any plans, and I know Oliver will get up first and bring us both coffee, and if I ask him to, he'll go out for croissants that we can eat in bed, flaky pastry falling on the covers.

'Yes,' I say. 'We can go to bed.'

59

TEN YEARS FROM NOW (NOVEMBER 2024)

I'm in a car. Oliver's driving. I look across at him, wondering how he'll react when I do this. When I say this thing I've never said to him, this crazy thing that I know he'll find so hard to believe. Rain lashes hard against the windscreen. There's a song playing loud and Oliver's singing along, and then he looks at me and grins, reaches across and puts a hand on my belly.

'You okay, baby?'

And I don't know whether he's talking to me or whether he knows something I don't. I look down to where his hand is. 'Oliver,' I say.

'Yes?'

'You're going too fast.' He is. He always drives fast but in this weather, on a motorway, it's scary. He touches the brake and we slow down a bit.

'Sorry.'

I see a sign and realise we're on our way to my parents'. I close my eyes briefly, will myself to say it. I can't carry on like this, living in two lives simultaneously. I need to stay where I belong, in the present. I'll have to find out what happens in the future when I get there, like everyone else does. I think about Mum, about how we might find her when we get to the end of this journey. But I won't be here to see it.

'I need to tell you something,' I say.

He looks over, fast, and the car lurches to the side and someone beeps, long and loud. He can tell it's something big. 'What is it? Is it the baby?'

So there is a baby. I swallow, feeling like there's a stone lodged in my throat. Tears spring to my eyes. I will hold this knowledge tight, while I wait to get here.

'No, nothing like that. It's strange, really. Hard to know how to explain it. There's this thing that happens to me, where I see visions of the future, and I'm in one right now. For me, it's really 2014, and...'

He's frowning, glancing back and forth between the road and my face, and I see that I shouldn't have done this now, that I should have waited until we were somewhere safe, because the rain is coming down hard and I see before he does that all the cars ahead of us have their brake lights on. And then it all bursts, like a bubble popping.

60

NOW (NOVEMBER 2014)

It isn't until Oliver pulls away from me and looks at me with concern that I realise I'm crying. And it's like a flood. The tears won't stop.

'Maddy, what is it?'

'God, I'm sorry, it's nothing, it's...'

'Is it about Charlotte? The baby?'

It isn't, of course, but I can't explain it and this seems like a reasonable excuse. 'I guess so. It's just a lot, you know?'

'Believe me, I know.' He gets out of bed, and the sun streams through a gap in the blinds, bathing his naked body. And then he's gone, and I hear the water in the shower.

I go in straight after him. Mum and Henry are due in half an hour.

'We won't say anything to them, right?' Oliver asks.

I'm getting dressed and he's brought us both a coffee. 'No, of course not. I mean, we'll have to eventually, but not yet.'

He runs a hand through his hair. There's a sort of manic energy to him.

'How are you feeling this morning?' I ask.

'Shellshocked.'

'Do you want me to make up some excuse, about the swimming? I can say the pool's out of action and we only found out at the last minute. And then I can take them out for brunch and you can stay here?'

Oliver crosses the room and cradles my head in his hands. 'No, we're good. Swimming with Henry will take my mind off things.'

I tell him I need ten minutes, some fresh air, and I grab my coat and my phone. On the street, I call Priya, and I'm crying again as soon as she answers.

'How did it go with the baby stuff?'

'I told him,' I say, trying to hold in sobs.

'About the visions?'

'Yes, this morning, while I was in one. And it stopped it.'

'Well, isn't that good news? Isn't that what you wanted?'

I wish she was with me and I could look in her eyes. She always calms me, and I feel frantic, untethered. 'We were in a car, Priya, and he was driving too fast, and then I told him and he was distracted and I think...'

'What? You think you crashed?'

'I think so. But I don't know because it stopped. I don't know whether it stopped because of what I said or whether something happened and he's...' I can't finish, but Priya knows what I'm saying.

'Oh god.'

'What shall I do?' But as soon as I ask the question, I know the answer. I have to have sex with him again, see whether I've really stopped the visions for good. If I haven't, then at least I'll know that future Oliver is safe. If I have... Well, I'll have to deal with that when it happens.

'Hold on,' Priya says. 'Now that you know, you can make sure the crash doesn't happen, when you get to it. Just make sure neither of you are in a car that day.'

Is she right? Or would it just happen in a different way, if it was going to happen? I'll never know whether I made sure Isla was conceived or if she would have been conceived no matter what I did. 'Maybe.'

I tell her that I have to go, that I can see Mum's car turning onto our street, and she tells me to take care, to call her if I need to.

Soon after, Mum and I wave Oliver and Henry off and go into the kitchen. I'm trying to act normal while inside I feel like I'm being ripped in two. I know that Mum can tell.

'How are things, with you and Oliver?' she asks.

How can I answer this? Oliver's having a baby and not with me. Oh, and he might die in a car accident in ten years' time. And then a new thought hits me. What if it isn't him who dies in the crash, but me?

'He's the one,' I say, and it's the truest thing I've ever said.

Mum narrows her eyes slightly. 'I hope you're right, but remember you haven't had much experience.'

As if I could forget. 'When you know, you know.'

'You know it won't all be easy, don't you? Even if it's the right person, you'll still face challenges along the way.'

'I know.' Don't I know.

I want to tell her I don't know how long we have, because there are things lurking in our futures that I've seen glimpses of. Me and Oliver. Me and her.

'Are you staying for lunch?' I ask, hoping she'll say no. I need to get to the bottom of things.

'No, I think we'll get back. Alan wants to take Henry to the cinema this afternoon. Listen, Maddy, are you okay?'

I am not okay. I'm not. But I can't tell her why, so I give her a weak smile and pretend I am.

And soon Oliver and Henry are back, coming through the door in the middle of an enthusiastic conversation about Marvel superheroes, Henry laughing in a way that makes him seem younger than he is.

'Good swim?' I ask.

'Great swim,' Oliver says. He ruffles Henry's hair and Henry grins and there's something in that small gesture that makes me feel so sure. This is my man, in front of me. Perhaps we don't have decades, but we have years, and we'll make the best of them.

'Right, we'll get off,' Mum says. 'See you both soon.'

'Sure thing,' Oliver says.

Mum leaves Henry for a moment and goes over to Oliver, gives him a hug. 'I hope you know what this means to us. All of us.'

He looks taken aback, but he hugs her in return, and I just hope all this goodwill will go in his favour, when we have to tell them another woman is having his baby.

My phone buzzes with a message from Priya:

PRIYA
So? Do you know more yet?

MADDY
Not yet. I'll call you tonight.

PRIYA
I'll let you know when I'm home. I have a date.
It's that guy Josh who helped me move.
Remember? I ran into him in Tesco.

I stare at my phone, a small smile breaking across my face,

despite everything. I tell her I do remember, but I don't say anything else, because I don't want to spoil this for her by letting her in on the way it's going to go.

When Oliver comes to sit beside me on the sofa, I reach for him, kiss him. I have to know.

'Maddy Hart, are you trying to seduce me?' he asks.

I push back tears. Nod. Pull him into the bedroom. He's gentle, careful, taking his time, and I feel like I might just disappear, just melt into particles and sink into the floor. 'I love you,' I say, and he kisses my eyelids and then he's inside me and... nothing. Not nothing; sex, sweet and slow. But no vision. No future.

Afterwards, we lie in each other's arms, and I feel a long way away from him.

'If there was anything I could do to change the way things are, I would,' Oliver says.

He thinks all of this is about Charlotte and the baby. 'I know you would.' *And I wouldn't want you to*, I think.

He sits up, then. 'I was up in the night,' he says, and it's news to me. I passed out and slept like a log until this morning. 'And I was thinking. And all the time I was out with Henry today, I was thinking. I love you, Maddy. And I can't pretend to fully understand why you're being so amazingly chill about what's happening, but I appreciate it so much. I can't think of anyone else I know who would react like this. And that made me realise that I can't think of anyone else I know who I like as much as you.'

'Well, I like you too, Oliver Swanson.'

'Maybe this isn't the best way to do this. The right way. But it's my way. I want to show you how much it means to me that you're sticking by me.'

It hits me, what he's going to do, and I feel a warmth gush through my body, starting at my toes and working its way up to my face, which I'm sure is flushed. And then it's chased by a cold wash of sadness. I sit up too. Reach for his face, stroke his cheek. 'Oliver.'

He shakes his head at me, as if to say 'no interruptions'. I guess it will be my turn to speak soon enough. 'Maddy, will you marry me?'

He doesn't have a ring. Of course he doesn't. He only thought about this last night. And all I can think, in the seconds after he gets those words out, is that I don't know whether I was married to him, in the visions. I don't know whether I wore a ring. Why did I never check that? It makes me feel panicky, like I don't know what the right decision is without being able to see it play out. And then I check myself. I do know the right decision. I know because of the way I feel, the way this man makes me feel.

'Yes.'

He throws his arms around me. And I'm laughing, and he's laughing, and I think we might be crying, too. I close my eyes, bite my lip, try to unsee the lashing rain, the slowing cars.

'In ten years from now,' I say, and I'm not sure whether I'm planning to tell him, but the words get stuck in my throat.

'We'll be married,' he says. 'Happy.'

He doesn't need to know. It's bad enough that it's hanging over me. 'You'll have a nine-year-old daughter.'

'We will.'

It means everything, that inclusion. I think of Isla, of the way her hair falls into her eyes when she runs and the way she gets the words asparagus and avocado mixed up. I ache to hug her, but I know I just have to wait. And in the meantime, there's so much to enjoy.

* * *

MORE FROM LAURA PEARSON

Another book from Laura Pearson, *The Beforelife of Eliza Valentine* is available to order now here:

www.mybook.to/BeforelifeBackAd

ACKNOWLEDGEMENTS

I am so thankful to my agent, Jo Williamson, my editor, Isobel Akenhead, and the whole team at Boldwood Books for everything you do for me and my novels.

Huge thanks to Le'anne Lory and Hayley Hodgson, occupational therapists who answered some questions for me about Henry's injury and recovery. And to Mandy Berriman, who has personal experience of spinal injury in a child and was so generous with her time and advice. To Emily Plumtree and Mia Pickett, for their expertise in acting. Any mistakes in these areas are my own.

Thank you to the writing community, with a special shout out (as always) to Lauren North, Nikki Smith and Zoe Lea. Thank you to PBC. Thank you to my family for the endless love and support: my parents, Sue and Phil Pearson, my sister, Rachel Timmins, my in-laws, Sue and George Herbert.

Thank you to Paul, for always being up for a plot discussion. Thank you to Joe and Elodie, for everything.

ABOUT THE AUTHOR

Laura Pearson is the author of the #1 bestseller *The Last List of Mabel Beaumont*. She founded The Bookload on Facebook and has had several pieces published in the Guardian and the Telegraph.

Sign up to Laura Pearson's newsletter to read the first chapter of her upcoming novel and a free short story.

Visit Laura's website: www.laurapearsonauthor.com

Follow Laura on social media here:

facebook.com/laurapearson22

x.com/laurapauthor

instagram.com/laurapauthor

bookbub.com/authors/laura-pearson

ALSO BY LAURA PEARSON

The Last List of Mabel Beaumont

I Wanted You To Know

Missing Pieces

The Day Shelley Woodhouse Woke Up

Nobody's Wife

The Beforelife of Eliza Valentine

The Many Futures of Maddy Hart

Boldw⚭d

Boldwood Books is an award-winning fiction publishing company seeking out the best stories from around the world.

Find out more at www.boldwoodbooks.com

Join our reader community for brilliant books, competitions and offers!

Follow us
@BoldwoodBooks
@TheBoldBookClub

Sign up to our weekly deals newsletter

https://bit.ly/BoldwoodBNewsletter

Printed in Great Britain
by Amazon

59675458R00174